Across Country

Stories from Aboriginal Australia

ABC
BOOKS

Published by ABC Books for the
AUSTRALIAN BROADCASTING CORPORATION
GPO Box 9994 Sydney NSW 2001

First published 1998

This project has been assisted by
the Commonwealth Government through
the Australia Council, its arts funding
and advisory body.

National Library of Australia
Cataloguing-in-Publication entry
Across country: stories from aboriginal Australia.

  ISBN 0 7333 0687 X.

  1. Aborigines, Australian – Anecdotes. I. Davies, Kerry.
  II. Australian Broadcasting Corporation.

305.89915

Compiled and edited by Kerry Davies
Cover art by Robin Cowburn
Cover design by Robert Taylor
Maps designed by Geoff Morrison
Designed by Jim Shepherd
Set in 10/12½ pt Cambridge by
  Midland Typesetters, Maryborough, Victoria
Colour separations by Finsbury, Adelaide
Printed and bound in Australia by
  Griffin Press Pty Ltd, Adelaide

5 4 3 2 1

A most exciting anthology ... indeed worldwide interest should be shown in this book of thirty short stories by eighteen Aboriginal writers from all around Australia ... There are beautiful tales of relationships in this anthology, mostly between younger members and older members of the family ... But most of all these are all men and women (and children too) who push aside all the petty racism of their lives to stand up equal among their neighbours. This book, in the words of the wonderful storyteller Herb Wharton 'gave me the sense of belonging too, being part of, not owning' and I feel sure that other readers will feel the same.

Archie Weller

*A*cknowledgments

The search for contributors to this collection of stories produced quite a deal of enthusiasm from writers and their supporters. Those who helped to spread the word and who provided invaluable assistance include: Graeme Isaacs of Mayfan; Robert Eggington of Dumbartung Aboriginal Corporation, Perth; Terry Whitebeach, Indigenous writing project officer in Central Australia; Bruce Pascoe of Pascoe Publishing, Apollo Bay; Bruce Simms, Jill Walsh and the rest of the staff of Magabala Books, Broome; Wal Saunders and Sally Dray of the Indigenous Unit of the Australian Film Commission; Marion Debitt of the Northern Territory Writers Centre; Mona El-Ayoubi of the Northern Territory University Faculty of Aboriginal and Torres Strait Islander Studies; Sandra Phillips and Sue Abbey of the University of Queensland Press; David Horton of Aboriginal Studies Press, Canberra; Donna Ifould, Pat Torres, Sava Pinney, Margaret Brusnahan and John Lonie; Anne Brewster of Murdoch University; Roulie Rankine of Arts SA and Marianna Annas of the National Indigenous Arts Advocacy Association. Thanks to all for your help and support.

Also, a special thanks to the Aboriginal and Torres Strait Islander Arts Board of the Australia Council for supporting the initiative of ABC Books in commissioning the collection.

Contents

Preface

Throughout the history of Australia's colonisation, and still in this time of decolonisation, there have been repeated attempts, from non-Aboriginal perspective, to categorise Aboriginal people and their views.

There have been various definitions of Aboriginality: full-blood, half-caste, quarter-caste, coloured, mixed blood; various definitions of cultural expression: traditional, tribal, contemporary, derivative; various assessments of political clout: dynamic, self-serving, clever, power-hungry.

But this apparent need to categorise, in attempt perhaps to understand or, more often than not, to justify yet another swing of policy, keeps taking that perspective deeper into its own dilemma, and further from understanding.

Over the fifteen years I have been involved with Aboriginal people, as journalist, publisher and friend, I have come to realise that such definitions have little significance for Aboriginal people themselves.

As with the Dreaming, an entity melding ancient past with present, the nerve of earth with the politic of justice, the law of creation and of being, proper way, the definitive edges are blurred.

Categories are not so important in the wider scheme of things – of looking after country, of being part of an Aboriginal nation, of re-asserting a respected place in your own country, of determining the future and wellbeing of your own people.

More and more Indigenous people are now committing their ideas and experiences to paper, entering the literary world, their writings as varied as their own cultural backgrounds and life experiences, each significant in its own right.

This collection of stories comes from across Australia, from young and old, men and women, bush people and city dwellers, experienced hands and emerging writers. Their writing comes from their own traditions and communities, from harsh realities, from family stories told and remembered, from the realms of imagination.

There is no specific common theme. Though if a theme were sought it might be that of coming to terms with a past that did not treat Aboriginal people with respect or afford them dignity; of families living in fear of the Welfare; of children trying to understand why they were dealt with as different, and lesser; of battlers getting by, getting on. These are stories celebrating life and expressing a hearty optimism.

These are Aboriginal voices reaching across country.

Kerry Davies
Compiling Editor

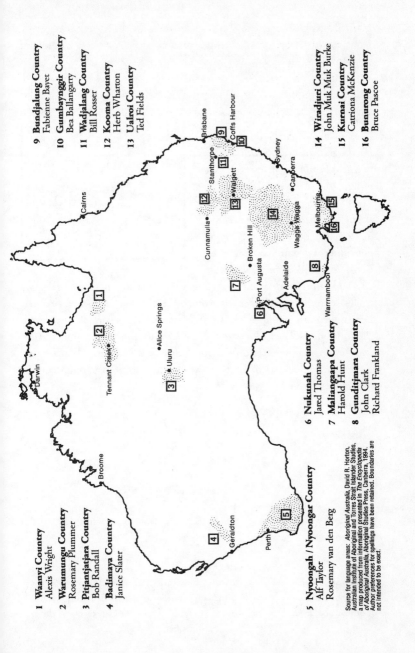

9 Bundjalung Country
Fabienne Bayet

10 Gumbaynggir Country
Bea Ballangarry

11 Wadjalang Country
Bill Rosser

12 Kooma Country
Herb Wharton

13 Ualroi Country
Ted Fields

14 Wiradjuri Country
John Muk Muk Burke

15 Kurnai Country
Catriona McKenzie

16 Bunurong Country
Bruce Pascoe

1 Waanyi Country
Alexis Wright

2 Warumungu Country
Rosemary Plummer

3 Pitjantjatjara Country
Bob Randall

4 Badimaya Country
Janice Slater

5 Nyoongah / Nyoongar Country
Alf Taylor
Rosemary van den Berg

6 Nukunah Country
Jared Thomas

7 Maliangapa Country
Harold Hunt

8 Gunditjmara Country
John Clark
Richard Frankland

Source for language areas: *Aboriginal Australia*, David R. Horton, Australian Institute of Aboriginal and Torres Strait Islander Studies, a map produced from information presented in *The Encyclopedia of Aboriginal Australia*, Aboriginal Studies Press, Canberra, 1994. Author preferences for spellings have been retained. Boundaries are not intended to be exact.

Beatrice Ballangarry

Gumbaynggir Country

BEA BALLANGARRY was born in 1943 in Bowraville on the mid-north coast of New South Wales, of the Gumbaynggir nation. She moved to Western Australia in 1974, where she studied for her Bachelor of Arts, returning to NSW in 1996. Bea is a prolific writer and performer, a prominent education-ist in Indigenous cultural studies and constantly in demand as a guest speaker in this field. She is also a tireless community worker for women's health and domestic violence. Bea is currently living in the Coffs Harbour area where she works for the Indigenous Tracks Program, which aims to improve support services and employment opportunities for Indigenous students. 'Wattle Tree Town' first appeared in Out of the Box, *an anthology published by Murdoch University Press in 1996.*

Glossary

budda	brother
cullung	exclamation
fulla	alternative spelling for fella
gaminin (*also* gammin)	pretend
giggay and gnarlgun	head and ears (sometimes interchanged)
gubba	white person
ngear	yes
tidda	sister
wark-wark bird,	warning birds, also known to children as ghost
doolygaarl bird,	birds, wark-wark a crow (which should not be
mook-mook bird	heard at night), mook-mook an owl, and dooly-gaarl a spirit being

Wattle Tree Town

'MA CAN WE go to the wattles again ... please Ma?'
'Ngear daughter-girl you can play over there in the clump of wattle tree, but *feel* the first chill of the evening, then it is time for you to come inside. If you miss that first chill then *listen* for the ground and the birds to tell you. When you *see* the dark that is not good because it is safer and healthier for you to be indoors before dark.'

'Yeah Ma, I will listen for the wark-wark bird to tell me, because sometime he's mumbling away by himself for a long time before dark, but when he starts his bird-call, I will bring my buddas inside.'

We played for hours, using the trees as posts between gaminin houses, and gaminin streets, sometimes using twigs, broken glass and small pieces of pretty material to make cubby houses, feeling totally secure in the knowledge that home was right next to this clump of wattle trees. Buddy made cars and trucks fom the twigs which fell from the wattle trees. If he broke a small twig, that was a car; if he broke a big twig, that was a truck. Allen drew the streets winding around the trees, sometimes making a hill by putting a handful of earth over a stone and patting it into the shape of a road. I made cubby houses at different points along the road in Wattle Tree Town.

'Get away from my house Allen, don't you know that the house is built first, then the roads are made to wind in and around the houses?'

'No ... joo wong tidda.'

'Say who?'

'Tay me, cause I know wenja make a town ja make all da woads pirst, denja build allda houses long da tide-a woad.'

'Cullung, Alley that might be the way the gubbas do it, but we not gubba people ... we build it right for Wattle Tree Town aye?'

'Budda Buddy why we gotta do tings tidda's way?'

'Cause she's the oldest ... Ma and Daddy always say listen to the older.'

'Che's ony tinchy binchy oder.'

'Don't matter none ... she's older.'

'Do I gotta mash my woad den wait till she's weddy to build a house?'

'Reckon.'

'O r r r i d e.'

Even though my very young brother had difficulties with this concept, he played along and we eventually fell into a peaceful threesome play. We had other places that were used in this way, but the wattle tree area was a sacred place for us three. We built towns or houses at different times depending on our moods. There were also times when my two brothers and I would hide in this clump of trees, not needing a town or a house, but just to sit in a huddle out of reach of the official-looking strangers who sometimes came to see Mum or Dad.

'Wark-wark, wark-wark.'

'Quick Buddy and Allen, run quick and follow me inside.'

'Cullung, that was close aye Mum. That doolygaarl bird was in the wattle trees again.'

'Well the idea of us telling you to come inside when you feel the first chill in the air, or the ground tells you, or your gut tells you in another way, are all the reasons for you not to be playing in the clump of wattle trees after dark. The doolygaarl bird is there to help us help you to remember all these things.'

'Yeah Ma ... but it still sounds scary to us, the same way that the mook-mook bird makes us frightened.'

'Well the mook-mook bird is saying that you should well and truly be inside, because he only come out after all the day birds have gone to bed.'

'It's the sound Ma ... you know ... a sound that makes a picture for me ... of some *big* ugly monster coming straight up from inside the ground to eat us. I can't see a little bird ownin' that sound Ma.'

'You will in time, it's only a matter of time and you'll know that this bird means this, and that bird means that, and so on. It's the same as the ground – daughter-girl if you are not meant to play in a certain area then the ground will let you know through a gut feeling, a knowing. A knowing that makes you take notice.'

'Well that's why we ran quick-way inside just now ... cause we don't want the wark-wark bird to tell you we don't listen. We want to show the bird and you we listen. Granny tells us all the things too. She tells us the things we mustn't do, and to know when things are there for us to listen and learn.'

~

'When the day sky is finished and the night sky has not turned to dark remember not to sweep the floor. You mustn't sweep anything out the door – leave it until the day sky comes again.'

'But why Gwanny?'

'Budda Allen we must listen to what Granny is saying, otherwise we get told the same thing in another way, but maybe not so good way next time.'

'Yeah tidda ... dontcha let dem fullas get me aye; you tell me till I know like you know.'

'Granny why does it always have to be me to listen good and make sure I keep an eye on the boys to listen?'

'Cause you listen good daughter-girl ... ngear ... cause you first child 'n ya must listen good. You firstborn 'n got good giggay and gnarlgun and know how to use 'em.'

'I know a lot of what not to do Granny. I know not to sweep out after dark, not to whistle after dark and what time to come inside and all that stuff, but when I go to school who will do the watching over the boys?'

'Next one down till you get home, then the next and the next.'

The three of us were curled up in our blankets on top of the bed watching all Granny's facial expressions, listening to her changing tones, respecting the silences for what they were, joining in when it felt right, all before a blanket of solitude settled over us and filtered through our little bodies and minds taking us towards sleep. A knowing that the learning for this evening was at an end.

~

Hot and agitated from the heat of the day we tried hard not to get too noisy, but were unable to control the escalation of hot frustrated feelings. I could see my mother's hot and weary body sink to the edge of the verandah, a faraway look in her eyes when they met mine. I now know that she was pregnant with her fourth child and almost due to deliver. Even as a young girl I was conscious that she found mothering a difficulty and right then I knew I had to slow my brothers and me down. I learned from my parents all the little short-cuts to parenting, especially the fun ones.

'Come on Buddy and Allen, let's call Daddy home.'

Calling Daddy home was sitting around the guitar on the floor, plucking at the top string to make a sound that was similar to the truck that Dad travelled in every work day. So we settled around the guitar that lay on the floor and I gestured for Buddy to pluck at the top string. Buddy looked, then he plucked the string. *Bung ng ng ng.* We let the sound die away to nothing.

'See buddas, he is at the last big mountain now, so what about you call Daddy now Allen?'

Bung ng ng ng. Again we let the sound die away to nothing.

'There you go see, now he is at the first bridge so not long to go now.'

We sat silently basking in our own images and listening to our own sounds of the big truck bringing our dad home the way it did every afternoon. To bring Dad to the gate at the roadside I plucked the top string real hard to make the sound last longer. *Bung ng ng ng ng.* We knew Dad was by now at the gate so we raced there happy in our knowledge that we had brought him home.

Walking up the hill was a very tall, very tired-looking man. Our dad was home facing our shrieks of excitement and laughter, plus gaminin sore-hurts on an arm or a foot seeking first attention. Our dad was home. We three jostled to be the closest one to him as we walked towards the back verandah which we used as our entry to the house. Dad bent down and picked Allen up allowing Buddy and me to walk as close as we liked to him the rest of the way.

'See Ma, I helped the boys bring Daddy home so he can play with us.'

I saw Ma and Dad exchange a look. I remembered the frequent looks they exchanged on similar days with similar requests from us. I later learned my Dad was glad to be home and anxious for a quiet sit on the verandah with Ma before he played with us. It didn't always work out this way for him, but occasionally us kids went to Wattle Tree Town and had no need for grown-ups.

'How you doin' Ma?'

'Not too good Dad, the kids were a bit much today.'

'Soon daughter-girl will be off to school so you'll get a bit of a break with only the two for a while.'

'Which will still be three at home in a week or two.'

'Yeah I know Ma. Ya know I'm doin' the best I can to stay in a job and I can't help it if the hours are far too long. I'm glad tomorrow is Saturday. If the day starts out to be as hot as today then we'll walk s l o w l y down to Grassy Bridge and stay near the clear water till late. I'll mind the kids while you rest under those willow trees there ... you know the ones ... on that western bank side ... yeah. The water's not too deep, you can sit in it from time to time if you want while the kids and I collect mussels, catch fish and I'll swim around with them in that shallow part up near the bend in the river.'

Mum nodded in agreement with the next day's arrangements before going indoors to make a billy of tea for her and Dad.

~

'Ya ya look here comes Aunty Ginny and Granny, I'm gonna beat ya to 'em first an' the last one is a rotten egg.'

'You don't have to race him Alley-boy, he's always wantin' to be first. Take my hand, we walk slowly.'

Buddy raced on ahead, arms up in the air yelling excitement as he went down the hill towards the gate that Aunty Ginny and Granny just walked through. When we caught up he was dejected to see we didn't fall in with his play.

'Orhh why did I have to race by myself, why didn't ya run too?'

'So Allen wouldn't cry, that's why.'

'But he should be gettin' big like us so he won't cry when we play races.'

Our little baby brother started crying at this point watching this angry interaction between his older siblings.

'Oh stop sookin' Alley, you jus cryin' cause we talkin' bout ya, stop it na ... stop it.'

'*You* stop it Buddy, don't you see one of us has to keep an eye on him when he's not near Ma.'

'Yeah well I'm not the girl so I don't havta mind him like a ma ... see.'

Aunty Ginny and Granny hugged each of us before we walked slowly back up to the house. They each carried a bundle of something tied in a big piece of cloth with a loop in the knot to hold as the handle. When we reached the verandah Daddy was straightening up from bending over the stove. He had a strange look on his face, but said he was real glad to see his mother and sister. They all hugged the one hug before anyone spoke.

We kids stood in silence at this exchange ... like a knowing that something is serious. Dad asked us to play, but the seriousness of the moment glued us to the verandah on the eastern end. Granny went and brought a blanket out from inside, spreading it double on the floor before Buddy, Allen and I sat down on it to begin talking quietly among ourselves. We tried to keep our eyes away from the other end of the verandah where the stove was and all the activity that was happening there. Seemed like everyone was working purposefully and in a strange compatible silence.

Soon there were more relatives. Granny started singing lingo, stopping every now and then to let the chanting from the other women join in. We heard Ma makin' funny gruntin' sounds, sometimes leading into a yell, then a quiet. We didn't notice time or see the changing colour of the sky from day to dusk to night. Our bodies showed our tiredness from the unexpected. Allen dropped off into a sleep, then Buddy did the same, but I held my eyes stretched wide open till they hurt.

Someone came with an outstretched hand, which I took no time to take, and led me to where Ma lay on the bed, lifting me to sit next to her. Ma looked beautiful. She smiled at me, but I wasn't sure how I felt at first. She smelled like she'd just had a bath; the room had a special smell ... a smell that filled my senses and one that I knew would travel with me in my lifetime ... a smell that held me to the moment. A moment of wonderment. For a brief time someone showed me a little bundle of something live and movin' and makin' little sounds, then moved away from the bed.

Ma was hugging me, caressing my whole body, my fingers, my toes and my face while my older women-kin were doing the same to her. The soft candlelight in the room, the good spirits floating around, the unspoken love passing from one to the other, the warmth off the women's bodies from the recent event, made this time a time for me too special to even know where to begin with an understanding of its significance. I fell asleep there in my mother's arms.

Next morning I awoke in my usual sleeping place, not jumping out of bed the way I usually did, but staying where I was, staring into nothingness, knowing I had something special to remember. That's right! The warm room where Ma lay on the bed, someone lifting me there to be included in the event. Did they include me because I was awake still? Would they have woken me if I had been asleep? Did my family think I knew what was happening? For me the day, the evening and the night is still wrapped in a cocoon of time that belongs on its own.

∼

The next few months us kids saw some of our lives through this new little girl in our family.

'If you sit quietly there you can watch when I give bubby a bath.'

We sat quietly watching Ma bath our baby and I would float to my other world ... you know ... the one in the cocoon. Was it this baby smell that took me there? Does this smell belong only to babies? There were so many questions now, all cramming in my head. I was especially happy about my sister because now there were two of us girls, so the boys couldn't use numbers for gain. Lots of relatives came to see our baby sister and spend days staying over helping Ma with us kids. By the time my sister could sit up Ma was doing everything by herself again.

~

'Hello school-girl, did Ma make all those pretty curls so you could go to school?'

'Yeah Daddy, and today Buddy has to look after Allen till I come home aye?'

'Yes they have to be good boys and look after each other, the way we all look after each other.'

'But Daddy when I'm home I havta look after the boys; when I'm not home they look after each other, why is it that way?'

'Because you born a girl my baby, and girls know how to do that best. Boys need each other to reach the same as girls do in some things.'

Miss McLocklin saw me coming through the school gate stretching out her arms as I raced for her, then scooping me high in the air giving me a big hug before putting me back on the ground. I liked my teacher because none of the school kids would play with me. They called me names and were nasty to me. Then came the day I was taken from the state school to the convent school at the other end of town. The convent school was where all my cousins went so it was said that I must go there too. Ma was unhappy about me going to the convent school, which caused many arguments with our extended families. Ma and Daddy started arguing about my schooling as well.

'Eric, I am getting sick and tired of being caught in the crossfire of our family, the schools and what I see as important for our children.'

'So you want us to just pack up and leave ... and go where?'

'Out to Eungai, that's where. Nana said to come if it got too much.'

'Then you want for us to leave my mob and go to yours ...'

'The mission mob interfere too much in our lives. Every time I make changes for us to live a little bit like the gubbas, you fullas say I do wrong so I am faced with "everybody reckons this" and "everybody reckons that" all the time. No matter what you think, we still gotta learn how to use their money, an' buy from their shops an' all. Too much for me now.'

'Ma, don't you know our lives are not our own to operate freely from? It never will be as long as we live in this country.'

'Yes, I keep hearing this talk from you, but I don't agree. We gotta keep searching to work the two ways or break free and learn the gubba way.'

'Come on then Ma, we go to Nana and try a different way.'

~

Browns Crossing at Eungai Creek was a name given to the place where the creek water ran over the road and became impassable during the rainy period. As soon as you crossed this point there was a little road leading off to the right that brought you to a sliprail gate of a fenced-off property.

Once through the gate and to the right a bit, was Nana's house. Nana's house stood on top of a small culvert that overlooked a deep waterhole. Nana called it the 'devil's hole'. A stream ran from it which fed some of the water into the creek at the bottom of the road. Nana reckons this was the devil's hole because there was no bottom. I reckon this was her way of keeping us kids away from there because from the house you couldn't see it except when you walked to the edge of the culvert. So to the grown-ups it was too dangerous for us kids to be there unsupervised. This waterhole also provided the daily water supply.

On the other side of the culvert living in a tent was Uncle Ansel, Aunty Vera and their children. Richard, whom we called Rip, was approximately my age, Angela was Buddy's age; Louis was Allen's age, and so on. Uncle Dooley, Aunty Gracie and their children Winnie, Dennis and Cyril, similar ages to us as our first cousins on the other side, lived in a tent behind Nana's house furthest away from the culvert. So from Uncle Dooley's tent you couldn't see Uncle Ansel's tent. Ma and Daddy pitched our tent between Uncle Dooley's tent and Nana's house.

This was my first permanent living in close proximity to our first cousins on my Ma's side of the family. Life here was very different as far as who played with whom. The boys here had already established that they had games which didn't include the girls. The girls too kept 'cubby houses', a girl's game. There were some days I missed playing with my two buddas, and we didn't have our wattle trees here, and it seemed so different without them ... naked different.

Fabienne Bayet

Bundjalung
Country

FABIENNE BAYET was born in Adelaide in 1970, while her family comes from Bundjalung country in northern New South Wales. She has worked as a researcher at Parliament House and for the Aboriginal Legal Rights Movement in South Australia and is now working on a novel. Her work has been published in Southerly *(1996) and other journals.* 'Public Notice' *was first published by Pascoe Publishing in* Australian Short Stories, no. 55, 1996.

Public Notice

S TUCK ON THE glass door, in the front of Lucas's, one of two supermarkets in this one pub town, Coober Pedy. I walk past it, turn around, staring, realising who it belongs to. The sticky tape is peeling, yellow and perishing from the dust on the glass. The paper glowing gold from the orange sunset flowing through the door. The edges of the paper ragged. The warmth from the sun touches my face. Dust particles float on the golden air, touching everything, leaving a film of dust all over my body, not to be removed until I wash back in Adelaide, but by then the dust has seeped into my pores, settled into every crevice, sunk through the layers of skin, and is now part of my blood. I stare at the notice, realising that it's about my Nana, about someone I know, someone who shopped here for twenty-three years of her life.

Came in the back way, down the hill. Everybody knew her, so it didn't matter. It was all part of the ritual.

Except on Thursdays. On Thursdays the truck would come in and block her. Packers would be ripping boxes, trying to restock the empty shelves before the hordes would come in, demanding more. Wanting to know where the Jarlsberg cheese was, the fresh olives, the vacuum-sealed bacon, the rare and very expensive fish.

I worked as a packer occasionally, with my mother and aunt, hating every moment. The smells, the ripping of fingernails on cardboard. Cold fingers, standing in the fridge, restocking, repacking while impatient customers stood behind me demanding new stock.

'Get me the vanilla custard, no the big one, at the back. Here, get out the way, I'll get it myself.'

I used to think *How undignified, how demeaning, how unsophisticated*, wanting to be back in Adelaide. But now I realise, dignity comes from the mind, not from the location. And I only hated the work because I wasn't very good at it.

On Thursday Nana would come through the front of Lucas's. Through these doors, and even before, when these doors weren't glass, but rollers and this place a tin shed.

I stare at the notice. I stand for a moment, remembering . . .

The priest reads, about a woman unknown to him. We are not churchgoers, and neither was Nana. Who needs to go to church when you have faith and humour in life at home? Father Paul, an old local, understood Nana. He understood all of us. He once talked my sister Sandra out of Catholicism, as a favour to Mum. But he's not here by the grave. 'God' has sent him away from Coober Pedy, from his home for so many years. This new priest knows that he has a long haul before he's considered a 'local' and he bears his alienation with dignity.

He reads . . .

'Mabel was born in New South Wales in 1922. She met and married Lindsay Gordon Williams . . . *That's my grandpa, I think to myself, surprised* . . . when she was twenty-one and bore seven children . . . *Ten actually, the triplets died as babies, although it's never spoken about* . . . When the marriage broke down . . . *I'd been told my grandfather went to war – Egypt, Papua New Guinea – saw his friends killed, came back, unrecognised as a returned soldier because he was Aboriginal. And took to the bottle in madness and for comfort* . . . she travelled to Tennant Creek to be with her mother, and worked at the local hospital. There she raised her kids, who grew up with great love, devotion and respect for her. She also met and fell in love with Bruno Giacommelli, who was a welder at the mines in Tennant Creek.

'In 1968 Bruno decided to try his luck on the opal fields. So he established himself and sent for Mabel and the twins ... *They were the youngest* ... In 1970 she moved to Coober Pedy to become an opal miner's wife ... *She came here the year I was born* ...

'It was not uncommon to see her fossicking through the mullock dumps looking for that little bit of extra money, as many of the opal miner's wives did. She was always supportive and caring about her family and friends. She had a wonderful laugh, full of life and warmth ...'

The service rambles on. Through the tears, the heaving sobs, there is something within me, standing apart, not really believing, looking at the sun, the blue sky, searching for her spirit and I'm thinking *These words mean nothing. They say nothing about her, her soul, her life. Isn't this what any family would say about their grandmother, their matriarch?*

But these words are all we could think of. Numbed with shock and grief – it is all we could say, all we could share. We are not of the great poets.

Around the grave we are all trying to be on our best behaviour yet our frailties and our faults are solidified in that moment. A fragment when we try to be our best in Nana's memory. Even the sunlight and the tears could do nothing to burn out the fact that no matter how different we all are, or how similar, we are a family who have lost someone we all love – love being a word that does nothing to explain the depth of our emotion.

Orchids, roses, native hops, carnations, lilies, banksias, proteas, daisies, she loved them all. We smother her in flowers.

And now I'm standing in the front of Lucas's, the sun streaming on my face, with a defiance that is raised after a loss, like the way we Australians are so ridiculously proud of Gallipoli.

She is now laid to rest, everybody that needs to know, knows. I tear off the notice, hoping to capture the gold of the sunset in the paper, hoping to capture the dust settling on me, the moment.

Later, my uncle finds the notice between my magazines, stored and hidden from embarrassment. He had put the notice up, being the dutiful son, trying to keep as busy as possible while working with his own grief. He looks at the notice, at me, but says nothing.

The dying sunlight streams through the doorway, slowly turning red. The sun is in my eyes, but I do not blink, I do not close my eyes, let it burn into me, burn into my retinas. People pass at the edge of my vision. I turn to do the shopping. There's no need to look for her in the dusty aisles, she's not here. She's in the glow of the sunset and the dust on my skin and in my blood.

John Clark

JOHN CLARK was born in Warrnambool, Victoria, in 1953. He is a member of the Gunditjmara community, and attended the Framlingham Aboriginal Settlement School before moving on to various parts of the country during his youth. John works mainly as a labourer and he has worked with Aboriginal organisations over many  *years. Many of John's stories have been published, and he also writes poetry and was involved with an oral history program with the Wathaurong Aboriginal Community. He is currently attending the Koorie Art and Design course at Gordon TAFE, Geelong, and hopes to continue work in this field. 'Johnny Cake Days' first appeared in* Australian Short Stories, no. 46, in 1994, *and 'A Handful of Beans' in no. 57, 1997, published by Pascoe Publishing.*

Glossary

budda	brother
gammin (*also* gaminin)	pretend
gubba	white person
tidda	sister

A Handful of Beans

THE FOG LINGERS in the deeper ferntree gullies of the Southern Victorian ranges. Further out on higher ground, beyond the fringe of mountain ash and stringy-barks, the mist has long withdrawn from the first mean rays of the sun.

Here where the evergreen forest was long ago sacrificed for the richness of the rust red soil, an extensive patchwork of ochre brown fields stretches far and wide on rolling hills to the north-east. The panorama is dotted with farm buildings, dams, apple, peach and cherry orchards, with paler green patches of potatoes and beans.

~

The sun rose like the lord of the mist and flared defiantly at the battlers and knockabouts in Riley's bean patch. Heads down, backs bent, the pickers move steadily forward, harvesting row after row, filling old kerosene tins with long fingers of fresh green beans. About five buckets fill a bag and for a few shillings a bag, you can get by if your back doesn't break.

Old Digger Stan blinked the sweat from his eyes and cursed the flies. He tipped his tin of beans into the hessian bag. 'Fair dinkum. It's hotter than the mustard in El Alamein,' he muttered as he tilted a battered akubra to scratch his balding pink dome.

In the next row, Stan's mate from way back, Reg Viney, peered from beneath the brim of his torn straw hat. 'Think of the rations in the ice-box, Digger. Something cold to wash that sand down your throat.' Digger Stan swooned at the thought of the beer.

'Too bloody right, mate. Better than a cool change.'

Reg raised his beefy frame and emptied his bucket of beans into the bag. Shaking the bag to settle the contents, his chubby face reddened with the effort as the familiar squadron of flies resettled on his sweat-soaked back.

Digger Stan sat on his upturned bucket and tried to roll a cigarette. He knew he couldn't. Digger's leathery fingers would not cooperate. Reg saw his mate fumbling with the makings.

'You right, Dig?'

'Yeah, mate.'

But Reg knew he wasn't coping and sensed Digger's growing frustration. Besides, Reg's well-intended reminder of their rations, four cold bottles in the cool of the hut, only heightened Digger's thirst. The old soldier fumbled and shook. Tobacco spilled from his fingers and finally the paper itself floated to the ground.

'Strike me bloody pink,' he snarled, snatching wildly at the slip of paper. Big Reg stepped over, calmly took the makings from Stan and rolled two smokes which they lit up.

Doreen Slater and her five-year-old son Sonny approached along the row opposite Reg. She picked one side of the plants while Sonny picked the other. They drew level with the two men. Doreen flashed dark eyes and smiled shyly.

'Good morning, Reg. Morning, Stan.'

'Good morning, dear, how's our cobber going?'

Reg smiled down on Sonny. The boy looked up with the same eyes as his mother.

'Good, Uncle Reg, we gonna pluck twenty bags today, hey Mum?'

Doreen laughed. Her fine white teeth brilliant in the darkness of her skin. Reg laughed too and admired the boy's enthusiasm. To be called uncle by an Aboriginal boy was amusing to Reg at first. Doreen explained to him one night at the huts that kids on the mission called the elders Uncle or Aunty as a mark of respect.

'Good on you mate,' chuckled Reg, 'you keep right on plucking.'

'Gawd, twenty bags ya say?' chuckled Digger Stan.

'You'll be a gun picker soon enough, I'll bet a shilling.'

Digger slapped a fly and drew on his smoke. He looked about him and marvelled at the many different people from faraway places in Riley's Patch. The Italians, Mario and Joe, talked non-stop as they worked nearby. Yabbering, Digger called it. There were the university students – Digger couldn't tell the boys from the girls – and those tight-arse Scotsmen. Noisy buggers. The gun pickers, old Tom Dooley, Willie and Beany Brown, straddled the rows like jockeys with their heads tucked in.

He watched Karl, the 'Kraut', heave a bagful of beans to his broad shoulders. A cheerful sort of bloke, thought Digger. Funny how things turn out. The world had turned too quickly for Stan. He felt the earth moving now, the way the ocean moved under a battleship and the changes made his head spin.

The shadows shrunk back to the trees as green turned to grey in the rising heat. Doreen fixed the scarf about her long black hair and said to Sonny, 'It's getting real hot now, Bub.' She still called him Bub out of habit. 'You go and sit in the shade with Alfy. See if he's feeling better.'

The boy looked to the line of trees where the truck was parked. The wiry figure of Alf Wilson sat propped against the rough bark of a pine. He'd been there since six this morning when he stumbled from the truck after vomiting all the way from the huts. Sonny set off slowly, dawdling down the long row.

'Go on love, it's alright.' Doreen had sensed his hesitation. Alf can be surly when he's hungover she thought, snatching at the beans. Just this morning he'd promised to pull his head in. Things will work out the way they'd planned, he'd said. After bean season there'd be other work and we can rent our own house and send Sonny to school. Doreen wanted Sonny to have an education. Something most mission kids never got.

Reg and Digger Stan eyed lanky Alf lying in the shade. They had seen the boy's reluctance and understood it. They'd seen Alf idle before, while Doreen and Sonny worked. They'd heard Alf shouting and swearing up at the huts. They'd heard Doreen crying too. The two mates glanced at each other. Reg spat and crushed his cigarette butt into the ground. Digger shook his toothless head.

'Fair bloody dinkum,' he said to himself as he bent his back to picking and cursing the flies.

～

Ashley Considine was a gun picker. Since he was fifteen he'd picked everything from peas to potatoes all over the country. Tall and quiet spoken he had a 'G'day' for everyone, but kept his distance. Ashley stood at the back of the truck with Jimmy Mack the foreman. Ashley hooked a bag to the scales and Jimmy Mack added the tally in the book. Just then Sonny came by.

'Howdy, Cowboy,' Ashley greeted him. The boy looked up and brightened.

'Howdy, Uncle Ashley.' Sonny had taken a shine to Ashley. The man's quiet friendship and gentle nature attracted the lad. To Sonny, Ashley was a Texas Ranger, a lonesome gunslinger out of the west. Sonny'd been badgering Doreen to get him a hat just like the mysterious Ashley's.

Alf Wilson smoked and ran his fingers through his slicked black hair. He scratched his back like a bear on the pine bark and shaped smoke rings as he watched Sonny talking to Ashley. Alf's bloodshot eyes drew a bead on Ashley Considine.

'Mister big shot.' The words hissed from his lips like venomous snakes. As if suddenly reminded of something he scanned the field for Doreen, saw her and flashed back to Ashley. Alf Wilson's eyes were glowing slits of fire.

A dusty green Land Rover approached, bumping along the track by the peach trees. Frank Riley with the morning smoko. The pickers ate and drank tea in the welcome shade of the pines. Boss Riley and Jimmy Mack discussed the quality of the beans and which field was to be harvested next. Doreen offered Alf a mug of tea. 'If I want something I'll ask,' he said sourly. Doreen decided to ignore him and passed Sonny a sandwich. Sonny asked for a cold drink then and when Doreen found the container empty she and Sonny looked straight at Alf.

'Aw love,' he whined, 'can't ya see I'm crook, for Christsake I had to drink something.'

'Alright love,' said Doreen thinking it best not to press him. The last thing she wanted was an argument. Especially in front of the others.

Alf had changed since they'd left the caravan park by the Murray River. The three of them were so excited when they packed up and Doreen couldn't wait to get here. She was willing to work her fingers to the bone for Sonny. She'd show them all on the mission that Doreen Slater could stand on her own two feet. Even if they are black.

Sonny dipped a biscuit in his tea and looked at his mother deep in thought. Sonny knew Alfy was naughty for drinking all the cool drink and he knew too that Doreen would not say any more to him about it. Sonny was growing accustomed to Alf's moods. The boy suddenly realised he'd been staring at the sullen Alf who glared steadily back at him. Sonny dropped his eyes.

~

It had been a good season for beans. They were still picking when March turned to April, then the beans started to thin out. A lot of pickers packed up and left in old dented utilities and vans, tooting and waving cheerful goodbyes. Doreen hadn't said so many goodbyes since she'd left the mission with Sonny. Goodbyes always made her feel sad and she put her arm around her son as they sat on the wooden steps of the hut. This was their last night on the bean fields. Where had the months gone?

Alf's attempts at finding other work went as far as the Valley Pub where he was heavily in debt for several boxes of beer he'd acquired 'on tick'. Doreen paid the bill. She told herself that Alf would be himself when they got back home and yet she knew too that he was more a stranger to her now than he ever was.

Doreen thrilled to thoughts of home but she would miss this place of crisp mountain air in the mornings with that earthy smell of freshly turned soil and dew on leaves. She loved to hear the cool breeze of evening stealing through the peach trees after work, and the hush and whispers in the giant pines above the huts reminded Doreen of the wind in the river gums back home.

Sonny sat with Doreen and wished Alf would hurry up. He could hear Alf's boots scrape across the floorboards as he moved about getting ready to go to town. Sonny was anxious to be away on the bus to Emerald Valley with his very own paper money and Doreen had promised him they'd look in the shops for a cowboy hat like Ashley's. The boy enjoyed a boiled lolly from a small brown paper bag. Jimmy Mack had given them to him at knock-off time.

'Here ya go, mate,' he'd said. 'You're a gun picker and a bonzer bloke.'

Sonny was swollen with pride. He felt he'd grown two inches as he stood on the back of the truck with the others. Everyone was in a good mood.

Even the old Bedford kicked off pretty smartly and everyone scrambled for a hold, laughing and cheering when Digger's hat blew off. Reg, Digger Stan and old Tom started singing a song Sonny'd never heard before. Some others joined in and the big German clapped his hands. Sonny held Doreen's hand and looked in wonder at their faces as they sang.

They were cheering and clapping when the truck rolled into Riley's yard and lurched to a standstill outside the pay office. There was a good feeling in the air and Sonny was swept up in it as he waited with Doreen to collect their last pay slip.

Ashley Considine collected his pay and made his way past the row of weathered huts tucked under the pines. He came by Doreen and Sonny and they exchanged hellos. Ashley accepted a lolly from Sonny and shook the boy's hand.

'Well, so long partner.'

He took Doreen's hand and held it.

'Goodbye Doreen, maybe we'll meet on the trail.' She and Sonny said they hoped so.

Her hand was warm and delicate in his steely fingers.

Alf suddenly swore from inside the hut. He'd cut himself shaving.

'Well, goodbye and good luck,' Ashley said and walked away.

Alf came to the doorway and saw Ashley entering his hut.

'What did he want?' he demanded, staring at Doreen.

'Nothing love, just saying goodbye, that's all.'

'Yeah Alfy, just saying goodbye,' Sonny chirped. 'Can we go now?'

Reg and Digger Stan shared the hut between Ashley's and Doreen's. Reg checked the oil and water in his rusted red van parked under the scaly limbs of the pine. They'd leave early in the morning. Digger sat slouched on a low stool by the front door of the hut. He had been sipping beer from a huge tin mug and was nodding off. Reg looked at his mate for some moments. The 'rations' was Reg's idea. It had helped him so why not Stan? Reg heard a door slam and saw Doreen, Sonny and Alf walking up the road to the bus stop on the highway. Reg ground his teeth as he watched Alf Wilson.

'That bludging bastard,' he grumbled and when Reg slammed the bonnet down old Digger nearly jumped out of his skin. He'd 'slipped away' and was in the trench with his mates when he heard the bang. Digger Stan sat there swaying and blinking like a dazed owl as the last hint of sunlight faded from the tree tops.

~

Pine cones caught alight and flared softly in Ashley Considine's fireplace. The door hung partly open and the electric light was off. It attracted too many bugs and anyway the firelight was good enough for Ashley. He was used to it. He turned from the fire and went to a dark corner where he lifted the top of a small record player. An old box-shaped thing he'd carried around for years with a few records, badly scratched and falling out of their dog-eared covers. The needle crackled on the disc and the tune began as Ashley sat in front of the fire. It wasn't often he played the records, but the music and the fire seemed to comfort him, like old friends, perhaps, and besides, Ashley was thoughtful tonight. He held up his hand, the one that held Doreen's a while ago and looked at it. He sat there like that for some time. Staring at his hand like a man bewitched, while behind his back a crowd of shadowy figures leaped and danced to every scratchy tune and rallied around his narrow bed as if to mock the man in his loneliness.

Sometime after dark the headlights of a taxi swept across the front of the huts. It drew up under the pines and purred like a cat on the pine-needle carpet as Doreen got out and guided a sleepy Sonny to the hut. Inside, a single light globe burned fiercely on the low timber ceiling. Doreen helped Sonny to bed.

'It's been a long day for you Mr Sonny James Slater,' she said gently. 'Goodnight now, Bub.' She kissed him but Sonny was already asleep. Doreen wiped her eyes. She'd been crying quietly in the taxi while Sonny slept across her lap. She went to the kitchen and flopped on a chair by the cold iron stove.

Alf had spoiled everything. He was not the easygoing Alf Doreen once knew. When they got to the hotel for tea, Alf said he wasn't hungry and shot straight to the bar. Doreen and Sonny ate in the lounge across from a group of elderly ladies who were quite taken by Sonny's 'lovely big brown eyes'.

Doreen was happy to chit-chat with the women until a frail lady in blue eyeliner leaned unsteadily from her chair and croaked, 'You know dear, speaking confidentially of course, I have connections with a wonderful welfare agency. Lovely Christian people they are, love. Should you find yourself in ... er, difficulties ...' The old woman droned on. They were all looking at Sonny now, as if he were suffering some incurable disease. Familiar waves of embarrassment and shame roared like the sea into Doreen's ears and she stood up, her face clouded with anger, frustration and fear.

'We have to go now,' she said abruptly and snatched Sonny's hand.

'That's a shame, dear.' The hags clutched their sherry glasses, smiling wrinkled smiles at Sonny gulping down the last of his raspberry lemonade.

Doreen told Sonny to wait outside while she went to get Alf. The bar chatter died when she walked in and started up again with a low wolf-whistle. Doreen felt all eyes on her as she walked up to Alf. She tapped him on the shoulder and he reeled on her.

'Bloody hell, what do you want, Doreen?'

'Can we go now, Alf? The shops ...'

'Well go on then, woman, I'm talking to ...'

'But you said you'd come with us.'

'Never mind what I said,' Alf banged his beer glass down. Doreen was taken aback at the anger in his voice. Alf glanced at his drinking mates who stared openly at Doreen. Alf turned to Doreen and slurred with menace. 'Well get going, girl. I'll be out soon, see?'

Doreen would never forget the look on his face. It was not

Alf's. She turned, eyes down, and made her way through the smoke and laughter to the door.

Sonny was looking into the lighted shop windows of Main Street when Doreen came out of the hotel.

'Whatsa matter, Mum?' Doreen felt herself falling to pieces. 'You sick or something?'

'No love, just tired, that's all.'

They came to McHarry's Boots and Saddles Store and found it had closed ten minutes ago. Sonny pressed his face to the glass, peering at the hats hanging up inside and Doreen started to cry.

'Never mind, Mum, we can get it tomorrow.' Doreen knelt and hugged Sonny. She felt she had let him down somehow.

'Bub?' she said tearfully. 'Is it alright with you if we go back to the hut now? I think I am a bit sick after all.'

'Yeah, Mum, I know.' The boy looked into his mother's face. Sonny knew alright.

~

A big round alarm clock ticked heavily on the mantle above the stove. Doreen heard the pines sway in the cool night breeze and the weatherboards creak and groan around her. She smudged yet another tear on her face and longed for someone to talk to. A small white moth flung itself relentlessly at the light globe and Doreen watched its frantic efforts to reach the light source, till it dropped exhausted to the table below.

Doreen Slater made up her mind. She was tired of banging her head on a brick wall. She was sick of crying. She would tell Alf these things tomorrow when he was sober.

Doreen slipped off her shoes and went to check on Sonny in the tiny back room where she drew the blankets around her son and kissed him. Laughter erupted somewhere outside and Doreen stood by Sonny's bed and listened. She recognised Digger's laugh and her ears caught the faint sound of music. They were welcome sounds and Doreen was drawn to them. She went to the door and stepped outside.

Doreen looked through the darkness to Reg and Digger's hut where a light burned low behind a ragged calico curtain. She stepped down to the cool ground and wandered into the inky blackness beneath the pines. Treading carefully, her bare feet sank in the soft needles as she moved like a shadow to within a few yards of Ashley Considine's hut.

The door was slightly open and Doreen saw the firelight dancing on the wall inside. She stood in the outer darkness listening to the music.

Every night I sit here by my window
staring at the lonely avenue
watching lovers holding hands and laughing
thinking about the things we used to do.

She thought about green-eyed Ashley. Was he lonely? Where did he come from? And Digger Stan. Has he a family? What would become of him and Reg? Big Reg, the jolly giant with a pot belly.

Doreen felt secure with her thoughts and dreams in the darkness outside Ashley's hut. So near, yet so far from the warmth and companionship she craved and her heart ached. Doreen closed her eyes and let the music carry her home.

She didn't hear the car. The headlamps ripped through the night as it swerved from the gravel road and crept to the huts. Dazzled and exposed, Doreen stumbled and felt for the huge trunk of the pine.

'Doreen?' It was Alf. 'Doreen?'

He called again with some urgency and almost fell out of the taxi. Alf cut a demonic figure in the lights of the cab as it reversed to the road. Clutching a green bottle, he wobbled and muttered to himself as Doreen approached.

'Where ya been, Doreen?' His eyes burned and fell to her bare feet.

'Nowhere Alf, you're drunk.'

He ignored her, gazing beyond to the music and light spilling from Ashley's hut. Doreen opened her mouth to speak when Alf slapped her across the face, knocking her to the ground.

'Black slut,' he spat, snake-eyed with hatred.

'No Alf, I never ...'

'You and that flash cowboy. You think I'm stupid do ya, bitch?' He lashed out at her again and Doreen buried her face in the pine needles, but it was Alf who cried out in pain and fell to the ground.

Sonny had woken and saw Alf strike his mother. The boy rushed from the hut and kicked Alf as hard as he could. Then he fell into Doreen's arms. They held each other, weeping, while Alf raised himself up and swore.

'You, ya little bastard. I'll fix ya.' Alf staggered forward and raised his hand to Sonny. Doreen screamed.

'That's enough of that Alf,' a voice in the dark said, and Ashley Considine gripped Alf by the collar and flung him to the ground.

'You two OK?' Ashley bent down on one knee to comfort Doreen and Sonny.

'I think so,' sobbed Doreen through swollen lips.

'Look out,' warned Sonny as Alf loomed from the shadows about to bring the whisky bottle down on Ashley's head. Ashley spun in time to see big Reg Viney grab Alf's arm and thump him on the head with a closed fist. The way a man might thump a cork into a bottle.

Alf buckled and fell in a heap at Reg's feet when Digger Stan stumbled into the scene hitching up the bottom half of his long johns and grumbling.

'What the blue blazes is going on?' Before anyone could answer he tripped over Alf's long legs in the shadows and went down.

Reg and Ashley went to Digger's aid as Alf stirred and sat up.

'Ya rotten mob a bastards,' he roared and swore as he struggled and finally stood up. Sonny had wrapped himself around his mother's leg and stared wet-eyed at Alf. Alf pointed a shaky finger at Doreen.

'You can have your flash cowboy man,' he snarled and staggered backwards against the wall of the hut. Doreen's head was spinning. She could only look at Alf; wanting to say something, but what? She was about to say, I'm sorry. She was going to cry again and then she remembered the moth.

'Alf,' her words were shaky but she was determined. 'Alf

Wilson, I never ... I won't put up with this, and you ... '

'Yous can all go to hell far as I care,' Alf barked at the stony faces around him. 'I don't care a handful of beans for none of ya's,' Alf said as he turned and limped into the night.

~

Magpies sang with the first splash of morning sun on the pine tops. Frank Riley's rooster crowed from somewhere across the road and Doreen opened her eyes. Sonny slept soundly beside her and she remembered falling into Sonny's bed with him last night. Last night. Doreen ran her tongue over her bruised mouth and recalled saying goodnight to Ashley, Reg and Digger. Telling them more than once that she was alright and that she and Sonny were going home tomorrow.

Sonny stirred under the heavy grey blankets and Doreen felt the warmth of his back on hers. She let her eyes close. Plenty of time till the bus leaves for town. Buy Sonny's hat. Book the tickets at the railway station. Mum and Aunty Jessie will meet us when we get back. All the kids. Everyone. We'll go out to Nan's place on the mission. Sonny is Nan's favourite.

Whenever Doreen received letters from home she read them to Sonny and Alf in the hut after teatime. Carefully avoiding Nan's repeated pleas and warnings. 'That young fella, he's no good for you, Doreen. His eyes too close together. Like a dingo. Please come home, my baby girl. Bring my Sonny boy home. Mixing with whitefellas only bring trouble ...'

Outside in the chill morning air, Reg fired up the pistons in the cranky red van. Doreen listened to it clatter past the hut to the road and with three sharp blasts on the horn Reg Viney and Digger Stan roared out of Doreen's life. And Alf? Alf was gone too. Let him go. Nan's words, the words Doreen never read aloud ran across her mind as she lay on her pillow in the cedar-scented dawn light. Let him go. We don't need him. Me and Sonny been alone before ...

A knock on the door jolted Doreen. Shot right through her and she saw Alf's angry face. Another knock. Louder this time. Was it him come back? Doreen swung her feet onto the cold floor. She ran her fingers through her hair, straightened her clothes and gathered what strength she had left. Sonny roused, mumbling something in his sleep. Doreen quickly tucked him under the covers and stepped into her shoes.

When Doreen swung the hut door open she was ready. Ready for Alf. If he wants a fight, well that's what he'll get then. But it wasn't Alf. It was two hefty policemen looking deadpan at Doreen and her heart dropped like it was on a string. Her first fear was for Sonny. The woman in the pub. The shorter officer spoke, revealing herself as a woman.

'Are you Doreen May Slater?'

'Yes.' Doreen nodded to back up her barely whispered reply and the policewoman went on to say that she had the unpleasant duty to inform Doreen of the death of Alfred George Wilson. Doreen caught snatches of information as she stood stunned, frozen in the doorway. Approximately twelve-thirty a.m. . . . Bus stop . . . Semitrailer . . . Alcohol level . . . Relatives will be notified.

The larger of the constables examined the outer surroundings and craned his neck to see into the hut behind Doreen. Both officers eyed Doreen now and she was aware of her fat lip, slept-in clothes and her hair.

'Been drinking, Miss Slater?' enquired the rubber-necked lawman.

'No I haven't.'

'What are your immediate plans?'

'What?'

'What are you going to do now? Are you working or . . .'

'I'm going home. We're going home,' Doreen said defensively. The police gleamed like trophies and stared at Doreen a full minute before they went to the car and heaved themselves into it.

Doreen shut the door. She put her back to it to steady her legs. Alf dead! She shivered in her woollen shawl and stayed there for some time; staring into nothing; seeing many things. Things she knew well but could never understand in a world of hurt where women want to take your children and men turn into wild wounded animals. A hostile place where decent people like Ashley lived by themselves and grew old alone or clung to each other like Reg and Digger Stan. These were Doreen's thoughts mingled with images of happy times with Alf and Sonny and Nan's words, 'Mixing with whitefellas only bring trouble,' ringing in her ears.

After a while, Doreen realised she wasn't crying. She'd done with crying. Doreen Slater would not deny her spirit any more than she would shed her skin and she shed no tears for Alf Wilson. Home, home, home. Every heartbeat said home and Doreen pictured the mission, the way it looked from the road and the smiling black faces waiting there with Nan, misty-eyed; arms reaching.

Yes, she'd go home. She'd go home prouder, stronger. She and Sonny had done it once, they could do it again . . . somewhere.

The alarm clock, the one that had sent them yawning to the bean patch every morning except Sundays, chip-chipped into Doreen's thoughts. She was Doreen Slater. She had a son to protect. There were things to do.

Doreen stood up straight and swept her hair back with her hands. She looked through the dusty window pane at the cherry trees, leafless, brooding, waiting for spring in lines that ran for ever on the steaming brown soil.

'Mum?' Sonny stood by the bedroom door rubbing his eyes. Mobs of unruly curls sprang in all directions and when he blinked at Doreen it was as though she was looking at herself.

'Mum, is Alf . . . is Alfy . . .?'

'Yes, Bub, he's gone . . . Alfy's gone now.'

~

Sonny held his mother's hand as they walked down the gravel road to the bus stop. Doreen carried a suitcase and a woven carry-bag on her shoulders. Sonny humped a satchel on his back like a swagman and his last two boiled lollies in his shirt pocket.

They walked in silence but there was something special about today. This was a day to start again and the sun on their faces was warm, healing and at last they were going home!

The roadside scrub and saplings still glistened, sparkled in the morning dew. A pair of lorikeets flashed across the road into the orchards as the sun cleared the highest ranges, dark-wooded and distant. Presently they heard a vehicle approaching from behind and Ashley Considine's blue utility drew alongside them and stopped. He'd just left Frank Riley's place where he'd heard the news about Alf.

'Howdy, Uncle Ashley,' Sonny said cheerfully.

'Morning, Ashley.' Doreen managed a smile for him.

'G'day, bean pickers, going my way?'

The truck bucked and they were away with Sonny in the middle, in awe of the gadgets and switches on the dashboard, thrilled with all the thoughts of adventures and mysteries a boy could hope for on a day like this. Doreen sat quietly. She accepted Ashley's offer to drive them to town and she knew, somehow, that he would say nothing about last night.

The intersection loomed ahead and Ashley shuffled the gears till they slowed and wheeled onto the highway. The bus stop was there. The old cut-out water tank for shelter. Doreen's heart caught in her throat. The truck that hit Alf had careered off the road scoring the bitumen and shattering white posts. It was bound for the market loaded with local produce, mostly beans. There were beans strewn everywhere. A man on a tractor and another with a shovel cleared the drain of damaged trees and shrubs.

Ashley braked when they saw Reg and Digger's rig parked there. The two mates had stopped to help clean up the mess and help themselves to a selection of unspoilt fruits. Besides, Digger was as crook as a dog. He'd stumbled over Alf's discarded whisky bottle last night and found it half-full. The wiry veteran drank it all despite Reg's requests to 'save it till tomorra, cobber'. Digger was doubled over and dry retching when Ashley pulled up.

'Well, g'day folks,' Reg said, looking at them with a slightly bemused look on his fat face. He held his straw hat in his big hands. It was almost full of beans. He went solemn and said to Doreen, 'It's a bad thing, luv, can I do anything for you?'

'Thanks, Reg, no.' Doreen had to force her words. 'We'll be alright.'

Ashley got out of the truck and Sonny jumped out behind him. The men stood between the parked vehicles talking and pointing here and there while Sonny scouted about the edge of the road and watched the tractor working. Doreen sat in the truck and fought off the dull ache pulsing through her body. She'd forgotten about the bus stop. She went numb when she saw it and that stopped her from crying but her eyes were wet just the same.

Doreen looked through the windscreen at scruffy old Digger and big Reg talking to Ashley and she saw them as her only three friends on earth. She would miss them. At least she could wish them well and ask them to write. Doreen opened the door and stepped down onto the roadside just as Sonny ran up with some beans and plopped them into Reg's hat.

Reg and Digger stopped arguing over something when Doreen came and stood with them by the road in the bright sunshine. In a minute or two the bean pickers said their goodbyes once again while the boy gathered beans from the asphalt. Doreen hugged Reg and kissed Digger on the cheek and you'd think he'd won a medal the way he stuck his chest out. Big Reg ruffled Sonny's hair with a huge paw while he held his hat full of beans in the other.

'Well then, gun pickers, we'll be off then.'

Lance Corporal First Class Stanley J. Barnett, as sick as he was, took Sonny's hand, shook it and saluted the lad.

'Good job, mate. Keep ya head down, son.'

Just then a covered semitrailer hurtled around the bend and the driver blasted the air horns as he swept past them in a storm of whistling steel and metal. Everyone froze and watched the truck roar down the road like some terrible iron beast.

It was quiet then. No one spoke but it was plain enough. The harsh reality of last night had returned with the chill gust of wind from that semitrailer and the driver grinning like the devil himself.

Sonny stared at the beans crushed and broken on the black bitumen. Doreen, Ashley, Reg and Digger all looked at the road as if Alf's body was lying there right in front of them. Then Sonny dipped his hand into Reg's hat and brought out a handful of beans. He turned and flung them high above his head and they fell in a pitter patter to the road. Digger scooped up a handful of beans and stepped forward. He tossed the beans onto the road and with a nod intended for everyone, dragged himself to the van and got in. Reg grabbed a mighty handful and Ashley dipped his hand in. Doreen was left with the hat and she joined Ashley and Reg, standing between them by the road.

Sonny looked up into their faces and knew instantly something was happening. The boy snatched a handful of beans just in time to fling them high into the sky with his mother, Ashley and Reg.

There were fresh green beans all over the place. Anyone would think these people were crazy throwing perfectly good beans away but these were not ordinary beans. These were beans for Alf. Big Reg turned and winked at Sonny.

'Alright then,' he said and made his way to the van.

Ashley turned to Doreen. 'Are you alright, Doreen?'

Doreen did feel alright. She felt better as soon as he asked her.

'I'm OK, I'll be fine thank you, Ashley.' For the first time she looked fully into his face, at his unreal green eyes.

'I'm going north, Riverland country. Don't you come from up that way?'

'Yes we do, a few miles across the river.' Doreen felt a stab of home sickness.

'You ever picked oranges, Doreen?'

'Well, no ...'

'I could teach you, I mean, I could let you know if there's work for you there ... and Sonny too.'

Doreen didn't hesitate. 'That's really nice of you, Ashley. I don't know what to say ...'

'That's OK, Doreen.' Ashley flipped his stetson on. 'You don't have to say anything. It's alright.'

Ashley climbed in behind the wheel and Doreen settled beside Sonny. The boy was propped up on his swag to get a better view of the road ahead. Ashley started the truck and as the motor grunted and vibrated under their feet he turned to them.

'Let's hit the road, partners.'

Ashley flopped his hat on Sonny's curly head but the brim

fell down around his ears and they laughed as they headed down the black highway towards the jungle green ranges beyond. Into the vast evergreen canopy where the night mists cling to the mightiest eucalypts in deep, damp gullies that smell of earth and new life and ages gone by. Secretive places where still, pearly waters trickle over stony creekbeds in mossy silence.

But they'll be back. The bean pickers will return to work and sweat on the dark brown blood of that ancient forest. Every year they turn up. The fringe dwellers, the outsiders, the wild and the lost, with their hopes and dreams, their wants and needs. These simple things that are worth more, surely, than a handful of beans.

The Black Rabbit

G RANVILLE ROAD REACHES north from the highway. Gradually rising and falling as it cuts across the endless foothills off the Great Dividing Range. A thin treeline follows the road faithfully on both sides. Held in check by the inevitable, unmerciful barbed-wire fence.

Beyond the fences red cattle are grazing on distant green slopes of bald hills and everywhere mooing dairy cows troop slowly to the yards for the morning milking.

After six or seven miles of steep grades and cuttings Granville Road veers sharp right, plunging into a deep valley to cross the bridge on Stringybark Creek. On the first rise past the wooden bridge a weathered white signpost points left. Blue Gum Road – No Through Road. Tacked to the post a faded yellow sign reads – Caution School Bus Route.

Steady overnight showers had eased at dawn and sunlight filtered weakly through the cloud screen over Blue Gum Valley. Refreshed by the cool night rain, the leaves on the trees by the road hung heavy with moisture. Cleansed from the dust of passing farmers' cars, the slightest breeze carried the scent of eucalypt and peppermint across the open fields.

The heavy milk tanker did not raise any dust as it thundered over the narrow bridge on Granville Road.

If the driver had looked down at the creek he might have seen the boy standing by the water's edge. Eddy Marshall saw the truck and listened to it top the rise. He looked down at his reflection in the water. A skinny lad, fair of skin, with a mop of dark hair like his father's. Eddy squatted down in his gumboots and tugged on a fishing line he'd set there the night before. He tested it and it jerked in his hands.

'I got one, I got one Rip,' he said excitedly.

As if by magic a red dog appeared from the jumble of ferns and tangled grasses and pranced about at Eddy's feet.

'It's a big one Rip,' the boy said, dragging on the line. The eel hit the bank thrashing madly about while Ripper yipped and barked at it.

'Shut up Rip boy.'

Eddy managed to place one foot on the battling slimy creature and clubbed it with his waddy. That's what his mother called it. A 'waddy'.

Eddy followed the creek towards the timbered end of the valley. Picking his way easily through the gloomy tea-tree forests. Avoiding the barbs of wild blackberry brambles and mindful of the double-edged blades of sword grass slashing at his legs. Eddy knew the valley well. He had a map in his mind and knew where a cockatoo's nest was. He knew where all the rabbit burrows were and the best place to catch a ringtail possum. He discovered a wombat's secret hide-out and didn't tell anyone. He knew the place where the leeches waited to cling to your clothes and drink your blood. Eddy knew it all and it was as if it was his valley.

Eddy had to see what was over the next hill, the next ridge. Many times he'd say 'Mum I'm going for a walk,' and he'd be gone all day. Scrambling through the scrub to discover another creek, a mass of granite rocks or an abandoned timber mill. He'd be standing on a hill miles from home. The king of the mountains. A gypsy. A wanderer. The boy could feel but not explain the sense of freedom and belonging the land gave him. He knew he just had to be here.

'Get back Rip,' Eddy warned the dog as they neared the traps on the fence line. The trap had been sprung and Eddy reset the rusted steel jaws, covering it with grass. The second trap was undisturbed, but the third held a large rabbit, wide-eyed and terrified. Eddy swung his waddy and the rabbit stiffened and kicked for the last time.

Eddy thought he should be returning home. He dropped the rabbit into the potato sack with the eel and swung the weight over his shoulder. He'd just jumped the fence when he saw it. The black rabbit was sitting right by the fence along Blue Gum Road. It was watching Eddy and when Ripper darted up from the creek the black rabbit shot under the wire and vanished into the thick mesh of bracken and fallen branches. Ripper dashed after the rabbit but Eddy headed for home knowing the black rabbit would escape, like he always did. He's too clever for Ripper. He's too smart to be trapped.

~

Rose Marshall stood above a pink washbasin looking into a cracked mirror. She'd listened to rain for a long time last night. Little Rachel hadn't stirred all night. Rose missed Ted badly yet sometimes she was glad he was away for five days a week. Rose picked up a hairbrush and stroked the fine brown strands cascading down her back. She wished she'd had thick hair like Ted's. Ted loved her hair but it was her skin that took his fancy. Rose remembered when they first met in Fitzroy. They'd been going steady for three months before Ted met Thelma and the others. 'I thought you were a Maori,' Ted said and they both laughed.

He'd better not come home drunk in the water truck tomorrow night, thought Rose. It's pay day too. Rose put the brush down and fixed her hair into a bun. After a thoughtful gaze into the mirror she shook it loose and went into the kitchen. 'Any more milk Mum?' Timmy Marshall said from the table. Rose poured milk into his bowl.

'You wash your face and comb your hair Tim. You look like a baby bird just fell out the nest. School bus will be here soon.'

The screen door banged on the back porch and Eddy came in soaked from the waist down.

'Eddy, I was just going to sing out to you. What you got today?'

Eddy held the bag open as Rose and Tim peeked inside.

'Biggest eel I ever got,' Eddy said smiling.

'Mmm that's a beauty. Your dad will love that rabbit too.'

Rose dropped slices of bread into the toaster.

'I want to go with you next time bush rat,' Tim said, settling behind his breakfast once more.

'Ya won't wake up an' ya too slow an' ya keep tripping over,'

Eddy told his younger brother. 'And who said you can call me bush rat?'

'Don't start now you two. You'll wake Rachel up. Look now there's the school bus going past, eat up. You've only got ten minutes till he turns around.'

'More milk please Mum.'

'Timmy we'll have to get a cow just for you.'

The boys looked at each other grinning. Tim dipped his spoon saying, 'Geez Mum this stuff sucks up all the milk.' Rose ignored him, clearing the bench of toast crumbs and breakfast cereal.

'Get moving Eddy. Change into your school clothes and comb those sticks out of your hair boy. Timmy stop chewing your fingernails.'

~

Bob Owen hummed to himself as he swung the school bus around at the end of Blue Gum Road where it ended at the huge gates of the Lansdale Stud Farm. Bob pulled over to pick up young Phillip Lansdale. The boy barely nodded to Bob as he lumbered on board. A rather large lad, red-headed and full of the devil. As Bob guided the bus along the potholed road he glanced in the mirror at Phillip. Phillip flicked a boy's ear as he went up the aisle. He kicked someone's bag over and made nasty faces. Phillip Lansdale was an unbearable bully and Bob Owen could do little about it.

'That's enough of that Phillip,' Bob said as the bus rattled over a stretch of bone-shaking corrugations and stopped in the gravel in front of the Marshalls' place. Eddy and Tim Marshall ran to the school bus shouldering their school bags, Eddy tucking in his shirt as he stepped on board. Tim followed, chewing a mouthful of something, milk stains on his collar.

'Morning boys,' Bob said as the bus moved away along Blue Gum Road.

Tim sat with the smaller children near the driver, which was as far away from Phillip Lansdale as they could get. Eddy locked eyes with Phillip sitting on the back bench seat with his giggling buddy Gerry Carson. Eddy sat down with Jamie Trenton, the leading goal kicker in the school team. Eddy had befriended Jamie after the first school match, when Eddy was selected ruck rover. The two boys often talked about the weekend games in Melbourne and they did so now.

Phillip Lansdale meanwhile was making loud noises on an imaginary didgeridoo, much to the delight of his tow-headed mate who clapped and laughed. Eddy was ignoring it but Jamie stopped talking and didn't seem interested any more. The Eggleston twins, known as the Stickynose Sisters, turned in their seat to stare at Eddy, obviously enjoying this game and other Abo things that Phillip tormented him with since that day Eddy was summoned to the headmaster's office. Eddy looked through the window at the fields rolling by and remembered the crackle of the loudspeaker booming out over the yard.

'Edward and Timothy Marshall report to the Aboriginal Education Officer in the headmaster's office.'

The Marshalls' contact with the Aboriginal agent was brief. The man seemed surprised as if he were expecting someone else, and he looked across at the secretary who nodded her head in confirmation. Afterwards when Eddy entered the classroom he noticed everyone staring at him, taking a good look. And later on the oval a boy said, 'If you're an Abo how come you haven't got a flat nose?' Others shouted 'Hey Eddy where's your boomerang?' After a week or so most of the schoolyard kids forgot that Eddy was a blackfella and didn't care if he was or not. But the visit from the agent had made it official, Eddy Marshall and his brother Tim were Aborigines and that was that. Besides, the loudspeaker let everybody for miles know about it. Phillip Lansdale would not forget it. Eddy glanced at the white skin of his knees as the bus rolled along the highway. He looked at his pale arms and tried to make sense of all this black and white stuff. Eddy pictured his mother. He could see her brown arms as she hung the washing on the line. The colourful teatowels with drawings of boomerangs and spears on them. She loved all the wildflowers but would rather Eddy picked her fresh gum tips to put in the big vase so the smell would fill the house.

There were those old photos in the biscuit tin, photographs

of old black people and old black cars. A torn picture of a group of little black girls in a swimming hole. One of them is Rose. Didn't Dad yell at him and Tim one night, 'You boys are lucky to have a home. Your Mum was born in a bark hut.' These thoughts went through Eddy's mind as the bus glided past the shop windows in town. Eddy knew his mother was black. Had always known in his way. He'd never given it much thought because it was never a problem. Not until recently anyway. Eddy's world had changed since that day in the headmaster's office. He felt different too, but why did it feel so wrong?

The bottle green bus rumbled through the schoolyard gates and children picked up their bags chattering and jostling as they streamed out onto the asphalt. The Stickynose Sisters showed off their new hockey sticks and a group of rowdy boys kicked a football. A blond-haired boy drew a circle of admirers with a new trick on his yo-yo and Gino Costello stepped off the bus bouncing his soccer ball. Phillip Lansdale snatched the ball from Gino and tossed it to Gerry.

'We don't play that silly game here golliwog,' Phillip said with a curled lip.

Gino went towards Gerry who threw the ball back to Phillip. Eddy watched from the shelter shed as little Gino went back and forth between his tormenters. Finally Gino flung himself at Gerry. Gerry quickly sidestepped and flicked the ball to Phillip as Gino crashed to the ground. Gino sat up frustrated to tears, beating his fists on the asphalt. The bell rang and as everyone walked away Phillip stood over the olive skin boy and dropped the ball on his head.

'There's your ball chocolate frog.'

Eddy made his way down the corridor to the classroom. If he learnt anything that day it was the fact that it doesn't pay to be different. Not to the likes of Phillip Lansdale.

～

The Marshall brothers jumped off the bus on Friday afternoon and raced each other to the back door, laughing as they tumbled into the kitchen. The boys pulled up quick smart when they saw a large black woman sitting at the table with a cup of tea. Before the boys could speak or move out of the way she was upon them squeezing and kissing the both of them at once.

'Boys this is my stepmother Thelma,' Rose said as she poured tea into Thelma's cup. 'Youse can call her Granny. She's going to stay with us for a while.'

'Well glory be, look at my deadly little boys,' Thelma said, stepping back to admire the red-faced youngsters.

Tim stood struck dumb and embarrassed. He still gripped his schoolbag and wiped away Thelma's kisses with his sleeve. Eddy was feeling the blood rush to his head like it did when he hung upside down on the swings. Was this huge grey-haired black woman with thick lips and bandy legs related to him somehow? She was black alright, the real thing. She was the truth smiling at him with moist brown eyes.

'Have another cuppa Thel,' Rose said. 'You boys get changed and cut some kindling for tomorrow.'

'By jingoes Eddy look just like his daddy, don't he Rosie,' Thelma said lowering her bulk on the chair. 'And my little Rachel, what you doing baby girl?'

Rachel played on the floor surrounded by pots and pans she'd pulled from the cupboard. Rose had fixed her fair hair into pigtails and her doll-like blue eyes peeped from behind her fringe. At the mention of her name she scuttled across the floor on hands and knees and clung to her mother's knee.

'She'll be walking real good soon Rosie,' said Thelma as the sounds of a heavy vehicle travelling up the road sent the boys scampering outside to greet their father.

Ted Marshall stepped down from the cabin in faded blue overalls stained with splashes of black bitumen from the new highway. The end of a long week on the roadworks, his body ached from sleeping in a rough bunk at the work camp. Not to mention the late nights playing cards and yarning with the gang. This fortnightly pay business is a bit rough but it's good money when it comes and about time too. A man could die of thirst working ninety miles from the nearest pub. Ted forgot his weariness when the boys ran into the yard.

'Hey how's my star footballers?' he said balancing a box of beer, lemonade and chips. 'How are you bush rat? What? Who? Will youse stop talking at once? Ripper will you shut up for Christsake?'

As Ted kicked off his work boots on the verandah Tim tugged on his father's sleeve, whispering 'Dad Thelma's inside and she's real black.' Ted's dusty face broke into a smile.

'You don't say, Ol' Thelma. She'll be good company for your Mum.'

The boys had never been so quiet at teatime. Eddy listened to the talk between Thelma and his parents, soaking up bits of information and storing it away to sort it out later when he had time to think. Right now Eddy just wanted to be near this fascinating old woman. Drawn by her warmth and dark mystery, Eddy sat mesmerised as Thelma waved her rough black hands about as she laughed and talked old times with Ted and Rose. Rachel was content to sit on Thelma's lap with her milk bottle till she fell asleep to Thelma's gentle rocking.

Later, in their beds, Eddy and Tim read comic books by a bedside lamp. The muffled sounds of talking and laughter drifted from the lounge. The snap and hiss of another bottle top falling victim to Ted's bottle opener. Presently, Thelma hobbled into the boys' room, scuffing her blue slippers with each careful step.

'Where's my babies?' She stood hovering between the boys. 'Eddy, I seen you when you was just a little one. Just a little skun rabbit you was.'

Timmy took a finger out of his mouth. 'Can you talk like a wild blackfella Granny?'

'Well jingoes, let me think now.' Thelma slowly settled on the edge of Eddy's bed. She sucked in a breath and began.

Oh Jacky Jacky was a very smart fellow.
Full of fun and energy.
He thought of getting married.
But the girl ran away you see.

Then Thelma sung a verse in a language unknown to the ears

of the young boys. Eddy lay back on his pillow gazing at Thelma in sleepy amazement as the words bubbled from her lips. The old woman stamped her feet lightly on the floor, clapping gently as she sang. Eddy saw a shine in her eyes in the half light and he knew she was smiling and looking away into the dark somewhere. Tim had listened quietly to Thelma while he demolished another fingernail and when Thelma had done singing he said, 'Gino Costello talks like that when he's mad.'

'Aw, he's from Italy,' said Eddy, annoyed by Tim's ignorance.

'Well now, time to sleep my little lambs,' said Thelma raising her bulk from the mattress. 'Don't forget to say your prayers.'

'What prayers Granny?' Tim said.

'What's this? By jingoes you poor little fellas don't even know one blessed prayer?'

The boys shook their heads dumbly.

'Glory be,' Thelma muttered to herself as she went to open the door. 'Fancy that, don't know no prayers.' She turned in the doorway. 'I'll have to teach you two the Lord's Prayer before I go back to Melbourne. You believe in Jesus Christ don't you boys?'

'Yeah, I do Gran,' Eddy said wanting to please her more than anything.

'Me too Granny,' said Tim slipping further under the covers as Thelma loomed above him. 'And Dad believes in Jesus Christ too Granny,' he said from under the blankets.

'Ha, Ted Marshall? That'll be the day,' chuckled Thelma.

'He does Gran,' Tim flipped the covers from his face and looked to Eddy for support. 'You know Eddy. Dad always tells Ripper to shut up for Christsakes.'

～

A cool spring morning revealed streaks of pink cloud on the horizon over Blue Gum Valley. A duck egg moon hung low in the west, fading as it dipped beyond the black ranges. Somewhere on the frosted hills a bull roared. His frustrated bellowing echoed throughout the valley Eddy Marshall loved to roam.

A kookaburra chuckled to himself as the boy and his dog

tracked through the long damp grass by the creek. Eddy was in good spirits. He had two grey rabbits in the bag and a small fish. A blackfish. Timmy will be jealous. Granny Thelma will say *By jingoes.*

Ripper bounded ahead, disappearing into the tangled scrub along the creek. He reappeared on the opposite bank, panting, the bottom half of him a layer of mud. The bush felt good to Eddy. The crooked trees, the creeks, the lonely timbered ridges draped in morning sun and shadows. The quiet magnificence of the rugged blue ranges drew Eddy like a magical charm and he sang as he made his way home. He sang snatches of songs he'd heard on the wireless and he didn't care if he scared the rabbits away or frightened the mobs of grey kangaroos from their breakfast on the green velvet slopes. The bush seemed to lay back in welcome to the boy and it had something to do with Granny Thelma.

Eddy couldn't remember all the stories she'd told him and Timmy. Why the magpie is black and white. How the echidna got his spikes. Granny Thelma told them of warriors and desert tribes, about spirits and the dreaded featherfoot man. Granny knew fantastic things and she knew a lot about Jesus too. Eddy and Tim could say the Lord's Prayer right through by now and what was the other one? *Gentle Jesus meek and mild look upon a little child . . .*

Eddy stopped in his tracks. He'd been tramping among dead limbs and tree trunks when the black rabbit ran across his path. Eddy froze and the rabbit stopped to nibble a blade of grass. Eddy stood still, bearing the weight of the bag on his shoulders, while Ripper rummaged about in the undergrowth, a mere stone throw away. Eddy stared. He'd never been this close to the black rabbit before. It lifted its head and shifted. Eddy admired the animal's ashen coat as the rabbit sniffed suspiciously and cocked an ear. Then it sat upright with both ears extended and looked straight at Eddy.

Ripper finally broke through the scrub a little way down the track and turned to see Eddy and the black rabbit. The dog bore down on the rabbit while it sat on its haunches just a dropkick away from the boy. The black rabbit merely sat there in the morning sun as Ripper pounced, and Eddy thought, 'We've got you now.' But the black rabbit simply vanished into the ground. A burrow entrance, hidden under grass by a pile of burnt logs, was where the black rabbit made his escape. Eddy Marshall marked the spot on his map as he trudged home.

Friday afternoons were usually rowdy on the school bus. Once, Bob slowed down to tell Phillip Lansdale to stop pulling Margaret's pigtails and please give Ricky's pocket knife back to him. Eddy and Jamie discussed today's inter-school match. Eddy had played well. Two good goals and high marks like Jezalinko. Eddy couldn't wait to tell everyone at home. Tell Mum, Dad and Granny too about Tim and the Stickynose Sisters in the yard this morning.

Tim was retrieving a stray basketball when the Stickynose twins and two other girls approached him. Pauline Stickynose said, 'Hey Timmy what did you have for tea last night? Snakes?' The girls squeaked and giggled while Tim stood looking at them in innocent bewilderment. Seeing no response from the boy Maxine Stickynose said, 'Are you a dirty little Abo, Timmy?' The girls went into fits of laughter but Tim merely blinked at them and suddenly blurted out, 'I am made in God's image.' This was true because Granny had said so. Doesn't matter what colour your skin is.

The girls seemed shocked by this revelation because they straightened up considerably and held their tongues. Tim knew then that he'd said something terrific, so he added, 'And so are you, for Christsakes, Amen!' Tim ran off with the ball and the girls stood there biting their lips.

At last the school bus squeaked to a stop in front of the Marshall place. Eddy and Tim stepped down onto the gravel and as the bus drew away Phillip Lansdale popped his strawberry red head from the window and shouted, 'Hey you two Abos don't forget to corroboree tonight. Ha ha ha ha.'

The Marshall brothers stuck their fingers up in reply and headed up the drive where they saw a black car parked by the shed. As the boys rounded the corner they almost ran into the man. A tall man they recognised as Stretch, one of their father's work mates.

'G'day fellas,' he said towering over them. He scratched an ear and ran his fingers through his silver hair before he said, 'Yer lil sister got a bit crook t'day.' He scratched his other ear and said 'She's OK, no worries. Teddy asked me to stay with yers till they git back from the hosp ... I mean doctors, so.'

'Is Granny here?' asked Eddy.

'No son, she went too.'

Tim followed Stretch into the house while Eddy went to let Ripper off the chain. Stretch turned and called, 'Hey Eddy, your dad said you'd make us a beaut fire after tea.'

By eleven o'clock the logs had burned to coals glowing low in the grate. Tim slept in an armchair with a finger in his mouth. Eddy lay on the couch looking blankly at the flickering television screen. In the kitchen Stretch flipped the pages of a newspaper and poured himself glasses of beer. A sudden flash of light lit up the lounge room and a car motored up to the house in the darkness outside.

It was some minutes before Eddy heard the car door slam, the squeaky screen door and the slow drum of his father's workboots on the verandah. Eddy looked at Tim who hadn't woken and listened to Ted and Stretch in the kitchen.

'Gawd almighty, Teddy. Here, have a drink mate, yer look like yer need it.'

'Bloody oath I do. Ta mate.' Ted's voice came low and strained to Eddy's ears. 'Aw, strike a light Stretch, she was as good as gold one minute and then ...'

'You'll be right mate,' Stretch said and glasses clinked and more beer was poured. 'That's the way it goes Ted. Yer know that cobber.'

After a minute Ted said wearily, 'You're right there mate. That's for sure. Listen Stretch, thanks for takin' care of ...'

'No trouble mate. I left them sleeping in the lounge there. Don't worry Teddy, I'll look after the dog an' you git yerself some shut eye for gawd's sake.'

Eddy listened to Stretch make his way outside and start his

car under an enormous spread of crystal stars over Blue Gum Valley. While the roar of Stretch's car faded in the distance Eddy sat and waited.

Presently Ted came in and sank back on an armchair. He looked at Tim and for a moment at Eddy. Eddy had never seen his father cry before. Ted leant forward with his hands over his face.

'Eddy,' he said, 'my big boy Edward.'

Eddy had heard enough of what the men had said in the kitchen to be alarmed. Something was wrong and it scared Eddy to see his father this way.

'Eddy, little Rachel got sick today, real sick, and they took her to the hospital, Eddy, but she ...'

Eddy, realising what his father was about to say felt his heart swell and the first tears ran down his face as his father said, 'We lost her Eddy. We lost little Rachel.'

Eddy's heart thundered. In a blur of tears he heard Ted's voice, as if from a great distance, telling him 'Take your brother to bed. Going to Melbourne in the morning. See Mum. You're a good boy Eddy. A good boy.'

~

The Marshall family had been at Aunty Ruby's for three days and each day Eddy woke to the drone of traffic on the streets. At the foot of the bed Tim slept with his mouth full of fingers and more than his share of blankets. Eddy was cold and his little brother's big toe had dug into his ribs all night.

Across the room, Aunty Ruby's boys, Wally and James, slept somewhere beneath a mound of covers. Aunty Ruby was a huge woman with a stern face which easily broke into laughter. Eddy took a liking to Uncle Punchy. He was funny and happy-go-lucky. When he came back from the pub last night with Ted he bounced around, shadow boxing, saying 'Look 'ere Eddy. I'll show ya how to knuckle up budda! Like this 'ere see.'

Punchy was light on his feet and Eddy admired his cocky style but Aunty Ruby held considerable power over her featherweight husband. Eddy saw it yesterday when she bopped Punchy on the head with the saucepan and told him to 'stop showin' off ya silly black fool'.

From his lumpy bed, Eddy heard the chatter of sparrows in the cobbled lanes. Pigeons fanned their wings and gathered on the factory roof next door. Soon the shriek of the whistle would scatter the birds as the foundries and mills fired up for the long grind.

Someone was moving about in the kitchen. It was Ted boiling the kettle on the bandy-legged stove. A cup of tea was all Rose would drink. She stayed in the room most of the time. When she did come out she'd hold her boys tight and cry till her tears soaked Eddy's collar.

Granny Thelma will arrive around ten o'clock and talk Rose into another cup of tea on the porch. Good old Granny Thelma. She was as talkative as ever and Eddy and Tim had to say the Lord's Prayer for her last night.

The street noises grew louder behind the heavy blinds as Eddy untangled himself from Tim's spidery arms and legs. Eddy had slept in his clothes and had only to tie his shoelaces and walk down the hall to the front door.

The trams fascinated Eddy. They trundled up and down busy Smith Street, just around the corner from Aunty Ruby's. The morning sun warmed Eddy as he stood by the butcher shop watching the massive steel wheels rumble by on the rails. Car horns blared and tram bells clanged. A fat man wearing an apron yelled 'hep banana, hep banana' and the smell of fresh fruit drifted onto the streets. Eddy threaded his way through crowds of little women in black robes, chattering and waving string bags. Passing the fish and chip shop, Eddy saw a dark man, with what looked like a dishcloth wrapped around his head, laying out strange-looking fish behind the glass. Eddy wandered past the bank, the real estate office and the little hunchback man's boot repair shop. Next, the milk bar with Tarax lemonade painted on the window. Eddy stopped by the espresso bar on the corner of Smith and Johnston streets. This was as far as he would go. Ted had warned him not to get lost.

'This isn't the bush Eddy. Lotta ratbags and no-hopers around, you hear me?'

Eddy stepped into the shaded doorway of the espresso bar. In the dim interior Eddy could make out a man wiping a bench and a group of men huddled around a table in the corner. The smell of rich coffee stung Eddy's nose and the twang of foreign music within spilled out into the hum of traffic and pedestrians.

Eddy took in all the hustle and bustle as traffic lights swapped colours and yet another overcrowded tram clamoured across the intersection. An ambulance appeared, wailing as it wove a path between the traffic and dashed by Eddy on the corner. A sickening feeling overtook young Eddy as the lights flashed across his face. The urgency in the siren's high-pitched screams, the paralysing howl of anguish, chilled Eddy and he thought of Rachel. Her funeral tomorrow. Smith Street suddenly turned cold. Eddy turned back down the hill, seeing only the cracks in the pavement and the feet of people passing by.

People stared and bumped into him more than once. The traffic snarled at him and the tram wheels threatened to jump the tracks and crush the life out of the boy. Eddy ran back to Aunty Ruby's.

At six o'clock it was settled. Thelma would mind James while the rest went to the pub.

'Just have a sip Rose,' Ted pleaded with his wife at the kitchen table. 'Get out for a spell. Do you good love.'

'Come on tidda girl,' said Ruby picking up her coat. 'The tram's comin' directly.'

Punchy shone his brand new point-toed shoes on the back steps.

'I can run faster to the pub than that friggin' ol' tram.'

'You will if ya don't hurry up Punch,' replied Ruby as she led the way down the narrow hall.

The three youngsters, Eddy, Tim and Wally, raced ahead of the others along the darkening street. Rose walked slowly between Ted and Ruby. Each had an arm around Rose as they passed the row of tiny terrace houses and the cracked stone wall of the steel mill.

The boys waited at the tram stop for the others to catch up.

The yellow eye of the tram grew larger in the fading light and Eddy looked back anxiously for Ted, Rose and Ruby, who were almost there. But behind them in the distance Eddy saw Uncle Punchy run around the corner and fall flat on his back. He was picking himself up when the tram, fringed with bright lights, glided to a halt and they boarded. It was warm inside. Eddy noticed a few people sitting at the far end. The bell rang and there was a jolt as they pulled away and a little black stick of a man came up to sell tickets. Wally sat quietly with the elders. Eddy and Tim stood up to see out of the windows. Eddy had forgotten about Uncle Punchy and looked back to see him dash by the butcher shop where he crashed to the pavement once more. Eddy pushed his face to the glass to see Punchy resuming the chase but he lost his footing yet again and Eddy lost sight of him.

'Serve 'im right,' Aunty Ruby said in answer to Eddy's concerned look. 'Big shot reckon he can beat the tram,' she said smiling. 'Well let's see then.'

The table wobbled. It was littered with peanuts and potato chips. A score of empty beer glasses, some not so empty and a brass ashtray the shape of a kangaroo spilled over with dead matches and cigarette butts.

'You said we were going soon Dad,' pleaded Tim, pulling on Ted's sleeve as another deafening roar erupted from the bar. Ted ignored his youngest son.

'No worries mate, good to see ya,' he was saying to an old black man among a crowd of people gathered round them in the smoky lounge. Tim shrugged and braced himself for yet another onslaught of beery kisses from strange black aunties and handshakes from men with names like Darky, Charcoal, Nulla and Mookeye. People stumbled in from the bar saying 'Rose, Harry just told me you was here.'

'Is that you Ted Marshall? Gawd strike me pink. Sissy get us a jug for me an ol' mate 'ere.'

'Mum, I wanna go home now.'

'No, I can't go back there Aunty Ruby,' Rose sobbed. 'I just can't go back to that house now.'

She broke into tears and slumped on the table. The women cried too and patted her back and stroked her long hair with their black hands.

'Dad can we go now? Can we?'

Eddy too was tired. He looked down at Wally asleep on the scarlet carpet between the legs of Ruby's chair.

'We're goin' in a minute,' Ted grumbled in his seat next to Rose.

Eddy could see people dancing by the jukebox in the bar . . . *let's twist again, like we did last summer. Let's twist again, like we did last year . . .*

Uncle Punchy was there twisting in his bare feet. His flash new shoes were just too slippery. When the record ended they cheered and laughed at each other while all the time a man and woman argued violently nearby.

Ringo Starr had just begun . . . *Well how come you say you will when you won't? . . .* when a loud smash caught everyone's attention and all looked toward the bar. A woman screamed and there were grunts and thuds, then a bar stool skidded across the beer-stained floor. People shuffled out of the way. They backed up into the lounge blocking Eddy's view.

Tim sat up straight and gripped Ted's sleeve; Wally slept peacefully.

'Kill the white dogs,' a woman screamed and Eddy slid from his seat to press his way through the crowd in the doorway but a hand was suddenly placed on Eddy's shoulder and a kind voice said, 'You don't wanna go out there budda.'

The strong hand turned Eddy round but Eddy had time to see the men on the floor. One with reddish hair and redder blood running from his nose and his mouth. He saw Uncle Punchy standing over them. His face hateful and bloodied. The big man Jock guided Eddy back to the table then a firm voice roared from the bar.

'That's it, that's it, I'm ringing the pleece, piss off ya bastards.' . . . *ah rock on George one time for me . . .*

Eddy Marshall yawned and tugged on the blankets. He rolled on one side to avoid his little brother's smelly toes. The drawn blinds flapped lightly on the window frame and after a while the muffled rumble of late night traffic died down and a steady drizzle fell on the city.

Eddy lay staring at the wall. They were still in the kitchen. Their voices grew louder and drifted down the hall. Ted, Aunty Ruby and Granny Thelma's soft tones.

'I can't go tomorrow Thel. I just can't.'

'Never mind Rose. You'll be right. We'll all be with you.'

A train tooted, scurrying into the night, and Eddy heard his mother crying and tried to picture the rainy streets. Deserted, silent and shadowy. Lonely it would be but for the winking traffic lights, splashing red, amber and green like wet paint across the tram tracks and shop front windows.

Where are all the people he'd met at the pub tonight? All the black relations who offered him and Tim lemonade and potato chips and a game of hooky. Everyone came from different places like Cumeragunga, Condah and Lake Tyers. Uncle Punchy left for a place called Framlingham to lay low for a while. Aunty Ruby packed his bag and told him 'Hit the road Punchy, friggin' troublemaker. You make me shame boy, screaming at the tram conductor like that. An' he's not a black Jap, he's a Pakistani.' Uncle Punchy is a wild man. He said he don't like cheeky gubbas. He must mean people like Phillip Lansdale.

Young Eddy Marshall, on the verge of sleep, wondered what all the black people were doing now. Did they miss their homes too? Maybe they came to Melbourne for a funeral like us and they never went home. Eddy fell into a deep sleep. The kind of sleep he'd have after a long walk in Blue Gum Valley. The boy was there now, standing in the long wet grass by Stringybark Creek. He was staring at the black rabbit sitting on his haunches in the sunlight streaming through the trees. The rabbit looked at Eddy and the last thing Eddy wanted was to harm that animal. It was black. It was different. It was clever. It had to be because it was black. 'No Ripper No.' Run away black rabbit. Run away from the dogs and the traps and the bullets. Stay away from the Lansdales. Stay home black rabbit.

Bob Owen was sweating behind the big windscreen. He steered

the bus down Granville Road thanking God it was the last day of school this year. Bob remembered why his head was aching. Phillip Lansdale was shouting and being a general pain in the arse and Bob wondered if he could stand another half hour or so. The bus swung around the corner on Blue Gum Road and as they passed the Marshalls' abandoned home Master Phillip screamed 'The Abos went to a big corroboree ha ha ha ha.' His chubby face grew pink with the effort he put into his laughter. A few children giggled half-heartedly as they bumped along Blue Gum Road towards Lansdale Stud Farm. Bob slowed as he approached and Phillip made his way down the aisle with his schoolbag over his beefy shoulders. Suddenly, what Bob at first thought was a cat darted under the wheels and Bob tapped his foot on the brakes. The bus jolted slightly and Phillip Lansdale crashed to the floor and slid head first to the front of the bus.

Bob parked by the Lansdales' gates and waited for Phillip to gather himself from the pile of bags, books, papers and pencils. The other children, who were squealing with laughter a moment ago were now silent.

'Are you alright son?' Bob had to ask but was having difficulty hiding his great joy at this memorable moment. Phillip was obviously flustered. He ignored Bob and stood rubbing his forehead. Then he puffed himself up and shook a hammy fist at the kids.

'I'll get youse. See if I don't.'

Phillip glanced wildly at Bob and stomped off the bus. As soon as Bob pulled away the kids rushed the windows, cheeking and jeering Phillip Lansdale for all they were worth. They knew he was going to high school next year and that is a different bus.

Bob Owen felt better as he drove back down Blue Gum Road. He laughed out loud once to think of Phillip tipping arse up and all because a rabbit ran onto the road. A black rabbit too!

What a wonderful world, thought Bob. He hummed to himself and the children sang as they roared past the Marshalls' empty house and only Jamie Trenton looked back at the house disappearing in a whirlwind of brown dust.

Johnny Cake Days

I HITCHHIKED DOWN the Princes Highway and walked along the back road that leads to the mission. It's a lonely road and you don't often get a ride so I jumped the barbed-wire fence and cut across the paddocks. I came at last to the riverbank and looked across at the mission on the other side. Granny Alice's house is a little wooden one with a red tin roof and I can make out the toilet and chookshed, the bungalow and wrecked car by the woodheap. I cross the river at the place we set the eel net. You can make your way across the stones if the water is not too high. I follow the cow tracks between the scrubby bracken and ferns, past the boxthorn bushes and into Granny's back yard. Aunty Faye is hanging out a long line of clothes.

'Ah Johnny boy, back already?' she says with a peg between her teeth.

Dogs and cats are gathered at the back door as well as chooks and ducks, all waiting for a chance to get inside. I slip smartly in, shut the door and there's a rooster on the table, a cat on the chair and two pups asleep at the foot of the big wood stove. The kitchen is warm and smells like there's a damper in the oven. Granny's in the front room by the fire with a cup of tea. My cousin Mouse and the kids are watching television as I settle down by the fire with Granny and we yarn for a while.

A lot can happen on the mission in a short time. Uncle Donny went mad with the chainsaw again. Speedy is on the booze in town somewhere. Charlie's locked up for fighting coppers and some racist idiots have been driving down the mission shouting out 'Dirty Abos' and shit like that. Aunty Faye came in with some school clothes to dry by the fire when the dogs started fighting in the kitchen. Mouse jumps up and Aunty Faye grabs the broom and together with a lot of swearing and cursing they hunt all the animals outside.

I cut wood till dark and looked at the stars for a while. Granny told me the stars are the campfires of our ancestors. Our ancestors must look down on the lights of the mission and wonder how it came down to this. Once the proud owners of this country, now a few thousand acres to call home. The moon is up now. Somewhere a dog is barking and I can hear the Hopkins River rumbling over the falls as it winds its way to the sea.

I woke up in the rusty red and yellow bus-bungalow and heard the magpies yodelling in the wattles outside. The sound of a car approaching, bumping along the wet mission road draws a mob of dogs out to greet it, yelping and playfully biting the tyres. A horn toots and voices. It's Aunty Violet. She wants to know if we want some tea or sugar from the store about four miles up the road. Someone calls out 'Book it up till Pension Day.' The car pulls away amid a chorus of barking dogs and then all is quiet except for old Billy, the goat, who calls out between mouthfuls of Granny's creeping roses. On my way into the house I pick up a handful of bark and sticks to light the stove. Granny is out in the back yard scattering bread and grain to a sea of squabbling hens, roosters, ducks, drakes and two white geese hissing and honking.

Inside, little David, Bernadette and Conny are eating porridge while Aunty Faye fixes their school lunches. She threatens to flog little David if he doesn't hurry up and get dressed. This is the story on most mornings, as little David likes to push his luck and stretch Aunty Faye's patience till finally she snatches the broom and rushes after him as he bolts out the door and down the road. Aunty Faye stops breathless and laughs, he's already halfway to school clutching his tomato sauce sandwiches.

I had grilled eel and damper for breakfast and I made a cup of tea for cousin Mouse. Mouse is still in bed breastfeeding her twins Ivy and Heather. They look up at me wide-eyed and blinking like baby mopokes. These two little darlings played up last night and Mouse is red-eyed and worn out. In comes Aunty Faye, 'Come on Mousie, help me clean up this place.' Mouse mumbles something about 'in a minute', as Aunty Faye collects Ivy and Heather and sets them down in the front room where they play in the sunlight streaming in through the windows.

Aunty Faye is mopping the floor now, humming along with Hank Williams on the radio. *Hey good lookin', what you got cookin', how's about cooking something up with me.*

Granny comes in the kitchen with some eggs wrapped up in her cardigan and I tell her I'm going shooting.

'I'll take the dogs for a run, Gran,' I say.

'Take the useless rotters and throw 'em in the river.' Granny is wild with the dogs because a fox has been snatching the chickens.

I felt for the rifle under Granny's mattress and pulled out an old .22 bolt action. That's where we hide the gun away from drunks – under the mattress. The bolt for the rifle was put in another safe place and nobody knew where. It took me some time to find it inside an empty jam tin along with six bullets and a pocket knife that needs a sharpen. I ask Aunty Faye, 'You know where the file is?' She's peeling potatoes at the sink and says, 'The kids had it last.' When you hear that the kids have had something last, you know that thing is lost forever.

Take these chains from my heart and set me free.

Granny stared hard through the window (she doesn't see too well nowadays). Old Billy the goat was chewing up Gran's white daisies. Old Billy has fiendish yellow eyes, a twisted pair of horns and with his long whiskers he roams about the mission butting the kids and smelling awful. I have seen him lift his leg and drink his own piss. Old Billy is under the kitchen window chomping away on white marguerites when he looks up and puts his evil eye on Granny. Granny screws her face up. 'I'll kill that mangy old bastard,' she says as she shuffles outside. 'Fetch the broom Faye.'

I slung the rifle over my shoulder and stepped out into the back yard. When the dogs see the gun they get excited, jumping up and down, carrying on like two-bob watches. The rifle is unreliable as it sometimes misfires so I take a posthole shovel to dig the 'bad habits' from their burrows. The dogs and I make tracks through the chook shit and pass by the front garden where Granny and Aunty Faye have exhausted themselves trying to chase the goat away with sticks and stones. Even the sharp end of the broom doesn't deter him. The women are flustered. They really don't want to harm old Billy, it's just that he's so wooden-headed. I said I'd be back by dark and left them there swearing, throwing buckets of water on Billy as he started in on the sweet peas.

Uncle Percy lives just a stone's throw along the road from Granny.

His little weatherboard house is painted blue and surrounded by leafy trees and garden. The dogs follow me through the gate, which is really a rusty old bed-end, past the woodpile and round to the back door where I leave the shovel and step inside.

'You home, Uncle?' I call and blink my eyes in the cool darkness of the hallway.

'Who's that there?' I hear him ask.

'Just me, Uncle Percy,' I call coming into the kitchen. Uncle Percy is propped in front of the stove toasting a thick slab of bread on the end of a long wire fork. The embers glow brightly in the dimness. A little ginger cat is coiled on Uncle Percy's shoulder, purring loudly into his ear. Uncle Percy is a true gentleman who hasn't changed much over the years, although he is a little greyer and thinner lately. He still favours dark pinstripe suits and hats. When he's dressed up and smoking his cherry wood pipe at the races he looks as flash as a rat with a gold tooth.

'Hot water in the kettle if you want a cup of tea, Jack,' he says.

Uncle Percy calls everyone Jack. So I stood the rifle in the corner and pulled a chair up close to the heat of the old black stove. We drank tea and talked about racehorses and bad luck while the Turf Talk Show babbled on over the radio. The warmth and familiar feel of this old place sets me thinking of when I was a little boy running about with my cousins when they lived here. It was a house full of people then but they moved to a Commission house in town. There were lots of people on the mission then and always something happening. I could go to anyone's house and be cared for.

'You Rita's boy?' someone might ask and that's all they'd need to know.

I remember small dim houses in candlelight. Mysterious black uncles and aunties telling ghost stories around the fireplace. 'So you kids don't go down the bridge or the headless man will get youse.' Drunks mad on red wine. 'Now stay away from Uncle Norman, he'll fall on yas.'

Things aren't the same on the mission. The magic of this haunted old place is gone, gone with the old people back to the Dreaming. Uncle Percy shifts in his chair and turns a page of his newspaper. The cat purrs on. A plum tree scratches at the window and the ticking of the clock on the mantelpiece winds my mind back again.

We kids would make sleds from sheets of corrugated iron and slide down the steep riverbanks, crashing through the tall bracken. Spotlighting was fun. We'd all race to be the first to stun the rabbits with our waddies. Spearing eels at the bottom of the falls in daylight or at night with a torch was always a good time. There were only about twenty of us kids went to our one-room schoolhouse. The teacher lived next door to the school and he would put on a do for Christmas. I remember someone playing guitar while he played bass on a piece of string tied to a broom stick and a wooden tea chest turned upside down. He'd thump away on it singing *King of the Road* and *Kingston Town*.

Only five or six kids go to the mission school now. They say they're going to close it down seeing as the weatherboards are falling off and the windows are broken. The little green shelter shed under the pines is falling down. We'd play kick the tin in the shelter shed where you could peep through the cracks and see where the other kids were hiding. Now there's more weeds and thistles than boys and girls in the playground and I wonder where all my cousins have gone.

I am roused from my daydreams by the loud snapping and snarling of the dogs outside. Uncle Percy is marking down the scratchings on his racing guide. 'What the bloody hell's going on, Jack?' The cat arched his back, spat and leapt to the floor, leaving a patch of orange fur on Uncle Percy's antique coat.

'It's them silly dogs. I'll round 'em up and get going,' I said, taking up the rifle. 'I'll save a rabbit for you, Uncle Percy.'

No doubt Uncle Percy will get a ride to town soon, park

himself at the bar and bet on horses. He is a keen punter and when he backs a winner he's as happy as a witchetty grub in a wooden leg.

'Watch out for snakes, Jack,' he says but I can hardly hear him for another violent outburst at the back door.

Sure enough, it's a dogfight. My motley crew have Uncle Percy's red kelpie bailed up in a corner. One of my hunters, Woofy, a big bandy-legged mongrel has the kelpie by the throat. I fear the eyes of the red dog will pop out as he howls in pain and fear. The rest of the pack snap at him mercilessly. The riot stops the instant I appear with the gun. As if struck by a magic wand the mangy mob turns and follows me out into the road.

The thin blue metal road twists around and down to the bridge spanning the river. Cypress trees line one side of the road and from the odd patches of boxthorn I hear the chattering of willy-wagtails and wrens. The dogs string out ahead of me. Dark woollen clouds, drifting in from the south-west are slowly breaking up and huge rays of sunshine seep through the cracks to sweep across the land like big friendly laser beams. Winter is almost over and the magpies will soon be collecting twigs for their nests and sharpening their beaks on branches high in the gum trees. The gold will fall from the wattles and little grey joeys will wriggle from the warmth of mother's pouch to feed in the sanctuary of the bushland at the top of the mission. Like the kangaroos, my people have found refuge here. A place where the scattered children of Bunjil can regroup, grow and gain strength in the knowledge that we have survived as refugees in our own country.

Uncle Russell's shack overlooks the road and across to the riverbanks. Puffs of smoke spill from the sandstone chimney and I can see him standing in the doorway. He waves and I wave back. Already his lot of dogs is tearing out to meet us. The shack and cow-trodden yard are surrounded by a huge boxthorn hedge entangled with pink rambling roses. There is hardly a trace of the dairy that gave milk to the mission years ago. I remember as a boy, the fresh cream and jam and damper every morning. No trace of the pigsties but the old car bodies are still here, lying rusted and bullet-ridden under the pines. We kids used to play in the cars and gammin we were Bonnie and Clyde. It seems like yesterday but it was long ago.

The dogs prowl about the doorstep, growling, circling each other with tails up like question marks. Uncle Russell's little dog Minnie is crouched low to the ground whimpering as Woofy sniffs her intently up and down. He could swallow her with no trouble but obviously he has other ideas. Uncle Russ appears with the teapot in his hand. He slings the contents over the animals. 'Garn, get out of it ya silly bastards.'

'Good day Uncle, you look crook,' I say. I heard he was on the grog yesterday.

'Aw, I'm feeling alright now, bud,' he says in his gravelly voice.

He's wearing a red headband, a green shirt with one sleeve, baggy trousers and no shoes. I follow him inside.

'Drink of tea, bud?' he says as he places the kettle on the flames.

'Yes, Uncle, thanks,' I say as I settle into a three-legged armchair. 'Don't chuck it on me though.' He throws his curly head back and laughs at that.

'How's your mum and dad going in that place down yonder?'

'They settled in OK, it's not bad for a Commission house.' He nods his head as he spreads golden syrup on a johnny cake and hands it to me. The black iron kettle bubbles and spits. Uncle Russ makes tea and pours it into a battered mug for me.

'No, I don't like that powdered milk,' I say. 'Here, Granny gave me your tobacco ya lost yesterday.'

'Oh yeah, I was lookin' everywhere this morning for that.' He starts rolling one up. He'd dropped his tobacco beside the road yesterday where he fell down and smashed his flagon. He's often found sleeping in the grass, drunk, his dogs huddled close around him like huskies around an Eskimo. He lights his skinny smoke with a stick from the fire and says, 'Did you know Devil bit Mary the other day?' Mary is my great-grandmother. A proud religious woman.

'Yeah,' I say. 'I heard about that.' Great-Granny Mary is ninety-nine if she's a day and she hobbles about the mission preaching the evils of the demon alcohol. She can talk the lingo too.

'Yeah,' I say, 'she went in to see Aunty Elsie and that mad one Devil's took a piece of her ankle.'

'Ain't he chained up?' asks Uncle Russ.

'He is now. The ambulance came out and took Gran to town to get stitches.'

'Ah, well, she won't be walking about the place for a while then,' says Uncle Russ, with a hint of satisfaction.

Uncle Russell picks up a boomerang he has cut from a blackwood tree. He's heating a piece of fencing wire to burn designs on his latest weapon. He will probably sell this one in the pub or give it to someone as a gift. I watch him working away while I sip black tea. Sparks crackle and jump from the fire. Wood shavings lie scattered on the floor with dog food cans and empty flagons. A hessian bag curtain flaps in the breeze. At the dark end of the room his bed, blankets tossed about, magazines and cowboy stories beside the kero lamp. It strikes me that I've never known Uncle Russ to have a steady woman. He's a loner like Uncle Percy. Uncle Russell coughs and splutters, spits in the fire and curses his wicked headache.

'I'll get goin', Uncle,' I say. 'I'll send one of the kids down with a rabbit for ya tomorrow probably.'

'Good, bud, see ya after,' he says as he hot-wires the boomerang, squinting his eyes from the smoke.

By the time I reached the steep slopes of the riverbank I was almost doubled over with a stitch. I rested, leaning on the shovel and cursed myself for eating too many johnny cakes. Below, the dogs have fanned out, sniffing and nosing their way about in the dense, dark green fernery. The river has cut a wide arc here and formed a small bay with a sandy shore. I remember when groups of mission folk would light a fire on the sand and fish for eels in the cool of evening.

Recovered from my johnny cake attack, I make my way along the trail, down through the bracken to the old mission swimming hole and crossing place. Here the water looks cool and golden, streaming across pink and grey stones, running into deeper pools, swirling and twisting, tugging at overhanging tea-tree and wattles.

I pick my way across the stones and the dogs follow, one by one.

Ringo, the old fellow with one yellow tooth jutting from his jaw; Sandy, the greyhound stretching from rock to rock like a caterpillar. Next, little Tommy Blackballs with his tail up high. Now silly Browny, his fox-like coat thick with burrs. Big Woofy crashes out from the scrub and leaps for the first stone only to lose his back legs and sweep downstream in the current. Snorting like a water-logged hippo he casually paddles to the bank where he emerges and shakes himself, flinging water all about.

Yips of excitement as Ringo and Tommy flush a rabbit from the grassy embankment. There's a short chase with Sandy making up good ground but the rabbit reaches the safety of the boxthorns. We move on following the course of the river upstream. Treading carefully through tall spindly grasses and tussocks in swampy areas and on through a rocky gully littered with huge boulders tumbled down from above. Every now and then a cloud is swept across the face of the sun and the scene is in twilight for brief periods. The wind is picking up a little. Up ahead I hear the pack barking in the heat of the chase but the 'bad habits' have the advantage in the blackberry brambles and nettles.

A rabbit appears in front of me lower down on the flat. Sitting upright in the swaying grass he makes a set shot. I slowly lower the shovel to the ground, and slip the rifle from my shoulder. I take aim, hold my breath and squeeze the trigger. A short crack as the echo is carried away on the wind. The rabbit flicks his ears and looks around. A gang of cockatoos, startled, cast themselves from their perches screaming in a flurry of white frenzy. I swear and select another bullet. The rabbit tucks his ears in and squats. Aiming at the eye I pull the trigger only to hear a dull click. Cock the bolt again, aim, squeeze ... click. Cursing under my breath I try again. Cock, aim, squeeze, crack.

The sound rings loud and true in my ear but the bullet strays. The rabbit flicks his ears and looks around. Again the cockatoos rise. Screaming blue murder they circle and reform to settle like a shroud of snow upon the limbs of a dead gum tree. In silent rage and frustration I consider throwing the gun at the rabbit but he is gone.

Ringo and Tommy Blackballs have returned to investigate the shooting. They sniff about and look up at me as if to say 'What, no rabbits?' They turn their tails to me and I follow them. The river runs deep and wide here, drifting through a shady avenue of knotty red gums. Shy blue waterhens dart from thickets of reeds squawking in alarm. A pair of wild ducks depart in a flap, creating rings of crystal on the mirrored surface. Metallic green dragonflies skim across reflections of the sky. The clouds are ganging up and the breeze is getting cheeky as I fight my way through sword grass and blackberry bushes to a clearing where the dogs are intently scraping at a couple of burrows.

A bunny springs from a pophole and Sandy snatches it by the hind legs. The bunny squeals and Browny clamps his teeth on the neck and pulls. The two dogs are effectively skinning their prey when Woofy, wild-eyed and crazed, rushes in and plunges his yellow fangs into the soft pink flesh of the rabbit's mid-section. Bones crack as the rodent is split three ways. Tommy and Ringo have their heads inside the burrows. Snorting, snarling and pawing madly at the soil. This is a good sign. I collect some sizeable rocks and block most of the exits. 'OK Tommy, look out now.' I start to dig, following the small tunnel until I have exposed a good deal of the tiny chambers. Pausing now and then to allow Ringo or Tommy to poke their trusty noses into the hole.

Tommy Blackballs is a small dog, black as tar and beady-eyed. He has his head down in the burrow, his hindquarters skyward. This is how he got his name, for his namesakes are exposed and displayed in comic fashion. Old Ringo looks on patiently. Tommy shows signs of desperation. Howling and scratching frantically at the small opening. I drag him back and feed a slender stick of bracken into the burrow. Sure enough, I feel soft flesh and movement. On the jagged end of the stock are fine slivers of fur. Kneeling down I reach into the chamber and grip the powerful hind legs of a full-grown buck rabbit. I break its neck immediately and slit the stomach. I throw the warm bloodied contents to the dogs, making sure that Tommy and Ringo enjoy the liver and heart. While the jackals feed I pull out three more pop-eyed rabbits.

Homeward bound as shades of evening creep round the river valley. The wind bites cold and sends a shiver down the glassy face of the river. The reeds and rushes sway in harmony with the trees. Clouds mill about like angry black bulls waiting to stampede. At the crossing place a mob of sheep take shelter in some low scrub. As we draw near they nervously disperse and this excites Browny and Woofy who launch into the round-up like old hands. I am reminded of the latest mission gossip about sheep being savaged by stray dogs and local farmers up in arms. I roar at the two marauders, throwing stones and cursing wildly. Ringo, Tommy and Sandy take heed of my threats and stay behind. Woofy changed course when a stone bounced off his ribs. He took to the river, swam across and headed home. Browny had a change of heart too. When I approached he flopped to the ground and rolled onto his back pleading for mercy. As no damage had been done I let him be although I imagine Browny and Woofy transformed into wolflike creatures under a full moon; thirsting for the blood of sheep.

We haul into Granny's back yard as darkness falls. The back door cracks open and light and sound spill out on the back porch. Little David steps out for a piss. He doesn't see me in the outer darkness so I sneak up close and say loudly, 'I didn't mean to scare you, mate.'

His little body jolts in fright. Fumbling with his trousers and flashing wide eyes at me he swallows a gulp and says, 'How many you got, Uncle Johnny?'

'I got four, buddy, here, take 'em inside for me.' He drags the corpses inside and I put the shovel in the pine tree for safe keeping.

In the warmth of the kitchen I stand at the sink pulling skin from the rabbits. A green-eyed ginger tom cat waits at my feet. Music and laughter escape from the lounge as Mouse comes in.

'Hey Johnny boy, they nice big rabbits.' She collects three blue cans from the fridge.

'Yeah, took me a while to get 'em,' I replied.

'Uncle Percy and Donny and Brenda in here,' she motions to the lounge. 'Mum said there's stew on the stove and come and have a drink.'

'OK, I'll just have a wash and a feed first.'

In the lounge Aunty Faye is in charge of the record player.

Selecting scratchy old favourites and playing requests. Slim Dusty sings something about driving a truck but the lights coming over the hill are blinding him. Granny has baby Heather cradled in one arm. Gently rocking in her chair she hums softly into Heather's ear as she has done for countless other children. Including myself. In the firelight a glass of beer glows golden amber on the floor by her feet. Uncle Percy sips from his glass and takes a pull on his pipe. He pushes his hat back and looks into the fire tapping his foot to the music. A nevous red kelpie waits faithfully by his knee.

Aunty Faye shouts, 'This one's for you Donny.' Uncle Donny, his left hand bandanged from a fight with a drunken fish tank, untangles his long legs and swings into his Elvis impersonation. With his jet-black hair brushed back he dances about can in hand, miming and making faces till his ankles collide and he stumbles.

'Sit down Don, sit down before ya fall down,' warns Aunty Brenda.

'Play it again, Faye, I'm just warmin' up.' Aunty Brenda pulls black Elvis down into his chair.

Little David, Bernadette and Connie roll about on the couch in fits of laughter at Uncle Donny's antics. Aunty Faye reminds them, 'School in the morning you kids, get to bed now, it's getting late.' She herds the reluctant children from the room and Mouse collects her sleeping babes and takes them to bed.

Uncle Percy refills my glass. In the break between records we hear the sound of light rain on the roof. After a while the music is louder, the drinks flow faster and everyone talks at once. From what I can gather the dog catchers came out today and took Devil away for biting Great-Granny Mary. Two fat coppers escorted the dog catchers while they picked up Devil and other dogs who chased the divvy van up the road.

'Just as well Ringo and Tommy went with you, budda boy,' said Granny. She has a soft spot for her two hunters.

'They all lucky they didn't get pinched,' says Aunty Brenda. We all agree on this and fill our glasses.

I stare into the fire and think of what could have happened. I have a vision of Ringo, Tommy Blackballs, Sandy, Browny and Woofy peering misty-eyed through the bars of their cold cells. Old Ringo plays *Swing Low Sweet Chariot* on the mouth organ, while Devil is led away to be strapped into an electric chair.

The rain is heavier now, drumming on the roof. Another log is reduced to ashes and the cold wind slips in under the door. Granny wants to hear *Me and Bobby McGee*.

'That's the one, tidda girl. Turn it up a bit.' Uncle Percy is telling us how he picked the daily double today. Uncle Donny reckons he was waiting on the results of a photo finish to win the quadrella, but by the time his horse got there it was too dark to take the picture. I'm almost too tired to laugh. Again my eyes are drawn into the glow of the coals and I dream my dreams only to see them go up the chimney in smoke. I say goodnight to all and step out into the darkness.

Freedom's just another word for nothing left to lose and nothing ain't worth nothing but it's free . . . The words are carried on the wind as I cross the muddy yard to the bungalow.

I light the lamp and flop my weary frame on the bed. The wind kicks up a storm now and the crack and rumble of thunder splits the sky. The bulls are stampeding. Hail stones sweep across the settlement in sheets of ice. The mission is lit up in electric flashes of lightning or is it Bunjil taking photographs? The driving rain is deafening in the bungalow. Uncle Russell must hear the same sound on his roof. I imagine his dogs gathered round his bed in the darkness, pricking their ears up at the sound of thunder. I wonder what Uncle Russell dreams of. Rain, rain, rain. What's that song Granny sings? It starts off . . . *there's a rainbow round the dear old Hopkins River . . .*

Ted Fields

TED FIELDS is a Ualroi man born in 1931 at Angledool, New South Wales. The Ualroi lived on the Narran River from Angledool to Narran Lake in the north-west. Ted assists with the Ualroi language teaching program at St Joseph's School in Walgett. For several years now he has been working with schools in the region, teaching

language and culture by taking groups of adults and students into the bush to visit sites and tell the associated stories. 'These trips are important in that they bring us into real contact with our origins. They tell us where we came from, where we are and, most importantly, where we are going.' The story of Mullian-ga was told to Ted by his father, a Ualroi man who lived all his life at Bangate Station near Angledool.

Mullian-ga

M ULLIAN-GA, THE FIRST man of the eagle hawks, was
a booral Wirrigan (powerful witchdoctor) who lived in a
giant yarrarn (gum tree) at Geera on the Barwon River. This tree
was so high it reached right up into the clouds. Mullian-ga had
worked his magic on the tree and it was so hard it could not be
cut with an axe; it was as hard as stone – mayadjeer.

Mullian-ga lived in this tree with his wife Gooleer and mother-
in-law Ngurroobarn, who were Mooday (possum). They lived
apart from the rest of the people, because Mullian-ga was illian
(against the people). He was a cannibal (bunna); he ate the people
from the surrounding tribes. All the people wanted to get rid of
him but he was too powerful (wirranggal).

As the people could not cut the tree down, they tried to burn
it down but the wind would come and blow the fire out. It would
come up out of nowhere. This was old Mullian-ga's mullie
mullie – his spirit (boolie wondah, that's what they call it when
the wind just comes up from nowhere).

So the people went to their booral Wirrigan. 'What can we
do to get rid of old Mullian-ga?'

The Wirrigan listened to them and went away to ask the spirits
what could be done. When the Wirrigan returned he called all
the people together.

'You cannot cut that yarrarn down and you can't burn it down
from the bottom, so this is what you must do. Get all the best
climbers of all the tribes and hold a contest to decide who is the
best. The best climber must take a firestick to the top of the tree
and place it under the goondie (house). He must climb up on
the shady side.' So all the tribes got together for the contest to
find the best climber: Geenbullaga, all the lizards and snakes;
Digayah, all the birds; and Goorangul, all the animals with fur.

These three mobs offered their best climbers. The Geenbullaga
nominated the tree goanna, Mungangarlie. He was a good climber

but gooribah (slow) because he was too fat and heavy. The people said he would take too long to reach the top of the tree. The best climber of the Digayah people was little Bibi, the woodpecker. He was gubbanbah (a light little fellow) and he went up the tree burpa (quick) but weil weil (all around the tree, not straight up). They wanted someone to go straight up quickly on the shady side of the tree. Little Bibi was no good either. The best climber of the Goorangul people was Goonyar, the tree rat. He went straight up, no trouble.

So it was agreed that Goonyar would be the one to take the firestick. All the people went to old Mullian-ga's tree and made a fire and Goonyar got a dull firestick. He went around the back of the tree – booroogah, on the shady side – and started to climb up. The people then went away and they stopped and waited – dooramillie – they waited to see what would happen.

Goonyar climbed up and up and up – gulleah. Up, up, up he went with the firestick. He climbed all day and the sun went down – booran. It got dark but it didn't worry Goonyar. He kept going in the dark. He climbed for days as it was a long way up to old Mullian-ga's goondie. When he got there it was nurrendah – dawn – just before the sun comes up. He planted the firestick in the middle of the tree underneath the goondie. He planted it warranbungia, with the butt first into the tree so the coal stuck out.

Then the wind started to come up. The sun came up. The wind blew the firestick alight. When the goondie caught fire underneath, old Mullian-ga and his family were asleep inside. Old Mullian-ga jumped up, 'Weebooran (I smell fire).' His family said it couldn't be fire burning – mayer, nothing. Then the whole goondie caught fire and old Mullian-ga and his family were burned. Old Mullian-ga and Mooday got out but were badly burned all over. That's why all the eagle hawks are now black and the possum has black feet.

Mullian-ga's goondie was destroyed and the fire and ashes dropped down into the hollow trunk of the tree and it started to burn from the inside. All the people watched from a distance as the tree burned for days and days; a long long time. The smoke from the fire blotted out the sky, the sun, the whole world, and the people couldn't see anything.

After many days the tree burned through at the bottom and after a long time it fell down – boondarnie – it fell down towards the south, away from the river. It hit the ground so hard the whole world shook – boorooee. The tree hit the ground so hard it went right across the land. The tree was gooloongooloo – hollow like a pipe – and the branches of the tree, as they fell across the country, cut all the channels of the Macquarie marshes, and that is how the marshes came to be.

One branch of the tree fell to the west and created Cuddy Spring and the water from the Barwon River flowed through the hollow of the tree and flowed into the marshes. And the old people say that if you dig down deep enough in any of the channels you will still find wood from old Mullian-ga's tree.

Old Mullian-ga's spirit now lives in Bullimah – sky camp – as the Morning Star and on either side of Mullian-ga you can see a dull star – these are the spirits of the Mooday.

Richard Frankland

RICHARD FRANKLAND is a singer, songwriter and filmmaker from the Kilkurt Gilga clan of the Gunditjmara nation in the south-west of Victoria. He was born in Melbourne in 1963. A former soldier and fisherman, Richard is also an accomplished performer, supporting Prince in 1992, performing with Archie Roach and  *Angry Anderson, and releasing his debut CD in 1997. He has also worked on a number of ground-breaking, and award-winning, television documentaries. Following his work as a field officer and investigator for the Royal Commission into Aboriginal Deaths in Custody, Richard wrote 'Way To Forget', which he adapted for film in 1996 (as No Way To Forget), also directing. The film was screened at the 49th Cannes International Film Festival and has won a number of major awards, including the 1996 Australian Film Institute Award for Best Short Film. In 1995 Richard founded the Victorian land rights organisation Miriambiak Nations, of which he is chief executive.*

Way to Forget

IT'S NIGHT TIME and I'm somewhere between Swan Hill and Melbourne. It's late, maybe just before midnight. Archie Roach is singing that song 'Beautiful Child' on a pirate cassette and my mind is drifting between the song and the road. The tyres squeal as I corner too sharply and I try again to concentrate on driving, try to hold out thoughts that keep running through my mind.

I take another sip from the drink in my hand and put the bottle on the passenger seat, another cigarette, another five or so k's done. Archie finishes the song and begins another. I'm glad I stole this tape off my brother and smile to myself at this small win.

I grip the steering wheel harder and increase the speed, wind the window down and beep the horn and scream at the stars, anything to stop me thinkin' about all the deaths, anything to stop me wondering what the fuckin' hell I'm doing in this job. Archie's singing about the land and the hurt that's been done, God he can sing ... few more hours and I'll be home, more interviews done, feeling good.

I decide to pull up on the side of the road and I get out and look at the stars. I know that they are like the land, they'll always be there. This job and the stars always make me wonder at my own mortality and the mortality of those closest to me. I get a little scared and cause I think I feel spirits close by I quickly (in a real slack attempt at being cool and casual), get back in the car, start up and churn up gravel as I drive off. The Archie tape finishes and I lose the battle of trying not to think about what I have seen, the tears I have heard and the pain that I witnessed.

'Oh Uncle,' this boy said to me, 'oh Uncle when I woke up and realised where I was, I looked to my future and seen me, getting drunk again, getting stoned again, hurting people again, hating again, and getting locked up again, and this was why Uncle, that's why I wanted to die, cause when I looked to my future I had none.'

Shake my head, try to shake out those thoughts, but it's too late, I've started the roller coaster ride through my memories.

'My father was a good man, he didn't hurt no one, he was sick, why did he have to die, what did he do to deserve that, he was only in there on warrants.'

'My son was a great artist.'

Tyres squeal and I guide the car with a beating heart back onto the road. I can feel the blood now, pumping through me, and the fear has made me more alert.

Even though it's warm I shiver and remember that saying, 'Someone's walked over your grave.' I wonder who is walking over my grave and I think of the people who I know so much about but never met, convinced that they are not resting in theirs.

Another cigarette. 'When we arrived, we examined the patient and concluded that he was drunk.' Ambulance officer in police cell. 'We could smell alcohol on him and he was speaking in an incoherent manner.' (A sign of diabetes I think.) 'We're not authorised to conduct litmus tests.'

'Good bloke for an Abo.' Watchhouse book in police station. This flashes through my mind like a neon light. *No NO NO*, Archie Roach snaps me out of it and seemingly fits into my thoughts.

I find that I'm in a small town and look for a motel, no more driving tonight, no more. No Vacancy flashes in front of me and another cigarette keeps me driving. I burst out of the town and into the inky night, all the stars are gone, covered with clouds maybe. My headlights can hardly cut through darkness and I compare it to my thoughts and moods. I find myself drifting off again and manage to fight myself and beat my thoughts into submission. The dashboard lights drag me into another time, another place again.

'I didn't know him well, cause we were taken away as kids. I remember the first time all of us together, all of us kids I mean. It was the same year he died. Did you fellas know that the same copper who arrested him that night arrested him for the first time about six years ago?'

I nod my head at my thoughts and laugh to find myself acknowledging my memories. I laugh again as I wonder if I'm going crazy, though nervously this time.

Another town has loomed out of the darkness and I search for a motel to stay the rest of the night. In frustration I keep driving knowing that I'll curse myself for my anger and impatience later.

Harold Hunt

HAROLD J. HUNT (Wymbitja) is of the Maliangaapa people of western New South Wales. Born in 1925, he spent a good part of his life doing stockwork, fencing, truck driving and shearing around the eastern states. In the mid-seventies he became an alcoholism counsellor for the Redfern Community Health Centre in Sydney and Chairman of the first National Aboriginal Campaign Against Alcohol and Drug Abuse. In his new role he worked with the NSW Health Commission and later the Department of Corrective Services, attending conferences, writing journal articles, lecturing in schools, hospitals and service clubs, and setting up alcohol rehabilitation centres throughout NSW. He continued this work in the mid-eighties in South Australia. Harold now lives in Bigga, NSW, where he works as a guest lecturer for the NSW Police Academy at Goulburn and Co-facilitator of Aboriginal Cultural Awareness workshops in regional communities for the NSW Police Service. He is also working on an autobiographical novel.

Guilty As Charged

THE THIRTY-FIVE-year-old Aboriginal woman stood in the courtroom dock in the little outback New South Wales town of Wanaaring. She was awaiting proceedings which were totally foreign to her. She was feeling extreme isolation, being the only Aboriginal person there, as well as being the only woman.

The courtroom was a rather large room, poorly lit and with highly polished brown benches and railings separating the gallery from the seating area provided for juries. A little further around was another bench, enclosed by a guardrail with a small gate at one end, this section normally to be occupied by the accused. Directly opposite was the box-type witness stand in close proximity to the raised bench occupied by the judge, magistrate, or as in this case a Justice of the Peace. This austere room, tucked in the bowels of the old weatherboard police station, had nothing to suggest that it had any connection with the outside world at all.

The only other occupants of the room were the complainant – an agitated, fidgety little man who owned the local store and managed the post office – a local grazier lounging casually on a cedar bench in the gallery and, sitting a little further along, a stoutly built, grey-haired, not-too-popular hotel keeper.

The man in charge of the proceedings about to begin was the manager of one of the biggest grazing properties in the State. He was a man of conservative manner who was noted for his limited dialogue with people of *any* standing. He displayed agitation, suggesting that he found the predicament he was in to be distasteful. He would have avoided it had the choice been his.

Proceedings got under way. The oath was dispensed with. The charge of assault was read out and the defendant pleaded guilty. Taking into consideration the evidence and the plea of guilty it only remained for justice to take its course. In accordance with statutory law, the sentence of 'two pounds or four days imprisonment' was pronounced.

There was dead silence. Not a murmur, not a movement of any kind to disturb the already gloomy atmosphere of the courtroom. After what seemed an eternity, the woman spoke.

'Well, I have no money to pay a fine so I suppose I will just have to go to jail ... and I suppose you men will take care of my goats, fowls and garden, as well as my five children.'

Here was an unexpected turn of events, which added to the already lopsided scales of justice. Whilst the case brought before the court appeared to have been dealt with, the real trouble had only just begun. Could the situation be reviewed? Could the sentence be withdrawn and altered? Thoughts like this must have raced through the mind of the man on the bench.

In this atmosphere of quiet turmoil, the Aboriginal woman displayed the calm dignity of her cultural upbringing. Her Dreaming taught her that to do nothing was to get nothing done, so that, after amusedly surveying the situation, when next she spoke, her words brought great relief to the very perplexed JP.

'Mr Henderson, seeing nothing is going to happen here, I might as well go home.' With the serene composure of her ancestors, May Hunt left the scene. She was quickly followed by the publican, who insisted she accept the two pounds he offered for the fine. He expected no repayment. It was his token of respect for a rare act of courage and common sense.

May Hunt was a battler – a battler of great integrity. Born at Milparinka on the first of May 1900, in the 'corner country' of New South Wales in the homeland of her Maliangaapa people, she was the second child of eight born to Jack and Hannah Quayle. Her parents travelled around that arid part of the State doing all kinds of bush work – fencing, horse-breaking, tank-sinking or shearing, or whatever was offering.

Despite having three brothers, May became her father's right-hand man whenever he was horse-breaking or doing similar work. She quickly learned all her father could teach her about the outdoor work. Her mother taught her to do the indoor things, like cooking, mending and cleaning. As well, while her two grandfathers were of British blood, her two grandmothers were traditional women, and May's mother was raised in the traditional ways of the Dreaming. This meant that she had the benefit of the training of both worlds.

Jack and Hannah never had any formal schooling. Nevertheless, they considered it important for their childern, so that, whenever they were working near one of the little outback towns, the children were always packed off to school. May reached third-class level – not much to some people but, to this bright youngster, it provided a base from which to learn to balance the whiteman's ways with that of her traditional ancestors. With her feet planted comfortably in both camps, she realised at an early age that this schooling would be necessary if she was to cope with whatever life had in store for her. Her early training with horses served May well in earning a living as she had to ride and drive horses at times; and the ability to hunt kangaroo and emu enabled her to feed her own family.

Big Jack Quayle often employed men on contract work such as tank-sinking, fencing and so on. When he employed the handsome young Irishman, Bill Hunt, romance soon developed into the marriage of May and Bill. From their union came eight children. They also adopted an orphaned niece, Myrtle, and in the ways of her Aboriginal ancestors Myrtle was simply and comfortably part of the family as a sister of the other children. May had lost her first born at birth, making Myrtle the eldest of her family. Next there was Roy, a couple of years younger, then followed Doreen and Harold spaced about twenty months apart, as were the others, Beulah, Eric and Rachel.

The going was tough during the depression years of the thirties and, to add to those already hard times, Bill was stricken with sandy blight (trachoma) and had to go to Sydney for treatment. This all happened at a time when it appeared the tide was turning for the better. They had just acquired the lease of a public watering place 200 miles north of Broken Hill, on the State's most western stock route. It catered for sheep and cattle being driven from the big holdings further out to the railhead at Broken Hill. This lease consisted of 640 acres or one square mile – not much land to graze two horses and two camels on. However, they strayed onto better pastures from time to time and, in that way, survived.

Life was hard but it was not long before May had tracked down some wild goats and turned them into milk and meat providers. Next, there appeared pigs, from God knows where! A garden was soon established, which yielded a healthy diet supplement to the damper brownies and fresh meat (mainly kangaroo, emu, goanna, rabbit and an occasional 'wild' sheep).

The goats would normally go out to graze each morning and return about sundown. One day they did not return and May's instinct told her that it was not their intention to return. So, after giving instructions to twelve-year-old Myrtle on how to care for the younger children, May loaded food and a swag onto a packhorse, mounted a riding hack and rode away. She tracked those goats over stony ridges, sandhills and creek beds until she reached the Koonenberry Ranges, the home of hundreds, perhaps thousands, of goats. There the trail was lost – but not May's spirit. After five days and four nights, she returned to her family, disappointed but by no means beaten.

Unhappily, shortly after Bill's return from Sydney, the marriage ended. It was a union which had survived many hardships and enjoyed much happiness, the growth of their children, the peace and privacy of the bush. May and Bill shared much of the domestic side of family life. People tend to work together when they live in tents and rough-built shacks. Their shacks were generally made of round bush timber lined with hessian, with the outside walls and roof made from flattened four-gallon petrol tins. They cooked on open fires, as a fuel stove was still beyond the Hunt family's financial reach. Earth floors and no electricity or running water made it necessary for all hands to participate in domestic chores. And May joined her husband in much of his work, particularly in the building of their camps and on fencing jobs.

Travelling around the backblocks in a camel-drawn wagonette with five children on board in search of employment, May and Bill must have bonded in a way that only that level of shared adversity could enable. But Bill's failing sight caused increasingly prolonged absences from the family and its struggles. May's proven ability to cope, unaided by her husband, strengthened the bonds with her children, as the threads of her marriage became thinner and weaker. All the marriage was doing now was producing more children, their youngest child now ten months old. To maintain the marriage *and* give the type of care she considered her children deserved, May felt was beyond her capability, so one had to go.

May was aware of the sadness the children would feel at not seeing their father, so she truthfully reminded them that their father was a good man, and that they would see him again. She explained that he had to stay in Sydney to get treatment for his eyes, and the family had to move on and get closer to their grandmother and uncles, aunts and cousins, and the kids could go to a real school and learn to write and then they could always write to their father until they could see him again.

May packed her bags and, with her children, moved to White Cliffs, where her mother and most of her siblings lived. There, disaster struck when, shortly after her arrival, her eldest son had a relapse of rheumatic fever, and was taken to Wilcannia Hospital, sixty miles away. Then her one-year-old son, after a short illness, died of gastroenteritis.

The days to follow were grim for May. Adhering to the traditional sunrise and sunset grieving, of wailing in the early hours and again as daylight was fading, she would be joined by family and friends from the near surrounds. This communal grieving would last several weeks during which time the deceased's name would not be mentioned. It gave her the strength to carry on and to care for her other children.

A short while after the passing of baby Ted, May's second-youngest child had taken ill and went off to the Wilcannia hospital where she spent two weeks. Not able to visit or talk to her sick child by phone, there were just messages from the hospital secretary, the usual hospital message, 'doing as well as can be expected'.

To supplement the dole, she did laundry work around the town and, with the help of her younger brother and one of her sisters, sold wood for ten bob a dray load to the townspeople.

After almost a year there was another move, this time to Wanaaring, the little town on the banks of the Paroo River, 120 miles west of Bourke. May's two older brothers, who had old but reliable motor lorries, helped her move. There they erected two tents and a boughshed on the riverbank a mile from the township, which consisted of a store, hotel, post office, police station and four private houses.

The camp was on an old garden site of four acres of Crown land. May negotiated the lease of it for one pound a year. In no time a garden was in the making. Then, seemingly out of the blue, there were goats and fowls. It was then necessary to make a journey of more than a week to go back to Coally Bore, her home prior to the breakdown of the marriage, to collect her beloved horses, as they were necessary for hunting animals to feed the family as well as for visiting relatives on a nearby station.

Comfortably settled, a new start, new hope – then tragedy struck once more. Sixteen-year-old Myrtle was stricken with rheumatic fever and taken to Bourke Hospital. Once there, she was totally isolated from her family, no telephone and mail once a week. Visiting Myrtle in hospital meant a journey of over 200 miles and therefore was out of the question.

That was not the end of May's worries, however. On a family visit to a brother some thirty miles away, yet another catastrophe occurred. May organised the boys and girls into two spring carts, while she travelled the way she liked best, on horseback. All went well until, on the return journey, the horse drawing the girls' cart, reacted to a broken piece of harness by trying to free herself from the vehicle with every bucking and kicking trick she knew. It was not long before the three girls were scattered along the roadside, bruised and shaken. The two younger girls got to their feet and went to the aid of Doreen, who was lying quietly with her right foot turned in the opposite direction to normal. It was a complete break. Boards were broken from the tucker box, a bed sheet torn into strips and a splint applied to the leg of the brave twelve-year-old girl, who gave not a whimper during the whole operation of securing, then lifting her onto the other spring cart and transporting her to a station homestead five miles further on. From there she was taken by car to Wanaaring, another twelve miles, where she waited for several hours for the local police officer to return from one of his routine trips to outlying stations. His vehicle was the only means of transport for the long drive to Bourke Hospital. Fortunately, despite the pain and the discomfort of the swelling, the X-rays showed that the leg had been perfectly set. All that was required was plaster and time to heal the break.

Myrtle, sick and dying though she was, found great comfort in the companionship of Doreen. She had yearned for the company of her family over the long months she had spent away from them, with no communication, confined to her bed. Myrtle would watch the visitors passing through her ward to sit with their loved ones on their daily visits, and occasionally someone would give a nod, if and when she caught their eye, and turn away in embarrassment. The priest and nuns would stop by to talk to her about God and the angels, and getting to heaven, *if* you were good enough. But in passing, Myrtle at least had the comfort of Doreen at her bedside, small indeed, but a link with her family as she departed this life.

With the death of Myrtle, once again May and her family were plunged into the trauma of grief and suffering. Through it all, their family unit became stronger, in as much as they found the strength, the courage and the tenacity to carry on by tapping into the spirituality of their Aboriginality – the quiet spiritual bonding never wavered.

So much more could be said about this beautiful, incredible, unstoppable, courageous, brown-skinned lady with a ready smile. Her soft gentle manner also portrayed strength, a strength carried with great pride by her family as they moved through adolescence to adulthood.

As time passed, her offspring moved to bigger towns where their own children would have better schooling and more opportunities. May moved to Bourke and set up yet another 'home base' for the family to visit and stay when they wished.

After almost seventy-four years of hardship, trauma, sadness, mixed with large doses of joy and happiness, May died peacefully.

~

God has her in His keeping.
We have her in our hearts

~

At seventy years, I am one of the four boys and girls who May Hunt, nee Quayle, so proudly reared.

Oh, about my mother's conviction that day so long ago in the Wanaaring Court, I'll tell you what the dreadful crime was. She was accused of, and pleaded guilty to, slapping the face of a man who ran over one of her pet sheep with his car, then abused her for having *her* sheep on *his* road.

You now, as she did then, can smile!

Catriona McKenzie

CATRIONA McKENZIE was born in Sydney, though her people are the Kurnai of East Gippsland, Victoria. She has worked as a writer for the last couple of years, having completed a Diploma in Writing at the Australian Film, Television and Radio School. She studied at the University of New York's Dramatic Writing and Film School in  *1996 and has had articles published in various magazines, including Reel Time, Tharunka and Film News. She has received several grants from the Australian Film Commission for script development and is currently living in Sydney where she is working on several feature film scripts, as well as her own projects.*

Kurnai Country

*W*ings

L A PEROUSE.
   I remember it was a beautiful day, not a cloud in the sky, the first time I met her.

I was walking along the coastline and I saw this old woman sitting, looking out to sea. I sat down beside her and we started talking. After that day I kept bumping into her, and we became friends. Some days she'd be sitting there real quiet, I'd sit down beside her, and she'd wipe a tear away from her eye. There was never more than one tear but it said things we never spoke about. We had an understanding that some stories are best left alone.

This one time, and it was years after we first met, and she was really old. And that's something I never knew, just how old she really was. And it was hot. I had shorts on and you could see this livid scar on my leg. Today I don't mind it, but back then I thought it was ugly, and you could tell.

It was a perfect day with the warm sun and a slight breeze, and the solitary figure of the old lady on the cliff waiting for me. I never wondered why she was there looking out over the waves to the horizon. Anyway this day she wipes one tear away and notices the scar on my leg. I'm shame about it and pull my sloppy joe over my knees. We sit looking out over the blue, under the blue. I look at her and for the first time notice she's beautiful. You know how you see someone then you really look and you notice things you never have before, and I notice her long grey hair, the breeze, her dark brown eyes. Then without looking at me she speaks.

'Nice scar, how'd you get it?'

I pull my sloppy joe down further and shrug.

She says scars are like maps. They tell you where you been. I mutter that I wish it could have been somewhere else. She sighs. 'Everyone has scars Bub. Let me tell you a story.'

And she tells me this story, her story, a true story. I know. I've seen the scars.

The old lady's parents had lived on the coast, and their parents before them, and so on. They had very much wanted children so when she was born her parents were the happiest people in the world.

The baby girl was perfect except for two small bumps on each side of each ankle. Her parents loved her so much they hardly noticed, for them she was their miracle.

As she grew bigger, those tiny bumps grew with her. Her parents didn't give it much thought. They made bigger shoes and longer skirts for her to wear. She loved to go walking in the bush, she'd take her shoes off and run barefoot across the land, free as a bird.

At night she'd come home to her mum and dad. She'd tell stories about what she'd seen in the day as they had their evening meal. Their lives were good and they laughed at how happy they were.

When she was twelve years old she started to disappear for longer periods at a time. Her parents never worried. They had a faith in each other which never shifted over all the years she was growing up. They'd just smile to themselves. They guessed where she was.

Those tiny bumps on her ankles had grown into small but strong wings which carried her high up into the sky, out over the ocean where no one could see her. She'd swoop down over the tops of the waves and tease the little sea horses who couldn't follow her up to the sun. Sometimes she'd play tag with the gulls through the clouds, before they all flew home in the evening.

This went on for years, until she was eighteen years old. One day – it was a beautiful day, like this one, with a warm breeze blowing over the water and the sun throwing out its gold – and she thought, 'It's a perfect day for an adventure.' She said goodbye to her parents, packed some fruit for the trip, and left.

Straight up into the sky, so high even squinting did you no good. She headed out to sea; she even left the seagulls behind and could barely see the tiny sea-whipped horses below. She went further than ever before.

Flying under the golden sun, over the deep blue sea she just happened, by chance, to look down and see the most handsome sea horse galloping over the waves beneath her. She flew down to get a closer look, and he must have spied her shadow on the water because he looked up and saw her.

'Come down and play with me,' he shouted over the roar of the waves.

She soared up and away because she was shy, but he called out again.

'Come and frolic with me.'

She looked and he was jumping high over the waves, kicking up his heels. She never gave it a second thought and swooped down over the water. They played for hours. She shared her food with him and he told her the secrets of the ocean.

Suddenly, out of the blue, a storm blew up. The skies went deep dark green, the waves grew trecherous and lightning started to strike the ocean. She was scared because she was so far away from home. The sea horse told her to get on his back and he'd outrun the storm.

'I can't, my wings,' she cried. 'I'll fly away and you can outrun the storm.'

She tried to fly but her wings were wet. Lightning cracked over their heads. Huge dark waves pounded them.

The sea horse cried, 'Quickly, the stirrups, or you'll drown and I'll die of a broken heart.'

'But my wings,' she cried.

'Forget them.'

In desperation she let her wings go and watched them sink down into the deepest waters. She put on the stirrups and off they raced, away from the storm, out to the deepest sea.

She stayed with the sea horse for years and they played and cavorted in the sea until one day she woke up and he was gone. She was all alone. Finally she dragged her body on to the shore and fell asleep in the white sand.

When she woke up she knew she was bound to the land forever. But she never forgot her wings.

Scars ache. So now she watches the horizon, and remembers how it felt, almost like a dream.

The old woman brushed the hair from her face.

'Now this scar on my leg,' I looked at her, 'let me tell you a story.'

The old woman smiled and leant back on her hands. 'Well, it is a beautiful day.'

I sighed. 'Once, when I was little ...'

John Muk Muk Burke

JOHN MUK MUK BURKE was born in Narrandera, New South Wales (Wiradjuri country), the son of an Aboriginal mother and an Irish father. His novel Bridge of Triangles (University of Queensland Press) won the David Unaipon Award in 1993. Muk Muk's poems have appeared in several anthologies including New Dreamings,  published by OBEMA at the University of Osnabruck, Germany. He has recently been appointed as a judge of the David Unaipon Award. John is currently on leave from his position as an Associate Dean at the Faculty of Aboriginal and Torres Strait Islander Studies, Northern Territory University, to complete his PhD.

Songs We Sing

'I AM THE RESURRECTION and the life.' Laurie noticed that the priest's gown just cleared the piled up clay. He remembered Tommy telling him of a child's show and tell: In the name of the Father and of the Son and into the hole he goes. Apocryphal. He had to laugh. Another urban myth. Other thoughts flitted about too. Barry's favourite song: *When the Rain Tumbles Down in July.* Funny that – here it is July, but a cold tea sun is pouring across the country graveyard, illuminating even the damp earth's waiting space. Waiting for Barry with his string-hardened fingers folded on his best ivory suit. The one with the satiny fringes and worked treble clefs. What bullshit it all is. Resurrection. What songs we make up to celebrate the delaying of the evil day.

It was on a rainswept July day that the white man and his black woman had wandered, starved skinny, into the mission. Her thin legs could hardly carry the weight of the tiny bundle who would soon be born – Barry's father. Water from the same river the superintendent dipped into to christen him also soaked his black curls when, forty years later, and a hundred or so miles upstream, he sank into his brown death. His corpse rose, bloated and strangely bleached, three or four days later: some said three, others four. All eventually agreed it was a Sunday. Whatever, the body rose, dead.

'And even though he be dead, he will live again.' The priest hitched his gown a little higher as he moved to sprinkle water on the coffin. Laurie himself believed that Barry would only ever live while anyone remembered. And as those who remembered became dead the life would fade that little bit more. Until no one remembered. *Them bones gonna rise again* only in the minds of the remembering living. Re-member-ing. Piecing back together. *Thigh bone connected to the knee bone* ... Songs again. Barry left heaps of tapes – thank Christ. Laurie blinked. Reminded himself that he wasn't blaspheming but thanking Someone for the good bits. Jack the Dancer was a bad bit.

Barry had always been a singer and a good dancer – a real natural sweet tone and a graceful mover. His voice had echoed something of the hobo songs, the union laments and the victory of Christ as sung in nasaly tones by the mission inmates within the tin chapel at Warangesda. Of course he'd been pretty little then, but the songs we sing are learned early. Especially the melodies. Laurie smiled as he remembered another Tommy story; the one about the little kid who said he *did* know his three-times tables, but only the tune at the moment. *Da da de da,* the boy had hummed. Perhaps a touch of the apocryphal there too.

How many years do tapes last? Put them onto CDs? More permanent. The dingo tooth necklace found at Lake Mungo had lasted about 15 000 years. The contents of some of the Dead Sea Scrolls found in 1947 at Qumran were believed to predate Jesus by perhaps 500 years. He'd read that some cow horns had been found at Catalhuyuk adorning what was believed to be some sort of altar. Neolithic – perhaps 9000 years ago. Could have been the first domesticated animals. Shearer Barry had been a buck-jumper too, and roped maybe the direct descendents of those old Catalhuyuk beasts. But what do we really know? We all put the jigsaw together different.

His sister had stood by the altar back in town and read one of her poems. He was surprised that he'd cried then. The priest had said something about Barry living on in his songs – didn't sound like the sort of Christianity he knew about. But surely Christianity too was another urban myth? Laurie thought it would be far better named as Paulianity. Urban Jerusalem re-member-ed at Qumran. So much jumble arranged and re-arranged itself in Laurie's head. As he thought about the re-member-ing of his uncle's life he realised that the whole story could never be told. Like the bits that Barry would never have whispered even to God back in the days when he believed in Him. But here he was, being sort of canonised, a puzzle pieced together to suit the tastes of the present living. A lot of shearers do more than merely *fleece* the sheep but the priest didn't actually dwell at all on that possibility. That wouldn't fit the big picture.

Laurie looked at the priest – that preserver, transmitter and subtle interpreter of a death of a couple of thousand years before his uncle's. And about 300 years after the death of that bloke in Jerusalem the songs that Constantine got his subjects to sing had a big change of tune too. The people were sort of missionised. *Istanbul was Constantinople. Sailing to Byzantium.* More songs. *Your cheating heart will tell on you.* Mary had worn a *Black Velvet Band* when she read her poem, *You Are My Sunshine.* Not very original Laurie thought, but then recalled Solomon. The priest's face sheened from last night's wine and today's sun.

Shirl struggled to get Barry talking about his burial. But finally he nodded from behind the haze of morphine and in his slow drawl agreed that it should be next to Pat. Jack the Dancer got her too. How he'd loved her. And written a real sentimental song from the depths of his heart when she went. *God Has a New Little Angel in Heaven Tonight.* And Tex – their shearer son. Worker with domesticated animals. *O lamb of God who takest away the sins of the world.* Go off into that other altar – the desert – and perish. Tex was just across the grassy path under some red stones and plastic carnations. *A White Sports Coat and a Pink Carnation.*

Laurie thought of the hundred or so records in the cupboard upstairs – not listened to since he bought the new player three or four years ago. He sometimes got out the Bach Double Violin because he hadn't found a CD of it. But the other ninety-nine – he left them in the cupboard. What remained in the caves at Qumran because Paul had his favourite bits of the songs left behind by Jesus? The Teacher of Righteousness. The Teacher of the Way. Jack the Dancer hadn't got him but the Romans had their own special dance steps. And Caiaphas sounds a little bit like cancer.

Shirl looked like she was about to faint. She'd forever thought of Barry as her little brother. The knowledge that he was dead and she went on living sat like a stone in her chest, a rock which wouldn't roll down and be washed through no matter how much she swallowed. Laurie had read *Lear* and now felt the rising gorge in his own throat. Why should a rat have life? Oh yes, Laurie had learned a whole new set of songs compared with those of his grandparents. Barry had been clever at school too but, like his father, he'd arrived in a great depression and school hadn't been long or stable.

Laurie moved to hold Shirl's hand. So Shirl grasped her son's fingers and the green leaves she held were now gripped by both of them. *I am the vine and ye are the branches.* Mary had handed everyone a green frond of gum leaves as they left the church. It was the *Aboriginal* way she said. And tomorrow they would all carry burning gum leaves through Barry's flat and smoke away the evil of his death. Laurie tried to remember where the galvanised bucket was: that would be the way to do it. Then he recalled that Barry had used it to vomit in. Doesn't matter – the fire will kill all that evil too. Gehenna, the rubbish tip outside Jerusalem, somehow got mixed up with ideas of Hell. Burn up all the rubbish. When Barry did speak of cremation, he drawled in his cowboy voice, 'No Sis, not for me.'

Laurie had been over in Geraldton all the time Barry was sick. He'd thought of flying across the desert to Wiradjuri country but told himself he couldn't interrupt his work. So he listened to Barry's tapes and drank whisky and water and tried to piece together some sense. Make his own myths. The hole he now stood near to would be the source of lots of Wiradjuri myths for perhaps the next sixty or seventy years. Until people forgot. Or perhaps the Singing Shearer would become a Clancy of the Overflow sort of bloke. One thing's for certain, thought Laurie, we sure won't know where he are.

But who is he? What if someone had cut off one of Barry's strong hands and then the other, and then a foot and then the other, and then the legs and arms and genitalia, and got right up until only his heart and brain were left? Would that be Barry? And if all the bits were sent off to different countries would Barry be sort of omnipresent? Laurie glanced at the grandkids and thought about those cattle in Anatolia and the ones Barry loved working with. What do we know? What is evil?

Some black crows were wheeling overhead and up on top of one of the concrete headstones a frilly was sunning himself. Sacred to the people around these parts. Some animals and fruits you can eat and some you can't – and some I for one wouldn't want too, thought Laurie. Then the sandwiches Mary had spread out under damp tea towels back at the house came into his thoughts. And the bottle of whisky he got yesterday. There was half of that left and plenty of ice. *Old Dogs and Children and Watermelon Wine.*

Barry's grandkids were here learning the rituals that go with death. They knew they weren't allowed to smile and should probably cry, and those over about six did. But the little ones had got wind of some sort of party later and were wriggling in their mums' and aunties' arms.

Laurie looked up at the slow-moving crows and noticed the sky clouding over. The priest closed his book and the men began to shovel in the dirt. Then the keening of the old women started and the people threw their green fronds into the hole and they were soon buried too.

The cars and the one-tonners headed back to town with their sad passengers – the present living. The sort of always living, Laurie thought. Then the rain fell. And Jesus it tumbled down by the time they got back to the house.

Bruce Pascoe

Bunurong Country

BRUCE PASCOE was born in Richmond, Victoria, in 1947. He was a schoolteacher for some years before setting up his own publishing company to publish the quarterly magazine Australian Short Stories *in 1982. His own novels and stories include* Night Animals *(Penguin, 1986),* Fox *(Penguin, 1988) and* Ruby-Eyed Coucal *(Magabala, 1997).* Fox *was runner-up in the Sandhurst Trustees Novel Competition in 1993. In 1997 he won the Commonwealth Bank Short Story Award, the Melbourne Times Company Short Story Award and the ABC Radio National Short Story Award. His great-grandmother was born in Bunurong country, South Gippsland, and Bruce is a member of the Wathaurong Aboriginal Co-op.*

The Master Race

WHEN THEY SHOT his mother, he ran straight past her. She looked up at him but he could see that the glance died in her eyes even before she fell to her knees. He didn't stop. His uncle was with him but he didn't stop either. He'd seen his sister out of the corner of his eye and that they'd almost caught up with her. It became a rush of confused images. His uncle dashed for a group of trees and he didn't see him again. As for himself, well he just kept running, past a grove of low trees, over the rutted track where an open cart was piled with bodies. The horse's eye whites were brilliant and mad, knowing by smell what it was being asked to haul. He ran past the horse.

But what he could never forget was that he ran past his mother. His stride didn't falter. They'd learnt that much about the new order – you don't stop. Even for your mother. Your legs run but your mind, or the better part of it, stopped where she fell. You know that the limits of humanity have been reached but your body, a mess of sinew, bone, flesh and organs, just runs. It doesn't know that eyes have seen the end of civilisation, the arrival of the master race.

I ran past my mother.

~

What could I do? I might have been weak but I wasn't a fool. The people had latched on to this idea of dominating the whole continent. The papers might express, occasionally, some mealy-mouthed sentiment about ensuring that the remaining members of the race be cordoned off in ghettos but it was too easy for the authorities to construe any such bleating as a call for extermination. The momentum was too great. The inevitability of profit from their demise was too obvious. The unspoken word was 'let's be done with them'. Get rid of the hindrance of another race, another ethic, another morality, another claim of ownership.

Ostensibly my position of office meant I was in control, but each new meeting, each new rally, assured me that I was there by the grace of the mob, to do their bidding, to give authority and respectability to genocide.

As Governor I had told the military that the idea was to bring the people into a central area where they could be readied for expatriation. But as I repeated and repeated the authority I had been given in writing it was obvious that the new regime could not reverse the momentum which greed had set in motion.

Even as I read out the terms of the Government's policy I was conscious that the look of the soldiers and their officers was simple contempt. They knew the real policy. Many of the soldiers and even some of the officers had been in prison just a few months before. It was obvious now that they had been released for the express purpose of performing those tasks that a career soldier might find unpalatable. How many, after all, are pleased to garrotte a child? We know there are some, history has always discovered some, but how many are they? Before this I'd always considered they were a minority criminal class but as I looked up into the eyes of the soldiers I could see the same light in most of them. They were hungry, eager, they would do their unstated task with relish. The designers of this policy must have known, even as they couched their orders in the fine phrases of the historian and scholar that there would be men who, though illiterate, would be able to read between the lines the meaning of the real message. And these soldiers knew their thirst would not go unquenched. Their eyes before me were dreaming of many heady draughts at this foul well.

I could see how things would proceed but what could I do? I had performed my duty and now history was out of my hands. The old institutions of law and public honour were to be ignored. How else could such an immense crime against humanity be achieved? The cut of their uniform was new, the design of their firearms modern, their tactics state of the art. We were a people believing our destiny was to capture an entire continent, to subsume its people for our own greater glory. Do not blame the little man with the stirring words – we were all to blame. So many of us thirsting to lift that chalice to our lips or, like me, prepared to turn away from the sight of my countrymen chafing to obliterate a race of people so that history would forget they ever were.

~

Part of me wanted to hide and part of me wanted to be seen so that the gun would be raised and I would be blown back into the universe, out of this world. I didn't want to live. I was only sixteen but ever since I'd been born members of my family had been shot before our eyes or they would simply disappear, never to be seen again. One after another they went until there was just the four of us. And now my uncle had disappeared, my sister had been caught – and I ran past my mother. I was the last. I should have stopped and held her to receive that last look, the last blessing a mother can give – and then waited to receive that other blessing – my own death.

But I ran past my mother and now I was hiding naked in vegetation beside a watercourse. This morning a frog swam to within reach of my hand and I caught it. Later a marsh hen mistook me for a log and I throttled her. I couldn't stop myself wanting to live. Despite myself I ate, I slept, I drank, I provided for myself the things which would keep me alive. And yet what was I going to do? Where was I going to go? There was nobody left. I was on my own and all the old reasons for living had been taken away.

~

I looked down at the lists of names. Mothers, fathers, children, aunts, uncles, grandparents, sometimes entire families. Cause of death? Well, here the language of the bureaucrat took over. 'Disease'; 'Misadventure'; 'Shot while attacking a member of the military forces'; 'Shot while stealing food'; and more often 'Cause of death unknown'!

But I knew. I'd seen them chained together, shuffling through the towns with their eyes downcast, shamed by their condition, mesmerised by the inevitability of their fate and that such a fate could be conceived by the mind of man. I'd seen them in the prisons standing completely still behind the bars, staring without even swivelling their eyes, staring at their captors. I'd seen them chained to trees and beaten with whips and sticks until they died. I'd seen them hanging from tree limbs, floating in rivers, starving in ghettos. When you read this you may have already become familiar with the details; indeed, if you read this it might mean the scheme had not reached the final solution, but I know that success or not we will have been guilty of barbarity never before exceeded on this planet.

Oh yes I am an intelligent man, a learned man – but I didn't lift a finger against those of my own race. I might have grimaced on occasions, groaned in my bed at night, stared at my hands as they rested on the lists of names but I did not raise those hands. I followed the orders I was given.

~

I cannot believe it was only months past that my uncles danced in the firelight and my aunts and sisters sang for the dancing, I cannot believe that we no longer divide our feasts amongst us as they've been divided since our ancestors told us that this is how food should be taken.

I have moved down the river to the estuary where I know there will be shellfish and herbs. I have gathered a handful of cress already, but I cannot believe my hands wish to continue these tasks.

From my new position I can look out over the shallow waters of the estuary to where they deepen against the cliffs on the other side. It is a place where food is plentiful, shelter is good and the movements of my enemy easily monitored, but it has one enormous disadvantage. I can see out across the ocean where the gulls and albatross glide across the water. It reminds me of the story my mother told me about how the seabirds find their way home, how if they follow the lines of waves for long enough they will find food and when they're tired they will find a beach. That will be home.

I told you I left my mind where my mother fell. And this is

how it is, I've truly left my mind behind. When I think of my mother's voice and how she sang to me by the fire I begin to think of how things are now. That I ran past my mother, that I ran past my whole family until in terms of the race it is only me that is left. I begin to think this as I look out to sea, I am on the brink of realising the enormity of that loss, that the land behind me is unpeopled by those of my own blood, I begin to grasp what my life will be from hereon in, and then that thought enters the space where the better part of my mind used to be and drops from sight. That's when my hands and eyes, against my better judgment search for food and a place to rest, for those things which will restore my body for another day ... and another and another.

~

'We got to a point above the river where it was impossible to proceed. It was difficult to move in that burse so there was a deal of manoeuvring before we could unsaddle and tether the horses. While we were doing this we were silent at our tasks, involved as we were in buckles and straps in the confined space. I became aware of a voice which I had at first taken for a bird. It was, indeed, a human voice and was singing some mad and wild plaint or hymn. It was such chaotic singing and so far off that I couldn't discern its language. I met Tauber's eye and we completed our task as quietly as possible.

'We moved with some stealth towards the singer until I became certain the language being sung was not my own. Even before I saw the person responsible for this unholy dirge I knew we had our man. And breaking into lighter bush we could see through the more widely spaced trunks to the banks of the estuary and there by a small fire was our singer. His whole head was covered in the white wash in which they smear themselves when mourning. Even his shoulders and chest were marked with it, but it was obvious he was black and more than obvious that he was mad. He'd eluded us for some weeks but it was him alright, the Aboriginal, Mung-to-rer, the last of his tribe. We did our duty for our King and country.'

Mammon

RONNIE AND I went a-walking. We've been mates for years. I met him in the bar of the Auburn Hotel – when Freddy Goldsmith was cellarman – in the days before they charged you $7.50 for a stubby of half-strength beer with a post-modernist label. Life wasn't any better but it was cheaper.

'G'day,' this bloke said, as I poured him a beer, 'I'm Ron Walker, businessman.'

He had a peculiar business in those days, Ron, before he was famous. He dealt in things which had arrived by ship. Well, not arrived as such, but nearly arrived. Goods which had completed nine-tenths of their journey, a point at which they intersected with Ronnie.

It was the sixties. We slept at the house we were at when weariness overtook. We ate and drank from the closest fridge. We all knew someone who'd spoken first-hand to someone who used to be a roadie for the Stones, the Blue Stones of Glenroy, a band that played hard rock – and weddings, goodbyes for aunties, commercials for Preston Motors, solos in their cells.

And we called the now famous Ron Walker, trader in goods still in transit, Long-Haired Ronnie. Ronnie the Interceptor.

I met him again last week in the Rob Roy Hotel. A few pots, renewed acquaintances, went over old times, showed each other our cartilage operations, went a-walking.

Oh yeah, this Ron Walker probably isn't the same Ron Walker that you think of when you see the word 'mammon'. This Ron Walker had a mid-life crisis – he went straight, cold turkey, honest as the day is long, egalitarian to the boot straps of his K-Mart runners. Yeah, chalk and cheese the two Ronnies.

'Come walk with me through the streets of Melbourne,' said Ronnie, 'and I'll show you something that's bound to blow your mind.' He always talks like that, Ronnie.

In Gertrude Street we savoured the leaden air spiced with the brake linings of the Coburg tram.

'Look,' said Ronnie, 'have a squiz in there.'

I peered through the doorway of a shop that had its window painted over with rough and angry swipes of whitewash. My angled perspective showed me a line of fifteen dry-cleaning benches steaming and thumping like a scene from *Hell, the Musical*. I knew it wasn't a Melbourne Theatre Company production because they were all in time. Perfect precision. And each face was Asian.

What had they done to deserve this? We know what actors do to deserve their penury, they're different.

Next door there was an empty Balkan restaurant specialising in flame grills. Ronnie shuddered. Then we came to another screened window and peering through the door you could see a row disappearing in a haze of cotton lint of at least twenty machinists making ghastly things. The window was screened by a buckled cardboard packing case and in a frowsy pit between it and the smudgy glass were displayed the kind of scrunchy elasticised hair rings you wouldn't contemplate giving a very naughty niece. They were awful. Turquoise, scarlet and splotchy brown – the designer of that material must dress Crackers Keenan or make the caftans you see at Camberwell Sunday market.

They were all Asians of course and a man with a ponytail appeared to be whipping them. It was probably his black BMW parked outside with the personalised number plates MAMMON.

We escaped Gertrude Street before we were dragooned into some kind of rationalised and internationally competitive slave labour.

As we turned into Brunswick Street Ronnie mused on the state of things, the state of things on the move.

'You know mate, I can't be convinced it wasn't a better world when you knew you had a job at the boot factory for life, you knew you'd get a bit of overtime and you knew you'd get three weeks annual leave and a bonus big enough to take the whole family to Kennett River.'

He might have said Kennett a bit loud because the greengrocer clasped her daughter to her chest and glared at us and the blokes in a queue at the CES threw themselves on the floor behind shelves of pamphlets offering jobs as waiters on Dunk Island.

'Sorry,' Ron apologised. 'Ray Martin and Kennett have got everyone a bit edgy. Look,' he said to me, 'here's the piece that should start the resistance.'

We came to a group of seats made out of the body parts of several ossified griffins. I knew it was art because they were terrifically uncomfortable.

'Have a look at the bloke on the seat opposite,' whispered Ronnie in his most conspiratorial manner. I shrugged and commented that the bloke looked like a clerk in his lunch hour taking a quiet five to read the paper.

'Not on your life,' said Ronnie in his stagy whisper, 'he used to be the manager of the Commonwealth Bank. He's pretending he still is. Comes here every day at lunchtime even though he hasn't had a job for six years. Scrap heap time. He's fifty-two.'

I looked at Ronnie fearing he was making it all up.

'Cross my heart and hope never to see another Black and Decker power saw,' Ron interrupted. 'I do a stint in the store at the Brotherhood of St Laurent. I've seen him sneak in there to buy his shoes. Seen him at the CES. He used to go to school with the old man. Mr Howard and Mr Kennett reckon he's work shy – shy, mate, this is the kind of man who hates leisure, he'd kill you for a job – it's the saddest thing I've ever seen. He's a bloke who expected he'd be giving his clothes to the Brotherhood, thought he'd be putting a five-dollar note in the Salvo tin every Friday night while he sipped his tiny glass of Foster's Light.

'We're creating a monster in this land of the fair go. That's why I've moved out of the redistribution of wealth business and started serving soup – most people are too poor to rob.'

We watched as people walked by our seats and the little bank manager tried to make his paper last.

I began to concentrate on the shoes and socks, the stockings and sandals passing before me. There was no in-between. There were either brand new shoes with twenty-dollar socks, glistening court shoes with stockings made from the opalescent threads of rainforest spiders or there were broken-down runners and holey shoes. And the two different sets of feet never walked beside each other.

Hooray, I thought, we've rationalised labour, some can work and most can't, we've created an army of unemployed just waiting for some charismatic with a working knowledge of explosives to unite them under a single banner. And what will that banner be? 'Fair Go for Workers', 'Share the Jobs', 'Buy Back the Farm'?

'No,' said Ronnie, 'eventually they'll unite under the banner of Revenge and it'll only take the sight of a fancy ponytail or pair of new Italian shoes and they'll go beresk. And the bank managers and school teachers will be up there with them. They won't care if you're Labor or Liberal because they'll know you've supported fifteen per cent permanent unemployment.'

We gazed across at our little man quietly panicking because he had only two pages of the paper to go.

'Anyway mate,' Ronnie said, 'I'm off to the soup kitchen, fending off Armageddon with a bowl of chicken noodle and a bread roll the rich decided they didn't require two days ago.'

I watched him become another pair of broken shoes on the footpath and knew I was going to write this story ... but I'll have to admit I've told ONE BIG PORK PIE – Ron's surname is not Walker – I don't know anyone called Ron Walker because I'm just an ordinary voter with very ordinary shoes.

Mammon II: The Poor Must Be Apprehended

THE POOR MUST be apprehended. At all costs. The police must convict them because you can't pinch the rich – they've got lawyers. Get the meek. Get those who don't know anyone who knows Ron Walker. Get them, screw their hip to a cake stand.

Get those who leave their licence in their only other pair of pants. Against the law. Fifty dollars. Immediately. On the spot. In my hand. Thank you pauper.

Of course their quaintly out-of-date cars have to be unroad-worthied because they can't afford new ones and we refuse to insure their old ones because they're simply not worth it.

'Insure an EH Holden little man, don't be ridiculous.'

'But if I lose this Your Honour I can't get to work at your clothing work house.'

'Walk, it's good for the poor. It's what they're used to. One-thousand-dollar fine for impersonating the rich.'

If the poor happen to have a little titchy window cleaning business – you know, high ladders, strong winds, little squeegee on a stick three floors up, dangerous work – well, they're fair game. Big office man refuses to pay? Well how can he? He's got three class-conscious kids in private school, a wife one jewel short of a coronet, a house in Monaco with dodgy plumbing – you know, a problem any of us can have – the swimming pool is too long. Small Claims Tribunal I hear you suckers say, not on your life, mate, it's not worth pursuing $750.

'What?' says our little man, tiny damp squeegee in hand. 'That's eight weeks rent.'

'Well you're wrong there preposterous little working class nerd, the Monaco villa is $2800 a day and the bloody pool is still too long – where can you get decent help these days?'

Oh, forget the window cleaner. Let him get a smaller house, sneak the wife and kiddies into a women's refuge, deliberately cut off his hand to get compo – there must be something proactive he can do. Forget him.

Here's another little chappie hauled up before the magistrate for questioning a courier company for charging GJ Coles $130 to ship two tonne of goods to Sydney and our little man $680.

'It's unfair,' the little piss ant says.

'It's free enterprise you cretin,' shouts the court. 'How dare you think you can ship goods to Sydney with the blatant intention of making ten per cent profit.'

And yet another urchin appears. 'Put him in the hulks. Send him to Australia. What's his pathetic little question?'

'He's been trying to intimidate the rich Your Honour. He says he's owed $1000 for building a flight of jarrah stairs in Sir Tawny Portnose's mansion – he's rung Sir Tawny on three separate occasions requesting payment.'

'Requesting? Three times? That's intimidation of a corporate figure. How dare you take advantage of a man in the very worst financial period of his life. Don't you realise Mr ... what is your little name, prisoner.'

'Smith, Your Honour.'

'Of course it is. Don't you realise that none of Sir Tawny's horses has won a race for a fortnight? Have you any idea the pressure he's under? Send Mr Smith's head to Australia.'

'He's in Australia, Your Honour.'

'Well send the rest of his body to East Timor. Your torso'll be well treated there Smith, an excellent chance for rehabilitation – time to consider the error of your ways, the common criminality of your soul, the stinking perfidy of your audacious belief in democracy.'

'Oh, look, here's another one. How dare a black woman enter

this court. What's her social welfare spirit want?'

'Raped by three policemen, Your Honour.'

'Well don't come in here planning to deceive the Australian public of paternity money. Back to the riverbank.'

'Hey fatso, I want the pigs charged.'

'Constable, bring the leg irons. Where's the neck clamp? Bring the Book of Humiliations. Ah, here it is – I've been sitting on it. Ah, yes, the Westminster System, look at the parchment, feel the gold leaf ... ahem, Chapter 3, Blacks ... the appropriate sentence for trying to perpetuate the course of justice is to be deprived of her children – for their own good.'

'All rise for the judgment of democracy.'

Rosemary Narrurlu Plummer

ROSEMARY PLUMMER is a Warumungu woman from Tennant Creek in the Northern Territory. She wrote her first poem, 'Tribal Woman', in response to her work in cross-cultural programs, 'so people could see and read about our side of things ... about how things have changed and how it hurts'. Rosemary has worked as a  Warumungu interpreter in numerous capacities, a facilitator in schools and cross-cultural workshops, and has participated in various linguistic and cultural programs. She is currently teaching at the Institute for Aboriginal Development in Alice Springs. Her poetry has been published in Australia and Canada in journals and anthologies, including Voices From the Heart *(IAD Press, 1996) and* Message Stick *(IAD Press, 1997). Her book,* Understanding Wumpurrarni Ways, *with Jane Simpson, was published in 1997 (Artplan Graphics).*

Singing Bonny M's Song

IT WAS A long weekend. Val asked Tanya to spend a few days out bush, using the back south road.

'Let's go!' said Val.

'Where to?' said Tanya.

'To Phoenix Waterhole.'

'Why Phoenix Waterhole? I wouldn't dare to drive that road at night. It's very scary. Besides, no one should use that road, they reckon.'

'Come off it, Tanya. Let's give it a go. People are always saying things.'

'OK, let's go,' Tanya said.

So they packed their luggage and started at five o'clock. Val drove. Tanya was still apprehensive driving the dusty, lonely road.

Val started singing Bonny M's song, 'Mary's boy child Jesus Christ was born on Christmas day'. Tanya had no interest in singing.

The sun was setting, night drew near and Val wanted to stop, to have supper. She asked Tanya.

But Tanya said, 'I wouldn't dare to have supper in the middle of the bush, because of the rumours.' Just then she saw something through the window, out in the bush. It was a light. 'Look!' she said to Val. 'What's that?'

Val didn't hear. She was singing Bonny M's 'Long time ago in Bethlehem / so the holy Bible says'. It was a lonely, dusty, windy road that stretched for miles that they were travelling. A huge red kangaroo hopped in front of them, suddenly.

'Ahhh!' Tanya screamed. 'A ghostly kangaroo! He's haunting us! Somebody please help us! Help! We're going to die!'

'Quiet, Tanya, it's only a kangaroo!'

Val stopped the car and watched the kangaroo disappear into the dark.

'Boy, he was huge.'

'Oh goodness gracious,' sighed Tanya.

They started driving again, up the hills, on to the stony, rocky creeks, through the scrub. It was nearly ten o'clock. They needed to be at the resort by eleven. Val kept singing Bonny M's song.

Hark now hear the angels sing,
A king was born today ...

They saw a man fixing a flat tyre on the way. He was going the opposite way. They stopped and asked him how far they were from Phoenix Waterhole.

'Before you reach Phoenix Waterhole, you'll see a big ghost gum with some old cars,' he told them. 'It's about ten kilometres past that.'

They thanked him for the directions and drove off.

'I have a strange feeling about that man,' Tanya said.

'Oh, well, never mind,' Val said, and went on singing.

While shepherds watched their flocks by night
they see a bright new shining star ...

It was getting late. The stars shone brightly. The Milky Way gleamed. Tanya yawned. When she looked back there was a bright light following them.

'Stop!' she yelled. 'There's a light following us! I don't know what it is.'

Val neither saw nor heard Tanya's cry. She was singing Bonny M's song, then humming the tune. Tanya watched the light. It made patterns of different shapes and sizes behind them. She couldn't believe what she was seeing.

'Val, turn around,' Tanya said, 'have you noticed what's behind us?'

'No.'

But then Val looked through the rear vision mirror and saw the light. It was making all sorts of fantastic shapes in the sky.

'What do we do now?' she asked.

'I don't know,' said Tanya. 'Look what it's trying to do! It's trying to stop us!'

The light hovered close to the back of the car, then it began to curl round in front of them.

'Ramp it up, sis!' Tanya yelled.

So Val put her foot down. As soon as Val speeded up the light faded. Neither woman could work out how it disappeared. Finally, they saw the lights of the resort in the distance. They were glad. Val began Bonny M's song once more, the verse about all the bells ringing out and tears of joy and laughter and people shouting that everyone could know there was hope for all to find peace. Tanya sat quietly listening to Val's singing.

'I will never use this road again,' Val told Tanya. 'I should have listened to you.' Then she sang another verse of Bonny M's song:

> *Oh my Lord you sent your son to save us*
> *Oh my Lord your very self you gave us*
> *that sin may not enslave us ...*

Val paused. 'You know,' she said, 'we could have rolled the car, but something saved us.'

At last they came to the ghost gum surrounded by old cars. Only ten kilometres to go, to Phoenix Waterhole and the tourist resort. They sang the last verse of the song together.

> *This day will live forever, oh my Lord,*
> *We have come to bow to you, oh my Lord,*
> *He is truthful ever, oh my Lord.*

Bob Randall

BOB RANDALL was born at Tempe Downs in Central Australia in 1934, of Pitjantjatjara ancestry. As a child he was taken to Croker Island, off the north coast of the Northern Territory, to the centre for part-Aboriginal children, one of many children removed from their families under the government policy of that time. When he left  Croker he worked around the Top End of the Territory as a horse trainer and buffalo shooter, among other pursuits, including songwriting and recording. Bob has appeared in documentary and feature films and works with the South Australian Film Commission as a consultant on Aboriginal issues. His work has been published in Identity magazine and in Paperbark: A Collection of Black Australian Writings, published by UQP in 1990. He returned to Alice Springs in 1994 where he works with the Language and Culture Centre of the Institute for Aboriginal Development.

Glossary

killer   beast selected to be killed for eating

Timor Ponies

IT WAS A little bit after the war. We'd just returned to the reservation on Croker Island from Otford in New South Wales. It was a boring kind of life on Croker, but there were a lot of Timor ponies on the island, and we always thought maybe if we were lucky we could try and trap some.

Sometimes the guys on the horses would catch one or two when they were rounding up the cattle on the plains but us boys used to be really hungry to have our own. Especially me. And I used to try and chase these ponies along the plains – this little boy chasing after twenty or thirty wild ponies with a little eight-foot rope along a flat plain and hoping to catch one and ride it back home. That's positive thinking! That's the way it was. We had so much hope, and hope energised us to do crazy stuff. No one in their right mind would do it today, but I think we were all a bit crazy in those days.

The weekend was coming up. Some of the older guys had built a yard at a place called Timor Springs, about fifteen miles to the south of where the mission station was. And we thought maybe this was the time we could go down and catch our own ponies. The dry season had been a lot longer than it usually was, so all the water places had dried up and the animals were only going to the special springs or watering holes to drink. And because a lot of cattle had gone wild, they'd built this big yard with wings running from the spring up into this strong holding pen. And when the older lads told us this, us boys with our imagination had gone wild and we could see ourselves catching every horse we wanted and bringing them all home. So we planned, and we asked permission from the white superintendent.

'Can we leave straight after school?'

We left at three o'clock in the afternoon to walk the fifteen miles to make camp. We were mad! Off we went, with just what food we could take. Heading south down the road to try and get there before daylight faded. We walked and walked.

We made camp that evening and it was a good bright moon. We checked the yards to make sure all the rails were in place, then we settled down for the night, excited, but we went to sleep. During the night, about 2 a.m., some voice whispered, 'Hey, there's something splashing water down the waterhole there.'

We listened and we could hear the sound of animals splashing in the water. So we went down as quickly as we could and as quietly as we could and slipped the rail into the blocking of the rail yard. And we had them. They were caught! We could hear the snorting the startled horses made as they smelt us and got frightened, then all these galloping sounds. We knew they'd be starting to circle, trying to get out. The dust started to rise, then they started racing up towards the race, through a laneway of rails, running up to the heavy holding stockyard. A couple of boys were hiding there and as soon as the ponies ran in the boys locked them in. About twelve ponies got caught that night. I ran up to the rail and I had my little rope in my hand and I said, 'Whichever one the rope lands on is going to be mine.'

You couldn't see anything, it was just a milling of bodies of ponies in the dust. So I just threw the loop in on top of them, and that was it. We went back to camp, really excited. When daylight came I ran up to the yard and looked over, and there was the rope around this little black stallion.

'Wow! That's the prince of all ponies!' I said. And so I called him Prince.

Next day we filled up the water for the holding yard, and said, 'Let's walk back now, and see if we can get the missionaries to help us with a truck. See if we can borrow a truck to cart them back.'

So we started walking the fifteen miles back to the mission. Everyone was hungry by late morning, and we'd had nothing to eat for breakfast except a scungy bit of meat that was left. So we saw this tree not far off the road – a cabbage palm. They're really good food when you've got nothing else to eat.

A couple of the older guys got out their axes and cut it down.

We split it open and had a good feed. Where the leaves come out is the part we eat – like bread, like cabbage. So we got our fill and then we walked. Kept on going. Made the mission by early afternoon.

We went to the superintendent's house and he said, 'OK, I'll send someone tomorrow to get you boys' ponies in.'

We were really excited, as only boys could be, after trapping these twelve little ponies. One of the older boys was told to get the truck and take a couple of boys down, on a school day. We were really disappointed because we had to go to school. We were waiting. We could hardly do our school work while we were waiting for the truck to come back. And after school we rushed down to the stockyards.

The superintendent was standing there and he said, 'Did you boys cut that cabbage tree down?'

'Yes!' we said, really excited. 'We were really hungry, we needed food.'

'Well, for that, I'm going to kill half your ponies.'

That was our punishment for cutting down a tree! We just couldn't figure out how these people thought. Well at least we'd get some. Half. I hoped they wouldn't pick mine to kill and feed the pigs with. We were allowed to pick one each and the rest, about half of those we caught, were put in a special yard, to be killed, eventually, to feed the pigs. But I was happy because mine was all right, my little stallion. One of the others had a little mare, a couple of the others had little colts and so on. We had enough.

The superintendent said, 'You boys have to look after them yourselves, you can't use mission property to keep your ponies in. We don't want them mingling with our horses.'

So we scrounged around for whatever scraps of barbed wire we could find, and rails, and built our own little yards, and we had to find troughs to water them. We tethered them with ropes for a while, then as they quietened down we shut them into these holding yards, and then we started training them.

In those days there was nothing like access to good things, like bridles, or things like that. You had to make everything. And after seeing the way the Indians used to ride their wild horses with nosebands I sneakily cut up all my sheets from my bed and made a bridle. Then I started training this little pony to work with the home-made bridles. We'd race each other, and have great fun.

From that time we started building up a little herd, because the mares had foals. We had our own now, these were *our* Timor ponies. And we'd go out with ours and catch others, and we built up a herd of about twelve, which us boys used to use for fun and to help round the cattle up. We became so excited about using the ponies that we even asked if we could go and get the killer in with them. Of course even the cattle thought, 'Are these kids walking or not? These are little animals they're riding!' Because we were the same size as them, sitting on our little ponies, we weren't way up. So some of the old bulls and cows didn't even want to move for us. We'd have to belt them.

'Come on, be frightened of me!'

They showed no fear of us whatsoever. But we meant business. So we'd muster them in and chase them around to have fun.

We built up our herd to quite a good number of ponies, and most of the mission kids learned to ride on our ponies with these home-made bridles, all bareback, because we had nothing. We were kids with nothing.

Later on I grew up and got married and had a little son and one of our little mares had a foal. So when my son could walk and ride I gave the pony to him.

I said, 'This is yours, and you can call him the same name I called my black stallion.'

Then I was banished from Croker Island because I had an argument with the superintendent over a fire he lit, which came up behind and nearly burnt the mission. The morning after the fire the mission bell rang and all the boys lined up near the store for allocation of duties, the same place we used to wait to get our rations. And because I'd been away, and had just come back that weekend from another shooting adventure – I'd gone over to Australia, and come back by canoe – I hadn't been there during the fire.

They were talking about the risk to the mission by the fire, why the workers hadn't contained the fire beyond the fire break, and I, not knowing what had taken place, said, 'Who was the stupid guy who made this narrow fire break, with this six to eight foot grass? The grass only had to fall over and the fire would spread.'

I didn't realise it had been the superintendent. I said it loudly, in front of everybody, because I didn't know the situation. No one else said anything. I opened my big mouth and I got banished.

I grew my little boy up in Darwin, with his pony still on the island. I told him, 'Later we'll go back and get him for you.'

A friend of mine used to run a barge to the mission, carrying supplies, so I worked out a deal with him.

'I'll give you two for one of mine if you bring the pony to Darwin from Croker Island.'

So he accepted the deal and we were able to bring eight ponies over. He had an empty load coming back, so he put them on the barge and brought them into Darwin.

You wouldn't believe the achievements of those little Timor ponies. They were the first purebreds that ever were brought into Darwin, when not too many people rode horses as a relaxation sport. So we started to enter into all the competitions, like gymkhanas and picnic races, and we did rides for kids, fund-raising things for school, we got involved in all of that. And my son and his little pony used to enter and win all the barrel races, even against the thoroughbreds. And we were challenged to all these special races at gymkhanas in Adelaide River and Katherine, wherever there were horse events.

We developed a good little herd of horses with the foals we got, and by catching more around Darwin. Those were the wild days, when Darwin was very small – twenty thousand people. There was wild country all around. So we built up our herds, and set up a riding school and taught a lot of kids and adults to ride, in a relaxed way. And because of the skills we'd learned catching wild horses and training them, we could do it. It was nothing for us to do that at any time.

And we had a beautiful big pony club eventually in Darwin. I used to teach people to ride, take them for joy rides, camping trips, all that, as well as breaking in wild horses for people on cattle stations. Our way, which was pretty bushy, pretty wild way, but we'd tame the horses down. I just sold my whole thirty-six head of horses and my school business, just before Cyclone Tracy.

So that was one little crazy boy and his dream of owning a horse. It led into so many things. One little boy on Minjalung in very tough times. And it was tough in those days, nothing was ever given to you. There were more obstacles than support, and you had to just really work hard to overcome those obstacles, if you wanted a better life.

And to think of the unfairness of losing half our herd because we were just too hungry, and we cut this tree down, this bush tucker, what we've always done. We didn't realise that because it was a tree white people saw it in a different way. We just saw it as a food. We didn't think about the prettiness of a palm, we just saw it there to be used as food.

I had that experience again later – looking at the same thing but seeing it differently. We were doing an archeological dig in the East Alligator River, and there were dozens of these wallabies around. We were meat eaters, we were hungry, and we were looking at this one wallaby from behind the vehicle, talking about it. I know what I was visualising – a beautiful wallaby roasting on coals, but a couple next to me, a white couple from New South Wales were seeing little Skippy. They wanted to pat it on the head – alive. We were looking at the same thing, but seeing a different picture.

But I didn't realise that till later, so when they said they really liked wallabies, I thought they meant they liked the meat. So I killed the wallaby and took it to them.

'What's that?' they said.

'That's the wallaby.'

'What?'

'Here it is, the wallaby you liked.' I handed it to them, to eat.

'We can't eat that. You're terrible! Why did you kill it?'

Well, I'd seen it too, and what I'd seen was a beautiful cooked wallaby and me munching on it.

Living, learning experiences. Meeting people with different interpretations from what I had, about the same thing. Major differences.

Another time we came across these beautiful water lilies in a pond. And these missionaries were with us, with their beautiful little cameras clicking away. And these girls rushed into the water pond to get the flowers.

The missionaries were saying, 'Oh, isn't it beautiful how the girls appreciate the beauty of the flowers?'

But then as the girls walked out they started munching on the stalks and throwing the flowers away. That was the only part they weren't eating! Then they came up with a stalk and handed it to the missionary, and said, 'This is for you to eat.'

'What? We wanted the flowers.'

'Oh.'

So the girls went and picked them up off the ground and gave the flowers to the missionaries.

The Old Songman

A T THE END of every wet season, when it was dry enough, we'd go and shoot buffalo. The church had a lease which would allow us to kill five hundred bulls. Apparently we used to send the skins to dealers in Darwin and they used to make leather out of them. But our job was to go out to Arnhem Land and shoot these buffaloes.

I was just finished high school. They couldn't send me anywhere else for further education. I was a brilliant student. It was nothing for me, learning. I never stressed out. It was so easy I couldn't understand what the problem was for some other students, struggling with subjects. But, as I'd finished with school, I volunteered.

The two who'd gone the year before didn't want to go again – they'd got scared from buffaloes. But me, straight away I put up my hand. Anything dealing with horses. No one else put up their hand. I don't know why, maybe they didn't like being away from the mission, whereas I didn't see that, I saw it as interesting, challenging, exciting bush adventure, away from this dull mission.

So there were a few weeks of buying up rations and we were gone. There was a boat which used to pull a punt with all our horses and blitz buggies across, and then we'd unload on the other side. The blitz buggies were trucks the army used to have, four-wheel drives, long before Land Rovers and Toyotas.

My bigger brother Jim was there, and me, and another brother, Dick. He was another shooter. We were supposedly the shooters. And I had to learn. I'd never really shot anything yet. I was just a good horseman. Then we went out and I learned to shoot buffaloes, and they introduced me to all our workers – the old men with their wives and children. Their job was to salt the hides after we got them. We had our team of skinners, they were the guys who could follow on the blitz after us horsemen had gone ahead and shot the buffaloes. And we'd have a driver, and he'd go to each buffalo and start finishing it off and then take the skin, take the hide off the animal.

I was a hunter. Right from day one, I learned to hunt. I didn't have sorry for animals – feeling – all I saw them as was a means to an end, to put food in my belly, or to get clothes on my body, to buy things out of the catalogues, good cowboy outfits! So I went over to Arnhem Land. I had my chaps, my hat, everything you need for shooting buffalo. My big gun belt, with bullets round it. You were forever loading those huge .303 rifles. They held about nine shots in the magazine. And you had to train your horse to go up to the buffalo and then to get used to the sound of shooting. My poor ponies! But I had two really good horses.

I was introduced to this old man, Beli Beli. He was one of the traditional owners of the land near Oenpelli (Gunbalanya). I didn't know what his job was, I was just told he was very important. Part of our staff.

He was the songman. As we worked, his job was to sing. He was employed that full three months just as a singer. At the end of every day you'd hear, sometimes the didge, and then the clapsticks would start. You'd always hear the clapsticks. Soon after the sun went down in the western sky, all of a sudden you could hear the song. He'd start singing. And he'd sing all night, till the morning star started to come up, that early morning star about 5 a.m. That's the only time he'd stop singing.

And that's the time our horse tailors, our youngest fellows, would go out and get the horses and bring them in. The women would get up really early and cook breakfast and before the sun rose we'd be heading out over this huge plain called Murgenella, in the opposite direction to where we'd been shooting the last few days. We'd go the other way, and we'd work different areas at different times.

In those days the herds of buffalo on those long plains were literally in their hundreds. It was unreal. When you galloped, you galloped among fifty to a hundred head of buffalo. You went from the side, picking out the biggest bulls. You'd finally gallop up alongside them and then Bang! in the spine, you'd shoot them. Bang! That one would go down – if he didn't challenge you. But in the big herds it was easy, because they'd follow, so we could just pick out the big bulls and shoot and shoot. You could shoot eight to ten in one run, and that was enough for the day. Sometimes we'd do twenty, if there was a good run. But if you ever hit the edge of the trees they'd get really cocky, those bulls, and they'd take you on, take your horse on.

Once, right at the edge of the plain, in the trees, my brother got in really close and that bull just moved over and threw him and the horse right over. Then I had to rush in and separate him from the buffalo. He was still stunned, he didn't know where he was running.

I said, 'Run over here! Jump on the back!'

I was used to running these girls, our friends back on Croker, and throwing them up on the back, so I said, 'Jump!' The buffalo was there, my brother was here (the horse had already bolted, a big gash on his leg, poor thing) and this bull was about to charge. I rushed in between them and grabbed my brother and threw him on the back and galloped off out of range. The bull was there, waiting to fight everybody. So I had to make him chase me. We'd do that, and then as they chased you, you'd lean back off your horse's tail and shoot them in the head, with a head shot.

A lot of things happened like that. But I believe that the lack of accidents and serious problems was because of the songman, because every night he'd sing the songs. It was his job, for the safety of everybody who was there, and to sing for all that country. He strengthened the relationships of all things.

It was the days when you didn't have access to stores, it was still bush and you lived off the land. You had a truck to use, to go to and fro, and you had rifles instead of spears, to get what you wanted for food. The waters would dry up and get lower and lower. We used to get huge barramundi, just from the waters drying up. So there was no shortage of food. We'd just fillet them and salt them and have them available all the time. These were the days when we never wore many clothes. The old people never wore clothes till even later. From 1948 till 1960 is the period I'm talking about.

We ran that camp. We'd leave the mission and go to Arnhem Land and organise the camp. The songman was part of the staff – the people would bring him with them, to that camp. The songman would just sit and wait. And he'd talk, and tell me things about that country, and ways to live right and to be strong. What he meant by *strong*, was to obey Aboriginal laws, which he'd teach me. No one ever got seriously injured, because of the maintenance of the law of country.

'You look after the old people,' he'd say.

He was an old man. I can still see him today. And that country. It was beautiful country, strange, wild, bush country. We could see Tor, one of the ancestor creators of that land.

The songman would say, 'Make sure, imprint in your mind where it is.'

Because sometimes you'd just gallop and gallop, you didn't know where to, because you were busy shooting. And the last bull you shot could be in amongst forest, and you're following him into the bush to shoot him again, so the skinners could follow. Then you'd wonder, 'Where am I? Where did I come from?' You'd galloped, chasing this animal, watching that animal. And it could go two or three miles and you'd still be galloping after him.

So I'd go to the highest point and look for Tor. And I'd wave at Tor in the distance, and I'd know, that's the camp, over there. Tor was the big rock that sticks way up there, and he was our ancestor creator that we had to look at to find our directions. And that old man taught me all that, because I was in new country, living out in the bush.

Sleeping with snakes. At night you'd hear this SSSSSSS and you'd look down from the straw beds – the women used to make them for us to sleep up off the ground. They'd make wooden platforms from paperbark, and then mattresses from reeds. And when the snake crawled on the reeds they'd rattle the reeds and go SSSSSSS and you'd grab the snake and just push him over! These big water snakes, so quiet, and they were everywhere! You had to be careful you didn't step on them when you put your boots on. Those were the times!

Beli Beli was my teacher. He was my grandfather on one side, but I also had a father – old Yidawarra. He was my father, in that country. He was the boss of the skinners, who looked after the hides. Made sure the meat all came off and put it out in the shade-sun to dry, not in the fast-sun. Stacked them all up. He took me under his wing, as his son, and taught me a lot, as well, about bush life.

Sometimes you'd leave your base – your main camp – and you'd go to a different area to shoot and you'd camp there, and then go another way, following up these pockets that went for miles and miles.

One time we were out at king tide, on this plain. We'd already been across Fish Creek. We'd made this bridge of three little saplings, across this saltwater creek. We went shooting and when we came back we realised the high tide had come and wet all this ground. We looked at it, and this time we had a load of hides, so the vehicle was twice as heavy. And this was the short cut! The long cut was to go right around.

We said, 'Let's give it a go.'

So we tried but the truck went down, four wheels deep in the mud, bogged, with a heap of skins on the back. And the nearest tree line, where we could go and get big trees to help, was a mile in the distance. So we had to walk and chop these tall trees and carry them back. And all we had to sleep on, in this fully loaded mosquito area was the ground, and the only clothes were the ones we wore. And the only fire we could make was with buffalo manure. So everything was cooked on buffalo manure. Beef, cooked on cow manure, and tea, boiled water. Ah, no. And sleeping that night, the skins were smelling and the dingoes were coming up. You had dingoes sniffing around you, and looking at you.

'Get away, dog, I'm not dead yet!'

After three days we got the vehicle up out of the mud but we lost all our hides. They'd all gone stinking. Once the rot set in, we lost them. We should have asked about the tidal movement.

We just didn't have that sort of knowledge. We'd tried to take a short cut.

So those were the sorts of things I went through. Living on the land, taking from the land the things you needed. It was a different way of thinking. Different ways of doing things – slower, but very effective. I remember making my own spears from saplings, digging the waterholes up, to water the horses, at the end of the dry season when all the surface water was gone. We all knew where the native wells were, and we'd carry a bucket and water the horses, then get a cup of water for ourselves once we'd dug the well out. Then we'd walk the horses to the point on the Australia side, so we could ship them back across to Croker, to the mission.

But it was the bush life, with the old people, that has given me a very strong knowledge about our ways, especially with old wise teachers like Beli Beli the songman. And that's why, today, I like singing stories, because that's the way I learned. But all those old people are gone, they are just memories now. Still very strong memories. And every time I go back there, which isn't often enough, I still see us there, and the memories of those days stay with me. Good memories.

Bill Rosser

BILL ROSSER is a celebrated Aboriginal writer, historian, poet and storyteller. He was born in 1927 at Toogoolawah in Queensland where he was educated to age eleven. He is a member of the Wadjalang people. He worked as a timber cutter and bullock driver until he joined the RAAF in 1943. He travelled widely around Australia and finally settled on Palm Island, where he wrote his first book, This Is Palm Island, *published by the then Australian Institute of Aboriginal Studies (AIAS, 1978). The stories presented here were written during his travels through Queensland researching for his subsequent books* Dreamtime Nightmares, *also published by the AIAS, 1985, and* Up Road the Troopers, *University of Queensland Press 1990. His work has attracted numerous literary awards, including the 1986 Stanner Award, 1987 New South Wales Premier's Award and Australian Human Rights Award, 1988 Queensland Premier's Award and in 1991 the Victorian RAKA Award. He currently lives in Ballina, New South Wales, where he is working on a new project.*

Stories of an Aboriginal Researcher

THERE IS NO place in the world like the Australian bush and I grasp every opportunity to lose myself in its vastness. Although the bush can be very trying at times, it is not *always* inhospitable. Far from it, it is a great feeling when you finally settle into your chosen campsite and the billy is on the boil and cheerily bubbling away, inviting you to chuck in a handful of tea. It's great to sit beneath a large she-oak tree, the cool breeze sighing through its wispy foliage and to hear your old bush chair creak as you sit and taste the rich black tea. Your ears strain at the sound of a high-flying jet, your only obvious link with civilisation. As you sit and watch, the fading afternoon sun turns the surrounding countryside into a velvet and brown sheen. The trees on the ridges and spurs take on the appearance of delicate lacework as they silhouette against the pink sunset and meld with the blue of the horizon. You hear the impossible brilliance of the warbling magpies and the crilling of butcher birds. From the distance your ears pick up the sound of kookaburras as they laugh in raucous merriment. Moments later the air is filled with the screeching of the sulphur-crested cockatoos as they wheel overhead and settle for the night on the limbs of a dead ironbark tree. Then, in the gathering darkness, your eyes are drawn to a million stars as they wink back at you. As you toss another log on the campfire a glowing shower of sparks springs up only to disappear among the leaves of the gumtrees, the musky aroma of the smoke flaring your nostrils.

The Clever Ones

IT WAS IN 1979 when I first visited the small west Queensland township of Dajarra. I had gone there to carry out some research about the lives of Aboriginal stockworkers during the early 1900s.

When I first arrived I knew nobody, but the residents of the town, being as friendly as they are, soon welcomed me into their homes. I was introduced to an old ex-stockman called Jack and made arrangements to meet with him the following day so he could tell me of his experiences. This, of course, was music to my ears; precisely what I was looking for.

The sun had barely cleared the hills when I ambled over to Jack's place. He was sitting on an old oil drum in his back yard, a lazy fire sending up wisps of smoke into the cold morning air. He was well rugged up in an old khaki army overcoat and, perched upon his head, was a high-crowned cowboy hat, the same style I remembered Tom Mix wore when I was a kid, as he rode across the silver screen shooting up the baddies.

'Bloody cold this morning, Bill,' he said, as he offered me his calloused hand.

'How do you live here?' I replied facetiously.

'Aw, you get used to it.' He smiled. I nodded as I wheeled another oil drum close to the fire and sat down, desperately trying to warm my hands. I looked closely at him and saw a face, heavily lined, which seemed to hold a perpetual smile.

We yarned about various things until the sun rose higher, warming up the morning air.

'I got a bit of a copper mine up in the hills,' he told me. 'Would you like to go up and see it?'

The Datsun started easily in spite of the cold and soon we were heading towards Mount Isa. After about ten kilometres he pointed to a side track which was almost overgrown with Mitchell Grass. After about five minutes Jack told me to stop.

'It's over there,' he indicated with his chin. 'We better walk from here.' I looked across and saw a hole in the ground about three metres square. As we arrived at the spot I could see a huge pile of first-class copper ore lying in the grass.

'We used to have good times around here.' A smile broadened as he waved his arm in a semicircle. 'I reckon you could still find a few empty bottles.' He laughed out loud at the memory and told me about the times he and his mates would come out here for drinking sessions years ago.

He moved over to a log and sat down, no doubt reliving his younger days. He suddenly sat upright, pointing to a tree-covered area about two hundred metres away. A frown crossed his face as he rose from the log.

'That's where I got crook once,' he said, pointing to a flat patch of ground. He shook his head slowly at the memory.

'What, crook from the grog?' A serious expression came over his face as he looked at me.

'No,' he replied. 'It wasn't the grog. I was "boned".' This mention of boning – a method of punishment, or worse, by the dreaded Kadaitcha man – captured my immediate attention. During my years of research among Aborigines I had heard many tales about the mysterious doings of these keepers of the law, the Clever Fellas.

'What happened?' I asked him. 'Can you tell me about it?' He frowned even deeper as he looked once again at the spot in the distance. He was clearly agitated and I gained the impression that he was scared. He remained silent for a few moments then slowly walked towards the spot he had indicated. I followed.

'There,' he said, pointing to the ground. 'When I got crook I lay down under those trees. This Clever Fella caught me.' He looked furtively at the surrounding countryside as if he expected to see something – or someone.

'Go on,' I prodded, indelicately. 'How were you caught?'

He began to explain. 'I was sitting around the campfire one afternoon. There were about five other fellas there, all laughing and joking about which one of us was going to cook tea. We had finished mustering for the day and we were having a bit of a blow. I looked up and saw this strange fella creeping slowly through the bushes.' He looked at me to ensure he had my full attention. There were no worries in that direction.

'As soon as I saw him I knew what he was.' He took off his hat and drew a hairy forearm across his brow. 'Course, I didn't say anything to the others; you don't do that. When you see that sort of thing you mind your own business. You don't get involved in that sort of thing.' He collected his thoughts before continuing.

'Now, I knew that something must be wrong but I didn't know what and I didn't know who he was after. I knew it wasn't me because I didn't do anything wrong but I couldn't speak for the other fellas.

'Anyway, I watched this Clever Fella come up behind the bushes. Then I saw his pointing bone. He started to point it at us and I thought at the time that he was pointing it a bit too close to me. But I wasn't worried because I knew I did nobody any harm. I found out later that one of my mates sitting around the fire had been mucking around with another man's missus. He was the one that the Clever Fella was after.' He breathed deeply and looked at me. 'But, you know, Bill,' he said, 'I knew he must have caught me instead. I was just going to jump up and yell out to him but he was gone. He just disappeared. I was real worried then.'

'What did this pointing bone look like?' I asked him. He pulled a face before answering my question.

'Well,' he replied, 'it's usually made from the leg bone of an emu. It's got a real point on it and a length of string made out of plaited grass tied on to one end and a bundle of emu feathers on the other. It frightens me to even think about it.' His hands shook noticeably as he tried to roll a cigarette. I offered him one of my ready-made cigarettes, which he accepted, throwing his roughly rolled tube of tobacco into the grass.

'I could feel myself getting weaker and weaker and that's where I fell down.' He took several hard puffs at his cigarette and looked down to the ground, shaking his head.

'I thought I was done for. But a funny thing happened. An old fella on horseback noticed me in the grass and came riding up to me. He got off his horse and looked at me for a while.

'"You bin boned," he said to me. "Why you bin boned? You good fella." I told him about what had happened and I think he already knew about it. Don't ask me how. And I think he knew me, too, but I didn't know him.' Jack looked at me quickly. 'I could smell him, though!' he said.

'Smell him?' I queried. 'What do you mean, "smell him"?' Jack side-eyed me and smiled slightly with a certain amount of smugness.

'He was an old Kadaitcha man,' Jack said. 'You can usually tell a Clever Fella by the smell. They smell ... oily.'

'Yes,' I told him. 'I've heard that before. Obviously he must have fixed you up,' I remarked. 'How did he do it?' Jack thought for a moment before replying.

'Buggered if I know,' he admitted. 'He told me to lie on my belly with my arms above my head. When I did this he sat across my back and I felt a slight stinging feeling in my side. I caught sight of his hands and they were covered with blood.' He was quite alarmed at the memory and I thought that he was not going to finish his story. I looked at him squarely, challenging him to do so. He waited for a long while before he continued.

'Well,' he said, a heavy frown creasing his forehead. 'He told me I could get up now because I was "fixed up". True enough, I was able to stand up, no trouble. I was strong again. When I looked at his hands I saw that he was holding a small stick, covered in blood.' He was shaking a little now as he relived the experience.

'When he opened his hand he showed me a small, red stone. He told me that this was the cause of my illness and that he had now removed the curse the other Clever Fella had accidentally put on me.'

I believe old Jack. Why would he want to tell me a load of bullshit? Actually, this was not the first time I had heard the claim that a 'little red stone' had been removed from a boned man thereby 'fixing him up'. No further explanation. And I've witnessed the Kadaitcha's magic myself, though not in such a potentially lethal display.

It was a rainy afternoon at one of the outstations of the Headingly Cattle Station. About seven of us were sitting around the campfire enjoying a well-deserved mug of tea. The young bloke who had lit the fire and put the billy on to boil was called Bootlace. As he sat among us he became silent and a vacant expression came over his face. One of the drovers noticed and touched him on the arm.

'Hey, where you at, Bootlace?' he chided him, jokingly. 'You gone all quiet.' The young man looked across to us and smiled.

'I was just thinkin',' he replied. 'It must be good for you married bloke. You just go 'ome and your missus there; your tucker cooked and the billy boiled. Wish I 'ad a wife.'

One of the men was sitting a little way off the main group. When he heard what Bootlace had to say he looked up and inclined his head slightly. He was an elderly man. His hair was quite long and very grey. His beard, too, was grizzled and grey, yet sparse enough to expose the deep creases which ran down each side of his broad nose. As he looked at Bootlace I noticed the steely appearance of his black, deep-set eyes. He nodded slightly towards Bootlace.

'You want a woman, young fella?' he grinned. We all turned and looked at him, wondering what his interest was.

'I reckon I can fix you up,' he told Bootlace. A serious expression had now crossed his face as he rose slowly to his feet. I think it was then that we all realised that this man was not the usual run-of-the-mill blackfella. There was something about his deameanor which somehow set him apart. One of the other men shifted uneasily as he looked closely at the old man.

'Hey,' he said, taking a backward step. 'You a Clever One, eh?' We all stared at him in disbelief. A Kadaitcha man was the most feared person in Aboriginal culture; a magical man; an oracle. Yet here was this man, friendly and docile, offering no threat or intimidation. Strange; very strange.

The old man dropped his head slightly and slowly nodded.

'You finish with all that stuff now?' asked one of our group. 'You no more?' The old bloke smiled and assured us that he was, in fact, retired as keeper of Aboriginal law.

He then ambled slowly over to his horse and removed a small bundle from his saddle-bag. It was wrapped in possum skin. From it he produced a small, blood-red stone and lay it upon a piece of bark. He turned his back to us and crouched over the object. We heard a low humming sound as he swayed over his mysterious bundle. He squatted there for almost a minute swaying and softly, very softly, humming his incantation. Suddenly, he stood up, wrapped up his mysterious paraphernalia, placed the bundle back into his saddle-bag and sat down again.

No one spoke. Bootlace cast a swift, cautious glance at the old man not quite daring enough to ask him if he was, in fact, fair dinkum. We returned to our mugs of tea, our conversation now very much curtailed.

'We better get 'em cattle out,' one of the group suggested, shakily. 'The boss want 'em branded tomorra'.' We sprang up, pleased at something to occupy our minds and take us away from what we had just witnessed.

We packed up our camping equipment and headed for the mob which was grazing on the next ridge. Except for the organising of the draft, very little was said for the rest of the day and, as we moved the cattle slowly back towards the outstation, each of us was consumed by his own thoughts.

As we rode into the camp we noticed smoke issuing from Bootlace's campfire. We drew rein and looked in disbelief as a young Aboriginal woman was busying herself over the fire, cooking something in a large, black pot. A billy was bubbling merrily alongside the fire. Bootlace looked on in astonishment. The rest of us looked at each other in utter confusion. Bootlace rode slowly over to where the woman stood, stoking the fire.

'G'day,' she smiled. 'You want a drink of tea? I just made a billy.' Bootlace dismounted and frowned as he gave his horse to Paddy, the ringer.

'Where you from?' we heard Bootlace ask her. She stretched out her arm and touched Bootlace on the shoulder.

'I dunno,' she replied. 'I just come 'ere.' We noticed Bootlace relax somewhat as he looked into the cooking pot.

'Meat all cooked,' said his new companion. 'Spuds too.' They both went into the tin shed in which Bootlace camped. We all rode off, dismounted and gave our horses to Paddy.

The Hunters

IT WAS ABOUT mid-1983 when I returned to Dajarra, to collect more stories of the Aboriginal station workers.

The sky was becoming dark as I arrived. I headed for the house of an old friend of mine, knowing quite well that I would be in for a mug of hot tea. My friend, Norman, liked his teas strong – very strong. I had no idea how he could drink the stuff. As I approached the house I was not disappointed. Sitting on a block of wood was my friend, gazing into a lively fire over which hung a blackened billy.

'How's things, Norman?' I said, as I came to a stop in the yard. He looked and smiled.

'Aw, take it as she comes,' he drawled. He motioned me to a chipped enamel mug upon an upturned box. 'Want a drink of tea?'

I walked over and poured myself a half-mug of tea and filled it with boiling water.

Norman had spent all his life on cattle stations but now he was retired, though still quite active.

'What you doing up here?' he asked. 'No gold here.' I told him briefly the reason for my visit. He nodded towards an old house further up the street and smiled.

'You remember old Ruby?' he asked. 'She's still there. She might remember a few more things that you want to know.' Yes, I remembered Ruby. I will never forget my first meeting with her years ago as she drove up and heard Norman say, 'That's the one I was tellin' you about.'

'Tellin' 'im what?' Ruby demanded to know. She was a plumpish woman of about fifty. Her skin was as black as coal, that is except where it folded at her elbows and armpits, where it was a smooth, silky tan colour. I introduced myself to her and told her why I was in the area.

'Yes,' she smiled. 'I can tell you how it was in the old days.'

After arranging to meet Ruby the following day, I drove off to a spot out in the bush to set up camp. I awoke just on dawn and heard the wallabies and several emus come down to their favourite drinking hole. They paid little attention to me as they stopped and picked at the fresh grass beside the creek. I did not bother to light a fire for a brew as I knew Norman would already have one made. As I entered the yard I passed quite close to an unsuspecting dog which was lying stretched out by the fire. The dog jumped to its feet, startled. It began barking and soon every dog in Dajarra was barking. I helped myself to a mug of well-brewed tea just as Ruby's vehicle turned into the yard.

'We'll have to go and get some meat for the poor dogs,' she said. 'The poor things are starvin'.'

'Where do you go for your meat?' I asked. It was a stupid question.

'There should be a few roos down at the five-mile,' she said. 'It won't take long to shoot a couple.' She looked at my Datsun. 'That'll be good to take.' She nodded towards my vehicle. 'My tyres are not too good.'

'No problem,' I assured her. She walked across to her Ford and took out a .22 rifle. She stood it up in the front of the cabin of the Datsun and got in. I leaned across and gently removed the rifle and lay it down in the back of the ute. She compressed her lips and glanced at me accusingly.

In the bush, just because a place is called 'five-mile' does not necessarily mean that it is five miles from your starting point. Ruby's 'five-mile' turned out to be almost twenty. We eventually arrived at a turn-off in the road.

'In 'ere,' she said suddenly. I was taken by surprise and I turned the wheel sharply to negotiate the turn but, because of the gravel surface, I put the poor old Datsun into an eighty-degree flat-arse spin. Ruby's rifle slid along the tray and the air resounded with a loud *crraaackk*!

'Jesus Christ! Was that rifle loaded?'

'I always keep it loaded,' she sniffed. 'Never know what you're goin' to see.' I brought the rifle inside the cabin and told Ruby to hold it upright between her legs, pointing slightly out the window. I lined the Datsun up with the road once more and we proceeded along the dusty road.

'Stop 'ere,' she demanded, urgently. I braked hard and came to a stop in a cloud of dust.

'See that windmill?' She pointed between the trees. 'There's a big water tank there. I reckon there'll be some roos there having a drink.' We both got out of the vehicle and quietly walked towards the windmill. I was about five paces behind, my eyes not leaving Ruby's rifle for a second.

Suddenly, two huge kangaroos bounded out from behind the tank and headed for the scrub. Ruby's rifle flew to her shoulder.

'Whack ... whack.' The small .22 missiles could be heard thumping into the kangaroos as they made their mad scramble over rocks and fallen logs in a desperate effort to escape the black huntress. One leaped high into the air and then dropped to the ground, lifeless.

'Got 'im,' Ruby yelled jubilantly. She raced over to where the kangaroo lay and began to wallop it with a big stick.

'Shit, Ruby.' I smiled. 'He couldn't be any deader.' She stopped her frantic attack and threw the stick to the ground and gave it a final thump in the guts with her foot and smiled sheepishly. Blood was everywhere; her legs, arms, face. All were covered with bright red flecks.

We dragged our quarry back to the Datsun and somehow, hauled him into the back. He was a huge 'old man kangaroo'.

'I'll skin 'im when we get 'ome,' she said, wiping blood from her face with a handful of grass. 'The dogs'll be right, now.'

The sun was high in the heavens by the time we returned to Dajarra. The dogs smelt us miles away and came racing to meet us. It did not take Ruby long to remove the skin from the roo. She kept hurling stones at the dogs to keep them at bay. When she was finished she removed the tail for her own use and chopped the kangaroo to pieces with an axe and threw it to the dogs. There was plenty for every dog but they fought furiously among themselves as they ate.

I met many more people during my sojourn at Dajarra. Although there was a well-stocked shop in the town, many of my black friends chose to 'go bush' and hunt for their tucker. Early one Sunday morning I was invited to accompany some blokes on a hunt.

'We goin' for emu,' they told me, selecting a variety of spears. We walked for quite some miles before seeing a mob of five emus grazing in a paddock. We all stopped dead in our tracks and sank silently to the ground where the long kangaroo grass hid us from their view. The hunters knew exactly what to do so there was no time wasted in planning the operation. The youngest of the hunters, a lad called Lionel, flattened himself on the ground and remained perfectly still. The others, crouching low with only their eyes above the grass, formed a semi-circle around Lionel with the 'open' part of the circle facing the unsuspecting emus. Not a word was spoken. The only movements were the occasional jabbing of a finger by the leader of the hunting group who then punched the air several times. I had gone with one of the others and he pointed to a spot for me to hide. I lay on my stomach, hardly daring to breathe.

After several minutes I heard a strange noise and I carefully lifted my head enough to see what was causing it. As I peered across I saw Lionel's legs kicking around in mid-air. For a moment I thought a big black snake had hooked onto him but I was reassured by a glance from my companion. Then Lionel began making a squeaking sound as he thrashed his legs about. The emus, of course, looked up suddenly, their long, brown necks weaving from side to side, trying to decipher what was going on. I was surprised to see that they did not run away with fright. Instead, they strolled slowly and casually towards Lionel's thrashing legs. They were completely perplexed. Still closer they went, their necks stretched to their limits trying to work out what these strange goings-on were all about. As the emus were closing in on Lionel I noticed the hunters were completing the circle around them until the emus were completely surrounded.

'Cunning bastards,' I admired. Suddenly, Lionel jumped up with a nerve-shattering yell. The emus fled in fear and panic but it was far too late. Which ever direction they took they saw a wicked spear aimed at them.

Three emus graced the campfires that night. What a feast we all had.

'Sticky-beaks, eh?' one of the hunters said to me. 'Emus are real curious. They want to know everything.' He smiled as he chewed on a drumstick that would make the Kentucky Fried mob green with envy!

Going for Goanna

IT HAPPENED out in the bush near Urandangie, near the headwaters of the Georgina River. I had been camped in the vicinity for some months, and had befriended some members of the Waluwarra family group. They were a happy and friendly mob and, once accepted, I became very close to them. Their ways and wants were quite simple: a dry bed, a good feed and plenty of land to roam around in. They were a lively lot and always seemed to be laughing – sometimes at me.

It was about May I suppose, and the weather was beginning to get a bit cold and ready food in the way of kangaroos, emus and bustards (plains turkeys) were becoming scarce, as they would be for the next month or two. Still, there were plenty of lizards and fish around so we did not starve. We walked for miles every day just looking around, playing and laughing. Around the campfire one night it was decided that we should go out and try to hustle up a goanna or two. Goannas, when cooked correctly, are quite good eating.

Our cook, a fellow known as Gammon Jack, had it down to a fine art. First, he threw the goanna – or whatever – onto the coals until its hide had been charred off then he placed the lizard into a one-metre hole, the bottom of which had been previously lined with very hot rocks. A small amount of greenery, usually tea-tree leaves, was moistened and thrown on top of the unlucky animal. Then the entire contents were covered with sheets of bark or tin, and then completely covered with soil. After several hours the hole was scooped out and the feast began. It would be cooked just as well as any holiday resort chef could cook it – juicy and tender.

The following day, after collecting an assortment of huge sticks, spears and stones, we headed off towards the Georgina River in search of a big 'gwanna'. It was a magnificent morning; the sun shone onto the dew-laden leaves of the black wattle trees so they shimmered. The air was fresh and the blood-wood smoke from the campfires still drifted lazily in the air. I remember wondering why I would ever want to go back to the city.

We chased up several lizards and wallabies but, as our stomachs were still full from our morning meal, we paid them no heed, preferring instead to let them grow fatter.

At last we wandered off in a more-or-less aimless direction but always mindful that the Georgina River, our destination, was somewhere ahead. The river was almost dry except for a few muddy waterholes where the dingoes, kangaroo and other bush animals and birds came to drink. A large flock of galahs drank and screeched, ever alert for predators. Suddenly, on spotting us, they rose into the air momentarily turning the sky pink as they wheeled and flew off, their screech reaching a crescendo.

We wandered along the riverbank for a while, searching every crack and hollow in the dead trees which lined the top of the bank. A breeze had sprung up and whistled and sang between the she-oak (casuarina) trees. It was decided to search the river bed itself, with half the group venturing off to the right and the other half to the left. I decided it would be prudent for me to remain on the top of the riverbank, not wanting to impede any mad dash, should any of the hunters spot their quarry.

They disappeared over the top of the riverbank and things went quiet. All talking and giggling had stopped. Hunting for food in the bush is a serious business. I sat on the ground, idly scratching away with a stick.

Suddenly, all hell broke loose. Yells and screams came from the direction of my left flank. I immediately jumped to my feet, more from fright than anything else. As I stood there, the yells were getting closer when, suddenly, over the top of the riverbank came an enormous goanna, racing at great speed, its belly high off the ground, its head aloft searching desperately for the nearest tree. Then the rotten thing spotted me! The stupid goanna thought I was the nearest tree and was intent upon climbing me.

Well, I couldn't just stand there and there was no way I could out-run it; so I took the only evasive action I could; I jumped ... high! Just as my feet left the ground, I felt its wet, dangling tongue drag across my foot.

The mob rushed up over the riverbank in hot pursuit, their enormous throwing sticks held in readiness to let fly at the frantic saurian. Upon seeing what had just happened they held on to their sticks and began to laugh. Their laughter became uncontrollable when one of the group reckoned that I lingered in mid-air for a full five seconds.

'You're a dangerous mob of bastards,' I said shakily. My remarks were not taken seriously and, to add insult to injury, they rolled upon the ground laughing their heads off. It goes without saying that the goanna lived to see better days, though I have no doubt that, by now, it has taken its respective place in the cooking hole of Gammon Jack.

Janice Slater

JANICE SLATER, of the Yamatji people from Badimaya country, is a prolific writer of short stories and poetry. She was born in Perth, Western Australia, in 1950 and raised on a sheep station about 430 kilometres away. Educated initially to Year 9, Janice returned to education in 1984 to gain her tertiary entrance. She has been writing intermittently ever since, working in the areas of Aboriginal education, employment and research. She now lives in the Coffs Harbour area of New South Wales and has four children and five grandchildren. Her stories 'Millie' and 'Black Knight, Black Night' were first published by Pascoe Publishing in Australian Short Stories in 1994 and 1995.

Glossary

bulai	look out
Nyoongah (*also* Nyoongar)	Aboriginal people of south-west WA
wajbulla (*also* watjella)	whitefella
yorga (*also* yorgah)	woman

Finders Keepers

I DON'T KNOW how long the holiday on the coast lasted. To get there would have been a long trip, no doubt uncomfortably hot and dusty, but I don't recall it. The car must have been cramped. It would most certainly have been tiring for all, yet once again my memory fails me.

No heat. No dust, no thirst or hunger or boredom. No memory. Gone. The travel part anyway.

What I do remember is the unfamiliar seaweed odour, the glare of the pristine sands and the prevailing whoosh of waves that never ceased. We knew only of our dry, red inland panorama. These strange grasses, birds, stunted dune scrub, tangled vines in the wind-bent bush; these things were all so foreign. Such cloudless memories now.

We hopped and skipped and yuckaied over blisteringly hot grey sand from small pools of shade to tufts of grass to towels when there was nothing else to save our feet. To the squelchy pig-face, to the wide white beach that stretched on forever, just as our young lives did. We flung down towels and kersplashed into the pellucid sea. Halcyon days! Black kids. Dry-red-dust kids. Cavorting, splashing, paddling. Ever bush cautious, never venturing out too far. We revelled in the sun with salt-prickly skin, salt-stiff hair. Even black skin burnt in the strident coastal glare. Dry mouths from constant salt water, empty bellies from fresh sea air and glorious activity, then home to campfire and fresh fish fried on an open fire. Impatiently hungry, picking tiny bones, each morsel ambrosia, replete with a large green enamel pannikin of warm sweet tea. Yes, these things I smell and taste still.

We found them one clear morning while searching for beach treasure. Saw them lying on the sand like a gift to us from the sea. Not a soul in sight. Just had to be ours. We stood staring at these profferings of glass and black rubber so black and inviting.

A snorkel and mask!

A snorkel and mask? Our windows to the ocean secrets. Ours? Yes, we decided, my sister and I ... ours. Nobody around, had to be ours for the taking. We took turns, she and I, all that morning. Ever cautious (we could not swim) we waded out to the shallow reef and discovered just below the surface of the ocean a world of marine treasures we had not imagined existed. The reef sprouted a miracle garden of colourful coral appearing nothing like the dried colourless pieces we had collected on the sand. Everything waved in gentle motion; rhythmically with the pulse of the ocean. A silent unknown world. Spongy seaweed, thin fragile seaweed, rigid rubbery seaweed, right there, just below the surface in those limpid subtropical waters; a revelation.

The reef appeared to us as a holder of secrets, with holes and nooks and crannies that held ... who knows what? Not but a few inches from the mask swam fish in colours we marvelled over. Startling black and white stripes, bright silver, glimpses of vivid colours appeared to us as some exotic marvel. We stared at them, and they at us. The fish so curious, we so awestruck. There were undulating ribbons of minute silver fish that shimmered with the morning sun's penetration, that flashed when startled, halted for a second, turned back in unison, then disappeared. Lone fish, reticent fish, innocently bold fish. What fortune, what luck to have these magnificent things that allowed us the privilege of witnessing this underwater shrine of mystery.

After deliberating for some time we decided to take home these wonderful, useful gifts from the sea. The best and only thing to do. We could not leave them where we had found them, they were now ours. Besides, someone else would be sure to take them, and we had found them, so they were ours. We rationalised and legitamised our decision. And that was that.

Finders keepers.

On the way back to the campsite, we passed our brother. Big mistake. We held the claimed behind our backs to no avail. What have U got? He demanded to see them. Just one look, he promised. He wheedled and cajoled. Could he please, please have them? Just had to have one go, wouldn't ask again, he promised.

Nuh! We replied ... Nuh, Nuh, Nuh!

We held them, one piece each. Tightly. Tossing our salt-stiff hair, we turned our backs and carried the prizes home, heads held high. Finders keepers, losers weepers.

Brother turned on us, said we were selfish, he didn't want to use the stupid old things anyway. Besides, he was telling. Ooowaah! Going to dob us in. For what? For stealing he said. But we found them, they belonged to us. So there!

By the afternoon we had eaten and washed and lazed, planned to go back to the magical reef tomorrow morning. The holiday had now taken a new turn. What stories we'd tell when we got back home. What would tomorrow bring? Mermaids, my sister intoned importantly. I believed her. I always did.

A stranger approached the camp. Bulai! Lookout! Wajbulla comin'! We heard the muffled voices of parents and wajbulla, glanced at each other with mild consternation. Naah! Didn't have anything to do with us.

Oh, yes it did!

You girls, we heard a parent calling. You girls better come here quick and give this man his things back!

Brother! Brother had turned traitor in envy and asked down at the beach if anyone had lost a snorkle and mask. Our brother had turned on us, turned Good Citizen. We, silent and shame, heads down, handed the mask and snorkel back to the wajbulla man.

Brother smiled self-righteously at the adults, accepting the 'thank you' virtuously. He gave us a smug triumphant smirk.

We reckoned that if he had found them, we wouldn't have told.

Maybe.

Black Knight, Black Night

S ERGEANT VERA STOTE and her new partner Gregory Fienberg cruise the streets of the coastal town in the patrol wagon; late winter 1967. Fienberg, the junior of the team, drives as Stote scours the streets for wayward girls. This she sees as one of her main duties. The straightening out of wayward young girls is her mission. She always says it doesn't matter if they are black, white, or brindle, if they are on the streets without good reason she would see to it that the Welfare got them into a home for juvenile delinquents, adding that of course the blackgirls are always the worst offenders, but you could only expect that.

'You've got to understand, Greg, it's in the breed. They're criminals by nature. The blackgirls start at it so young. They walk around the streets brazenly looking for boys. Next thing you know they're pregnant and soon they're working the streets for booze money.'

Constable Fienberg nods in agreement, although he can't think why Vera might have these opinions. He's been in the force for only a few months, never had contact with Aboriginal people before. This country assignment is seen as good grounding. They pay their dues and after a time, apply for a city posting to get back to civilisation.

Most officers, anyway. Not Vera Stote. This is her territory. Born and raised here. She makes certain that everyone knows. She is tough and unrelenting in her search for offenders, juvenile offenders, black juvenile female offenders.

Her straight black hair is cropped short. Her small black eyes are so deep set that she appears to be squinting at you. So deep set that you can't see what she is thinking. She doesn't want you to see what she is thinking. She doesn't want you to know what she is thinking. After years spent in the harsh climate her skin is sucked dry of moisture, dried out to a toughness that befits her. She stands tall and thick. No make-up for Sergeant Stote. It isn't permitted on duty, not that she will wear it off duty anyway. She may have been attractive in her youth. Her lips are full, though the upper now shows the fine downward creases of a heavy smoker. Her nose is slightly thickened and askew from a break after a cricket ball struck her in a social club game. Sergeant Stote spins a yarn to Fienberg that she'd been attacked by a truck driver when she'd booked him for a traffic offence. 'This,' she says solemnly tapping the side of her nose, 'is the price you have to pay for being an honest copper, Gregory.'

It is six-thirty on a Friday evening, still light from a low setting sun. Little eddies of paper and leaves dance in the street, choreographed by a gusty sea breeze. The main shops are closed, leaving the cafes and delicatessens open. The picture theatre will open soon. Hotels prepare for the Friday night crush. Fienberg wheels the dark blue, white-topped patrol wagon into the carpark near the beachside fish and chip shop. The wide spreading Moreton Bays drop small reddish-brown figs on the bonnet. The bitumen under the trees is a lumpy mat of red-brown squelched figs exposing tiny white seeds. A few seagulls stand one-legged in a circle of street light. They wait for the next handout of chips, squabble for space, as Sergeant Stote and Constable Fienberg stride over to the fish and chip shop. Lou, the garrulous Greek owner, greets them with a gold-toothed smile.

''Ow ya goin', Sarge? See ya got a new offsider. What'll it be tonight? Ees on the 'ouse, same as usual. Barra's frozen, but ees good. Gunna be quiet night, or what ya reckon?'

'Two pieces of barra and plenty of chips, Lou. You ever seen a quiet Friday night around here, mate? Never. We'll find something to keep us busy without even trying. And this is Greg Fienberg.' Vera motions towards her partner.

'Pleased to meet ya, mate.' Greg nods at Lou.

'Good town this, ay Vera?' Lou rolls the r's in Vera.

'Nothing here that a good cop can't fix, Lou.'

Greg Fienberg wonders how many other small perks there are. Could be that it might just be worthwhile doing a stint here. At least for a while. He thinks of the girlfriend he left in the city. He knows she'll wait for him. Won't stop him from grabbing a bit of fun, though. He's heard about the surfie girls around here. Might even get to a Stomp on a night off. It's cray season so he thinks he might have a fair chance of winning a heart, with most of the local boys out on the boats for the season. He rubs the blond stubble on the back of his head. All the blokes are wearing their hair long, he'd stick out like ... well, like a cop. He'll have a go, anyway. It's all this Beatle stuff, the cause of the long-hair craze. It'd never last, never beat Roy Orbison, his idol. He reckons that bloke can really sing. Not this long-haired hippie stuff the Beatles do. Can't make head nor tail of most of it.

'Ready? We'll eat in the wagon.' Stote startles him out of his thoughts. 'Got a girl, Greg?'

'Yep. Well sort of. Back home.' Greg doesn't really want to say they are engaged. He wonders if the rumours of Vera Stote and her capacity for men and booze are true. He can't imagine it.

~

Steven Bardich has been in town for a few days now, arrived from the city with his cousin in a Morris 1100, flashing money around, impressing the local gang. He notices Judy and asks around for her name. Sees her walking home from work. She carries a brown paper parcel of new clothes picked up today. It is her pay day. He drives slowly alongside her, keeps talking to her until she glances over, smiling shyly.

'What's ya name? You a solid lookin' yorga. Want a lift?' He stops the car. Judy stops walking, hesitates, gets in.

'I don't know you,' she says. 'You got no shame. Where you from?' Dark skinned, dark brown hair slicked back, curls spilling onto his forehead. An attractive, lithe, nineteen-year-old Nyoongah. He wears a black shirt with tight black jeans and black desert boots. His dark eyes dance and play with Judy's, then drop to her long brown legs. 'You a Rocker or what?' Judy asks, conscious of his eyes.

'Nah! I just bought these clothes cos they solid. Aren't they?' he shoots back at her teasingly. 'I bought these cos I've 'ad my eye on you since we come to town. An' I bought these, too, for you. Down at the jewellery shop. Steven Bardich at your service, Judy Gardener.' He reaches down under the seat and flourishes a gold bracelet, a gold necklace with a heart and some dangling earrings made of a single white bauble hanging on a gold chain. Judy is aghast. She'd never be able to afford gold jewellery.

'I can't take them! Mum'd kill me!'

'Don't show 'er, then.' He reaches over and presses them into her hand. 'Wear 'em to the pictures with me. Tonight.' He keeps holding her hand covering the jewellery with his other hand. Judy flushes but doesn't protest against his hands. She pushes the jewellery down into her bag. She won't tell her mother. All her friends will be impressed. She saw the girls eyeing Steven and his cousin. Everyone knows when strangers are in town.

'Come over 'ere.' He reaches over with an arm to bring her to the middle of the front seat. Judy slides over, long legs tangling with the gear stick in the floor of the car. He keeps one arm draped over her shoulder and starts the car up with the other.

'You can tell everyone you're my yorga now, OK?'

'You're a bit cheeky, I don't even know you!' Judy doesn't move, sits proudly beside him as he drives her home hugging her parcel of new clothes and the gold jewellery in the bottom of her bag.

'Drop me off at the corner of my street. I'm too shame. Don't want everybody lookin' at us. Not yet. See you at the front of the pictures at 'alf past seven.' She slams the door and runs up the street, waving back. The Morris 1100 roars off back to town, Steven singing loudly, crashing through the gears. A bigger car with more power would have been better.

'No wuckin' furries. We gunna 'ave a good time t'night. Flash yorga, car and we gunna 'ave a *good* time. Next time I'll borrow a Ford V8, for sure.'

~

Exhausted, Judy Gardener rests a while. The kitchenhand job at the guesthouse is heavy on her feet. More than once she is asked by the manageress to do extra, after the housemaid doesn't turn up. Judy curses the manageress as she massages her sore feet. The pay is just enough to pay her mum board and the rest she uses to buy clothes for going out.

Judy begins to prepare for the night at the pictures and who knows what else. They couldn't just go to the pictures. Oh, no. Steven will drive her around like a princess and he will be her Black Knight to be shown off to the rest of the gang. She hopes Steven is paying. Course he's paying, must have money to pay for the jewellery and the nice little car. Course it wasn't a flash car, not like the whiteboys round town with their hotted up FJs and Zephyrs. Didn't matter, she got a solid lookin' black rocker boy.

She had seen it in the window of the Co-op and wanted it; just had to have it. After six weeks of lay-by she has paid it off and tonight is the night to wear it, going to the pictures with her new man, Steven. Carefully she lays out her new outfit on her bed. The dress is made from two materials. The top is a dark pink ribbed wool with a rolled neck and cut-off sleeves and the attached straight skirt, bottle green corduroy with clusters of small dark pink flowers. A wide matching belt set in large loops hugs the hips. To complete the outfit, a jacket matching the corduroy skirt. Judy feels very Mod, though she worries about the white sling-back shoes, the only good pair she has. They don't match and look shabby. Shabby shoes show that you are careless with your appearance, her mum always says, even if they're old, you've got to keep them clean. Shabby shoes aren't enough to stop Judy looking forward to meeting her new boyfriend at the pictures. She worries that her Mod outfit won't go with Steven's rocker look.

Dreams of escaping the country town have risen up again. Her friends can't understand why she wants to move away. This is their town and they cannot see why anyone would want to leave family and friends behind. But Judy has dreams. She can't explain to them a restless feeling of dissatisfaction. She can't say that she wants to be an actress with glamorous clothes and fine jewellery and a two-storey house. They will laugh at these dreams, she knows this. Her mum just says that it's her dad's wandering spirit, and hopes Judy will grow out of it. But Judy still has dreams of a life somewhere else.

The Housing Commission has allocated her family a new duplex on the outskirts of town. It is surrounded by dry grey-black sand, which is trekked into the house and swept out again by her mother time and again. Judy's mother, Aileen Gardener, battles on with the kids. Tries to get a garden going. Pleased to get a new place. Sorry not to have good furniture to put in it. Judy spends less time with her family now as she is working and has friends in the town. At sixteen she has grown to be a tall attractive girl. Her father, a shearer, had gone off to find work years ago and never came home. Stories go around that he'd gone east. Judy misses her father and vows he will come back one day.

They get by now. Aileen manages with a Deserted Mother's Pension and help from her church friends. She joined the church and sends the kids to Sunday School. A good woman trying to do the best for her kids. Judy loves her mum and four younger brothers. When Judy tells her mother about Steven, the first thing she asks is, 'Who's 'is people, Jude? You gotta make sure ee's not related.'

'No, Mum,' she lies. 'I already asked him. They from the goldfields, he reckons. It's alright. Anyway, it's not like we're gettin' married or anything. I only just met him.' No point in spoiling this. She will ask Steven afterwards.

'Just makin' sure, Jude. And make sure you stay out of trouble. Watch out for Sergeant Stote. She'll get ya for somethin' soon as look at ya.'

'Mum, I'll be OK, promise.' She plans how not to let her mum see the jewellery. 'I picked up my lay-by today. I'll wear it out tonight. It's real flash, Mum. The girls are gunna be jealous!'

Aileen trusts her daughter, but not the crowd she goes around with. She worries that Jude will get into some sort of trouble. Her girl's thoughts of leaving the town also worry Aileen. No good will come of it. She is sure of this.

~

After finishing the fish and chips, Stote and Fienberg resume the patrol. Vera lights up a Camel and Greg winds down his window, coughing.

'Gawd, what are they made of? Camel dung, or what?'

'Get out of it. What are ya? Piss weak, or what? Nothing like a good strong smoke! Well, maybe one other thing.' She leers at Greg suggestively. He chooses to ignore her look. Oh-oh, keep it clean ol' boy, don't want no messiness, being new on the job. Old enough to be his aunty, at least. She sucks the remains of chips through her teeth. This irritates Greg.

Vera has been observing the young recruit. His muscular body shows beneath the crisp new uniform. There isn't a shred of uniform wasted, she notes approvingly with narrowed eyes through a swirl of smoke. Taut broad shoulders, taut wide chest, taut slim waist and mostly she notices ... taut behind. He walks with a taut, spring bounce ... oh yes, she notices his tautness.

The streets are getting busier. Young families with dressing-gowned kids eat fish and chips in the park near Town Beach. The salt-laden breeze is freshening after a warm day. Old couples walk dogs and teenagers begin to gather outside the Red Rose Cafe. The bass of the jukebox thumps and drifts with smells of mixed grills and coffee. The patrol wagon passes slowly and the teenagers all turn to look elsewhere. Some have the two-fingered sign up away from view.

'Look at 'em, Greg. Think we can't see it. The two-fingered salute. I'll book 'em one day when I've nothing better to do. Otherwise, I'll get 'em for something when they start hanging around the pubs. Speaking of pubs, let's go downtown and check out the Commercial. She'll be gearing up now.'

Greg wheels the wagon in a U-turn. A small group has gathered at the front of the hotel, both black and white. Some are gesticulating and jostling with voices raised. Country music whines and twangs out of the bar. They get out of the wagon and walk to the group. Vera singles an old man out.

'Alright, mate. Any trouble here?'

'No, nothin'. No trouble, Sergeant Miss. We just arguin' about nothin'.'

'What's this in aid 'v?' Vera asks an elderly woman who is standing with an unsteady sway.

'Who you callin' native?' the elderly woman crackles back in a high thin voice, trying hard to focus on Vera.

'Now don't get stroppy with me, Maudie, I didn't mean to offend you.'

'Up end me, ay, I'll show you. I'll up end you in a minute!'

Vera sees a confrontation looming. Raising gnarled black hands into fists, the old woman dances around, shaping up to Vera. Maude is ready to fight. Greg notices Maude's pink palms abstractedly. He stands by not knowing which way to look, whether to laugh or step in. Instead, he stands alert awaiting Vera's next move.

'Come on, Maudie, settle down. We'll have to take you down to the lockup to sleep it off.' Maudie still threatens loudly to up end the Sergeant as the two officers lead her to the patrol wagon. As they drive back to the station, Greg asks what they were taking her in for, and Vera replies, 'For her own good.' Maudie keeps up a racket shouting and banging on the rear window of the wagon.

'Do I also detect a bit of softness there, Vera? I thought you didn't like coloureds?'

'I don't,' she replies, 'I'm no bleeding heart, but I've got respect for age and it is for her own good. She could get bashed up and left for dead, old Maude. She's got a reputation for causing trouble. It's the booze. Pickled her brains. She'll get a feed before we let her go in the morning and she'll thank us. It's the young ones that get up my nose. What with their tight jeans and high young tits and flying hair. You should see the way men ... old and young. Leering at them. Married men, too. Ought'a be a law against flaunting yourself like that. Slightest reason and we'll have 'em down the station and report 'em to the Welfare. And Greg, don't go getting ideas about blackgirls. Forget it. Never know when you could get the clap or crabs. Besides, it isn't moral to mix with 'em. Stick to your own colour, I say.'

Greg absorbs all she has to say while driving back to the town centre. He tries to figure out this large opinionated woman. Is she jealous of female youth? She can't vent her anger on the whitegirls, so she singles out the blackgirls and no questions are asked from her superiors. Maybe she has trouble with men, too. He isn't too bothered with all her advice, just wants to get on with the job of being a policeman as best he can, save a few bob and get back home.

~

Judy dresses and hurries through the grey-black sand, getting her white shoes dirty. 'Damn!' she curses, and turns back to wave at her mum. Upon turning the corner, out of sight, she thrusts her hand into her bag and snaps on the bracelet. Walking hurriedly she fiddles with the clasp of the necklace at the back of her neck till it is secured. Last comes the earrings, clip-ons, the final thing to do before she meets her new man, Steven. She doesn't even know his second name. Dusk has settled all around, the street lights flicker on one by one. Oleander perfume hangs thick in the air. Judy feels the stiff newness of her jacket and the soft clinging top of her dress. Hugging the jacket closer to her she quickens to a jog. Not having a watch means having to guess, but she knows she is running late. 'I hope, I hope, I hope he waits. Shoulda give me a watch, not a bracelet.' She smiles then feels ungrateful.

~

On the way back to town, a traffic patrol sedan passes Stote and Fienberg from the opposite direction, sirens blaring, blue lights flashing.

'Cripes, that's Longie and Flash. Wonder what they're up to? It's not knock-off time yet.' Vera laughs. The two-way crackles out a message. 'Car theft. Break and enter. Two male youths apprehended. No assistance required.'

'Oh well, that's their work cut out. Bookin' will take a while. Carry on up the Khyber, Constable.' Vera settles back and lights up a Camel.

~

By eight o'clock Judy begins to worry. The milling picture crowd has filed inside at the sound of the session bell. Cold gusty salt wind wraps around her bare legs. Bare long brown legs now covered in goosebumps. The harsh glare of the theatre entrance causes Judy to shrink in to her new suit, made garish by the fluorescent lighting. Stands there searching up and down the street for Steven, feels exposed.

Light draws colour from her skin, a soft brown now turned sallow, hollows her eyes sockets, etches out the cheekbones. The outfit now feels inappropriate, gaudy. He'll be here soon, he'll be here soon, she intones to herself over and over to keep from walking away. A crushing disappointment settles in. She imagines that Steven might have met someone else. A carload of whiteboys passes by, slows to a crawl. They whistle and shout obscene suggestions. Ignoring them, she stares fixedly at the shopfront opposite. She'll tell Steven, tell her mates about those whiteboys, they'll fix 'em.

Once more, she glances quickly up and down the street. Decides to go home, change, and maybe come back to town to find her friends. She notices Sergeant Stote and her new offsider cruising past twice already. What could have happened to Steven? She twiddles the bracelet round and round her wrist, unsettled by the presence of the police. Please, please, God, I wanted to have a good time tonight. Where is he? Just a few minutes more and then I'll walk home. By eight-thirty Judy resigns herself to the fact that Steven isn't going to show up. Vera and Greg park the wagon further up the street. It is Vera's plan to watch Judy.

'She's up to no good, I tell you. Where the hell did she get those clothes? Must've cost a packet. I know her. She works at the guesthouse. Getting a bit uppity. Couldn't have bought those clothes on her wage. Just watch her.' Vera's eyes squint viciously and her mouth draws across her face tightly.

'Looks like a nice girl to me.' Greg ventures, 'Very nice.' He wonders what this is leading to.

'No such thing as a nice blackgirl, Greg. Look, she's walking after that group of old blokes. Move out, mate, I'm gonna get her for soliciting.'

Disbelieving, Greg moves the car slowly to the kerb as Vera leans out the window.

'Hey!' she calls to Judy, 'I'd like to speak to you for a minute, missy.' Judy, startled, comes over to the dark blue wagon.

'I'm just walking home. I'm not doing anything wrong.'

'Oh yes you are, missy. What were you doing following those men?'

'What men?' Judy is confused. What is this cop talking about? She scans around and notices a group further along the street, turns back to the Sergeant. 'What?'

'Don't come the dumb blackgirl with me. Get in, I'm taking you down to the station for questioning.'

'But ... ' Judy protests.

'Just get in or I'll have you for resisting.'

Vera gets out and holds the door wide with a flourish of a hand towards the car, 'After you, Madam.'

Judy protests. 'I'd rather go in the back.'

'You will get in where I tell you, and don't smart mouth me. Besides, you might like Constable Fienberg.' She emphasises the 'like'.

Resigned, Judy slides into the middle, crushed between the two large cops, pulling in to make herself as small as possible. Greg can smell her freshly washed hair. He thinks it odd that Vera put the kid in front, when she'd put old Maude in the back. It seems her way of operating varies occasionally. God only knows what she has in store for this kid. A cool one, too, this girl. Probably scared out of her wits.

They do not speak on the journey back to the station. Judy does not like riding up front. Doesn't want to be there at all. Worries that her mum will find out about this. She has done nothing wrong. Some of her friends gathered at the Red Rose Cafe see her travelling up front with Sergeant Stote and Constable Fienberg. They point and yell, 'Hey, sister, what's goin' on?'

Judy wishes she wasn't there at all. She thinks some of the girls, her friends, are giggling and laughing. Does she see Steven with them or is it someone who resembles him? This is too much for one night. She holds her head high, folds herself up inside, puts on a mask of indifference, removes herself from the situation.

At the station Sergeant Stote sits behind her desk and lights a Camel. Constable Fienberg stands to the side with hands clasped behind his back. Judy sits rigidly, awaiting questioning.

'Name? Date of birth?' Her voice has a smoker's rasp.

'Judy Ava Gardener. Twenty-third of October, 1951.' Stote, head bowed at the form, stifles a grin and shakes her head slowly.

'No doubt about these people. Mother likes film stars, does she?' Judy doesn't answer.

'Just what did you think you were doing? Waiting for a quick quid?'

'I don't know what you mean.' Judy answers in a flat tone.

'Soliciting is what I mean.'

'I don't know what that means.' Judy knows what it means. She never makes eye contact with Sergeant Stote, fixing her gaze on an old 'Missing' poster, fly specked and yellowed with age. Somebody's daughter is missing.

'Picking up men for money is what I mean. You should know, I'm sure some of your relatives do.' Stote has assumed a patronising tone, laced with sarcasm. Her elbows rest on the desk, fingers dovetailed. Judy remembers a child game: *Here's the church and here's the steeple, Open the door and here's all the people.*

'I was waiting for my boyfriend.' Judy remembers to put 'ing' on the end of waiting. She will not allow her thoughts to be tainted by the venom directed at her. She coughs as cigarette smoke is blown towards her.

'You work at the guesthouse. Can't pay much. Where did you get those clothes and jewellery?' She leans back in her chair, arms folded over the thick midriff. Judy hears the sound of thick-stockinged thighs rasp together as Stote crosses her legs.

'I bought the clothes at the Co-op. I've got a receipt. My boyfriend gave me the jewellery ...' Her voice wavers a little, uncertain for a second that she should have mentioned Steven. Sergeant Stote gets up and moves across for a closer inspection, grabs Judy's neck and roughly pulls hair back from one ear, exposing a white bauble on a gold chain. It hurts and Judy wants to pull away, but doesn't. Stote walks back to her desk, head bowed, hands behind her back, appearing to be absorbed in an important discovery.

'Well, well, Constable Fienberg. We have got a fancy one here. Boyfriend's name?'

'Steven.'

'Steven who?'

'I don't know.'

'I see. Fienberg, go check on the names of those boys picked up tonight.' She snaps her fingers, bristles with sudden efficiency.

'Right, Sergeant.' Fienberg hopes she isn't right. He is tired and looks forward to finishing up for the night. He strides back into the office.

'Steven Bardich and John Woodville. Both Aboriginal. Charged with car theft, Morris 1100, and break/enter of a sideshow carnival on the way from Perth.'

'One of them your *boyfriend*?'

Judy pieces it all together.

'Yes, Steven.'

'Yes what?'

'Yes, Steven, Sergeant.' Judy does not let her mask slip for one minute, welded to the chair. Her skin is a thin brittle shell with a maze of tiny cracks and minuscule pieces will begin to fall off any minute now, down to the floor one by tiny one, with a tinkling sound. She remembers a china jug belonging to her mother that has these tiny cracks all over it. Crazed, she recalls reading a description somewhere. Yes, it was crazed. It was a crazy night. Somehow it didn't matter about car theft and stolen goods. These things had no importance, no bearing on the fact that she was Steven Bardich's yorga. And she was going to leave this stinking town with him, one way or another.

'If there's no charge I'll go now,' Judy volunteers.

'You'll go nowhere until I say so, missy. Let's have another look at that jewellery.' Stote tugs Judy's arm, roughly pushing up a sleeve. Judy thinks about the long hot shower she will take to wash Sergeant Stote off her. 'Well, well. All that glitters is not gold, is it Judy Ava Gardener? That's just cheap shit stolen from a sideshow carnival.'

Stote laughs a phlegmy laugh and gloats over this for a few moments. She has no real interest in this girl any more, knows the girl has no real part in this. But now Stote is tired and wants to relax with Constable Fienberg.

'Take the cheap crap off and give it to Constable Fienberg. I'll send the Welfare around tomorrow morning. I could book you for receiving, or soliciting, but you obviously haven't got a clue. Stay away from this boy, for your own good. And stay away from town. Your mother's a good woman, I know her.'

'Can I see Steven?' Judy is brazen now, not caring. There is nothing to lose. She needs to see him. Needs to know if she is still his yorga.

'Absolutely not. Besides, he couldn't see you with his two busted-up eyes. Pity. What a waste of a pretty dress.' Stote sighs. Bored with this conversation, she yawns and dusts her hands together briskly, dismissing the whole business. 'Take her home, Fienberg, and be back here in fifteen minutes, and I mean fifteen minutes. I've got some overtime for you to do, *just for me*.'

She winks at him as he puts on his cap over the blond satin stubble she can already feel between her thick fingers.

Millie

MILLIE SAT ON her perfectly made bed, then quickly rose, aware of the crinkled bedspread. She smoothed out the wrinkles on the blue quilted silk cover and sat on the matching dresser chair. Her head ached and she stared at her reflection in the mirror. She twisted her long dark hair into a loose pile and secured it with plastic combs. Fine damp strands strayed down the back of her neck and over her ears. She lifted a hand to her face, touching the fine wrinkles around her eyes. Her beautiful dark skin now had a yellow pallor, the brown almond-shaped eyes veiled by thick lashes stared back from the mirror. The headache had dulled her eyes. Soon she would have to prepare the evening meal, the three children would be arriving home and, later, her husband Roger.

They had met while Millie was working at the venetian blind factory. Millie worked on assembly. The blinds hung by the pelmet which was attached to a frame suspended from the ceiling. The blind adjusted up or down so that as she threaded the slats into the plastic strips that held them together she could adjust the work to her height. Sometimes she would cut her fingers on the sharp edges of the metal slats. The monotony was relieved only by the different colours of the blinds. They came in pastels mostly, but sometimes a whole house order would be in white with gold stars backed by fine gold strands. She was proud of her job. She had come up from the south to look for work, and had found this job quickly. She made sure she was punctual and picked up the tasks readily. Jobs weren't that easy to get for a black girl.

Roger worked for a building company as a cabinet maker and had come to pick up an order for a display home when the truck driver was off sick. So it was by accident that they had met. He had noticed Millie from the start and made a point of coming over to her bench to check the order. Millie had shyly redirected him to the office. On the way out he ambled over and asked if she would like to go to the drives. Millie hadn't understood what the *drives* was, until he whispered, *drive-in*. They hurriedly, furtively, whispered a time for the date (the boss might be looking, she said) and he was off.

At seventeen, Millie hadn't been anywhere much, and it flattered her that this man should pay her some attention. Later, Roger would make jokes about *blind dates* and *love is blind* and Millie would laugh. Millie's grandmother gave permission for her to go out with Roger, as she thought it was wonderful that her granddaughter should be shown interest by a white man, and a decent one at that. She wanted her granddaughter to get on in life, have opportunities that she could not provide for Millie's mother. Roger was twenty-seven, ten years older than Millie, and already owned a block of land.

After a short courtship they were married at the Registry Office with Roger's brother as a witness. He had said that it wasn't necessary for anyone else to attend, much to Millie and her family's disappointment. But Millie was in love and proud of her new husband. Roger was short, though taller than the tiny Millie, stockily built, swarthy complexioned with startlingly clear green eyes. His skin was fleshy, as if it would go to fat in older age. At twenty-seven he had a sprinkling of premature grey at the temples. A scar, about three inches long, ran down his right temple. Millie asked him several times what caused the scar and each time he told a different story. At first when she pointed this out, he would become angry and the scar would turn a deep reddish purple, so she never brought it up again.

~

As Millie sat at her dressing table idly tidying hairbrushes and bottles of perfume, she thought back down through the years to when they had first married. His block was in the new northern suburbs and through his work contacts they were able to build a modern three-bedroom home with ensuite, family room and separate dining area. Millie didn't know too much about house design, so Roger did all the planning and decorating. Millie was happy just to have a bright, clean modern home. Sometimes Millie would have an idea about what she would like, but Roger knew best and would remind her that he was the expert on houses and she wasn't to forget that. She remembered how happy and lucky she was. No one else in her family owned their home. At times she would feel guilty about it, and vowed if she ever won lottery, the first thing she would do would be to buy a house each for her mum and Nan, then with what was left over she would buy all her nieces and nephews bikes and toys.

She thought about her own three children. The first, Roger, had come quickly, just seven months after the wedding. Roger had told her to tell everyone the baby was premature. But of course he wasn't, and Millie wasn't ashamed of being pregnant when she got married. In her family it wasn't considered a big shame, lots of girls had kids and never married. Roger, her first-born, resembled his father the most and was the apple of his father's eye. Wherever father went, son went, excluding Millie at times. Millie wasn't invited on fishing trips or to the football or to visit Roger's family. When the next baby, Jason, came a year later, Millie was glad to have Roger take the toddler out and give her a break. Jason had his mother's dark skin and his father's green eyes, a very attractive child. But for Roger nothing could take the place of his firstborn, and Millie could lavish her second with the love she was not given the opportunity to offer her first. Eighteen months later Michelle was born. A very welcome daughter for Millie, her daughter being the image of herself. Again, the new arrival was treated with the indifference shown Jason, and Millie again was secretly pleased, no one was as important as her baby daughter. While she was in hospital for Michelle, Roger had said that they'd better put a stop to this having kids, they were getting darker all the time, next thing they'd be having a full blood, ha ha. Millie had laughed nervously at that.

At first they were really happy. In the early days their time had been taken up with setting up house. Millie hadn't seen that side of Roger for a long while. She couldn't remember when it had started, really. Perhaps it was such an insidious progression that she hadn't noticed the change. In any case there was a time when she had blamed herself for Roger's outbursts. Roger had a stormy temper and she had learnt early in her marriage not to aggravate it.

When he checked the house for dust, she would make absolutely sure there would be none. When he checked the grocery docket she would make absolutely sure every cent was accounted for. When he checked the mileage on the car, it would always show no further than the shopping centre, as she knew better than to go any further, for that would make him angry. At first all the scrubbing and cleaning and checking then rechecking before Roger arrived home from work had worn her out, but he was pleased that he'd taught her how to do it properly, and when Roger was pleased, Millie was also pleased. He taught me everything I know, she would tell her next door neighbour. But now, Millie would no longer allow herself to be blamed for Roger's anger.

There was the time they had taken photographs of the lounge and sent them to Roger's mother in Melbourne and she had written back saying how pleased she was that Millie was able to get the hems straight on the curtains. That pleased Millie then. Now, the comment would only make Millie laugh. And the time Roger's best mate's wife visited and told Millie how impressed she was with the way her windows were clean and that it must be because Millie was different, one of the *better ones*. Millie hadn't enjoyed the visit, as all the visitor would talk about was what brand of soap powder to use, the best type of toilet paper, and all the time checking to see what Millie used and showing great surprise that everything was clean. By the time the visitor had left Millie had felt like the Welfare had just been to check on her, and wondered if she had passed the test.

Millie closed her eyes, resting her fingers against her temples, and smiled a small wry grin at the memory of that woman. Thank goodness they had shifted away. Roger had insisted that she be friendly to his mate's wife, but how could she when they had nothing in common. She couldn't say that to Roger, so it was better to say nothing at all.

She put a slim hand to her neck, remembering the time she did say too much. Roger had come home to find a dent in the car. It had happened in the carpark at the shopping centre while she was inside doing the shopping. Roger had turned a deep red saying that it was her own stupid fault for parking too close to other cars, did she think he was made of money? Pay for it out of the housekeeping, he snarled. Millie had shaken with anger at being so unjustly accused and raised her voice at Roger saying what the hell did he think, that she was a magician? Could the little money he gave her stretch further by magic. Stunned that Millie had answered him back, Roger had walked over menacingly, slowly raising his hands to her throat and squeezing, snarling into her face, so close she could feel droplets of spit. If she ever, ever felt that he couldn't provide for his family, she could get back to the gutter that she came from. She couldn't breathe, she couldn't cry out, could feel her body go limp. If it wasn't for one of the kids coming into the kitchen at that moment, Millie was in danger of passing out.

Her hand massaged her throat slowly and her stomach churned. Still sitting on the dresser stool, she opened a drawer. There folded neatly was the scarf that she wore for a week to hide the bruise on her throat. She slammed it shut.

She rose from the stool and smoothed her skirt. Turning sideways, she tucked in her tummy and checked her reflection. The crisp white cotton shirt tucked neatly into her slim waist encircled by an embossed leather belt. The jade green cotton skirt gathered lightly on her hip line, flattering her neat figure. Millie approved of her reflection, tucked some strands of hair up and repositioned the combs. Yes, she knew she was still attractive but did not feel so. Slipping on her leather sandals, she walked slowly through the house, deep in thought. Everything was in its place, so neat and tidy, every ornament placed carefully. Roger had taught her well. She knew that she would miss him, miss the house and all the familiarity of the way their lives ran. Millie also knew that there was something missing, and she longed to find that something.

She lay down on the lounge and closed her eyes and smiled

a little smile, remembering the time she had come home excited that she'd found a bargain ... a red-light special ... souvenir boomerangs painted with a tribal Aboriginal man's head and PERTH WA in bright yellow. Roger had said that *no way* was she going to put that ooga-booga stuff on *his* walls ... *no way!* And that was that. Millie had tucked them away to the back of the linen closet until the boys had found them and ruined them throwing them around at the park. It's in the blood, she thought. Her kids.

Jason was the creative one. Shy and sensitive, Millie worried for him most. His father had no time for him, calling him Mummy's boy because he didn't rough and tumble or play sport like his older brother. Art was Jason's love. He would sit for hours drawing, keeping his sharpened pencils and textas in proper colour order. He always got top marks for Art. You've got your talent from your Uncle Stan, my brother, Millie would tell him. And Millie would sit with Jason and tell him all about her brother, Stan, who learnt to paint in jail ... beautiful Aboriginal pictures she would tell him. And Jason would ask why they never saw their uncles and aunts and cousins.

Young Roger was a survivor. They hadn't shared a close relationship since he was very small. Roger had taken care of that. Now twelve, his whole life revolved around football, cricket and fighting with the boys at school. He had to be the best. Aggressive, loud, he showed little respect for his mother and idolised his father. He bullied Jason, calling him sissy and Black Boy. Millie had tried and tried to persuade him to see how cruel he was to Jason and that he should be proud of his brother's skin. He would laugh and say that Jason should stand up and fight like a man. His father would laugh in agreement.

Michelle was the perfectionist. From an early age, she had learnt that to keep everybody happy, you stayed clean, didn't upset Dad and kept very, very quiet. Sometimes, just sometimes, when he was in a particular mood, her father would take her on his knee for a cuddle, attempting to show interest in her school work or dolls. Michelle would stiffen and answer 'Yes Daddy' to his questions, and slide off his lap quickly. She was afraid of him.

Millie was the absolute in Michelle's life. Mummy cared for her.

On her last visit to her mother and Nan's (they lived together now) Millie had told them that she was thinking about leaving Roger. Both were shocked. How could she ever give up her nice house and a husband who didn't drink and was a good provider for herself and the children? Millie had seen the disappointment on their faces and said feebly that she wasn't happy. It was difficult to explain to them without feeling somehow it was her fault and that she should attempt to make the marriage work.

Outside the afternoon blazed. The venetian blinds were drawn. Inside the air was still and cool. Double insulation; Roger had installed it himself. Millie lay in the darkened lounge rehearsing over and over the way in which she was going to tell Roger that she was leaving with the kids. No matter which way she said it, Roger wouldn't accept it, that she knew. Perhaps it would be better to leave when he was at work. After all these years she felt she owed him more than that.

And then there were the children; Roger would either be divided in his loyalty or side with his father completely, Jason would go with his mum, as would Michelle. It would break her heart to have to leave her firstborn, and she regretted ever having allowed him to grow away from her. She knew now that she should have been stronger. Although her love for young Roger was as it should be, her husband had in some way made her feel inadequate as a mother. Her tender years at the time of his birth served to magnify this.

She thought about her house. More correctly, Roger's house. He had never put Millie's name on the mortgage. It was his house. It didn't even belong to the children in the sense that they were not allowed to bring friends inside the house. Among this regimentation, the children, not knowing any other way, were robustly healthy and obeyed the rules.

'You didn't teach me everything, Roger.' Indignant, Millie sat up. 'I happen to be a very good cook.' She was talking out loud now. 'My Nan taught me to cook, and she learnt from the people she used to housekeep for when the mission people got her that job. I know how to do things, even without you around. You've run my life for me for too long now. I'm not going to live like this any more. I'm not even allowed to see my people when I want to.' She rested her hands on the tiny bulge in her stomach. 'You're not going to make life hell for another child.' Roger did not want any more children. He said that it was obscene to have hoards of snotty-nosed children.

Millie was pregnant again; she had got her days mixed up on the pill packet somehow. Contraception wasn't something uppermost in her mind, because Roger hadn't been as demanding as he was in the early days. The relationship had eroded. Roger now went to bed early and Millie stayed up to do the ironing, clean out cupboards or watch television. But there was that night a couple of months ago, when Roger had a few unaccustomed beers with the next door neighbour at their barbecue.

Millie liked Barbara and Colin next door. They were so easy going and casual. Roger and Colin got on as well as Roger would allow it. Never, in all the years they were neighbours, had Roger shared any confidences with Colin. Roger was not like that. Barbara was open, gregarious and, Millie thought, a bit casual with her housework, but Millie admired this as she was not able to relax enough not to do her housework every single day. She marvelled at how Barbara could jump into their back yard pool and not care if her hair got wet just after styling it. Roger always said that Colin was a good bloke, but that filthy wife of his should take more care of things for Colin. Millie would never repeat that to Barbara ... ever.

Just that morning, Millie and Barbara had shared a coffee and Millie had told Barbara that she was pregnant. Knowing Roger's views on the matter, Barbara had said that she was glad she wasn't in her shoes, kiddo, and what the hell was she going to do, and that she and Colin had heard how he ranted and raved when he lost his temper, and yes, they knew that Roger hit her, they could hear everything. Millie had begun to defend Roger then admitted she was sick of living on the brink of Roger's temper. She was leaving. Barbara had called out to her as she walked out, 'I'm here if you need me.'

Dinner that evening began as a normal one. The children

chatted about their day, and Roger in his usual way would tell them to shut up and eat. 'Children should be seen and not heard, specially at the dinner table. Thank you.' He continued eating.

'Have you cleaned that car out, Millie?' Millie's heart pounded so quickly and heavily, she thought everyone could hear it. The knife she held clattered to her plate, her hand shook so much. The pulse in her temples pounded. To still her hands, she placed them on her lap. In her belly she felt a faint twitch.

'Yes, I did it after the kids left this morning.' Her voice quavered, and she cleared her throat to hide it. The children had finished and were now watching television in the lounge. She would have to tell him now.

'I've got a surprise for you, Lovie.' He always called her Lovie, even when he was angry. She didn't look at him, and for a moment flashed back to the time he had got angry over something, she couldn't remember what, and he had said 'You're a filthy black bitch, Lovie.' This tone tonight, though, was diffferent. What was he going to say? Please, don't let him be so nice. Not tonight.

'I'm going to get you a new little car.'

Millie watched the words come out of his mouth like slow motion bubbles that drifted out and upwards. She couldn't absorb the words. They bounced off her gently. What was he saying? He looked up from his coffee, quizzically. 'Millie, did you hear what I said? I said I'm going to buy you a new car. Not second hand. You deserve a new car,' he announced, somewhat perplexed at Millie's expression.

'I'm leaving, Roger. I'm taking the kids, we'll live at Mum's till I get a place,' she said in a flat voice.

'What?' His voice rose, incredulous. 'You're *what?*'

'You heard me, Roger . . .' She felt defeated, small, inadequate.

'Don't think you're gonna just walk out . . . like that.' He snapped his fingers. 'Just when the hell did this all come about? Your mother, that's it. I shouldna let you visit the other week. She's been putting these ideas in your head!' By now he had pushed his chair back violently and was pacing the kitchen.

Millie sat quietly, head down, much calmer now that she had said it. Roger's face twisted into a red-purple sneer. The scar on his temple protruded. Teeth clenched, he spoke in a low deliberate tone. 'And don't think you're taking the kids. Forget that, for a start. Roger! Jason! Michelle!' The kids came running from the lounge and stopped abruptly when they saw their father's face. They looked at Millie, still sitting with head lowered at the table.

'You're mother is leaving us. She's going back to her boong family. You'll be staying here with your father.'

'No! No! You're coming with me.' She ran to the children and hugged them to her. She felt young Roger pull away.

'Don't do this to me, Roger!' Hot tears welled, she pleaded 'Don't do this!'

Michelle was crying loudly, Jason cried silently and young Roger had a sneer on his face that Millie recognised.

'Well, we'll sort this out here and now. Do you kids want to stay with me ... or your mother?' Roger spat the word *mother*.

Jason and Michelle looked up to Millie sobbing. 'I want to stay with you, Mummy,' Jason sniffled. 'Me too,' Michelle said softly, her big brown eyes pleading. Young Roger strode over to his father and turning back to Millie said 'I'm staying with Dad.' He folded his arms and leaned against the sink, not a flicker of emotion, except for the set sneer Millie knew so well.

'In your rooms! *Now!*' Roger yelled at the kids. 'I've got some things to sort out with your mother!'

The three scuttled off to their rooms. Millie had begun to shake uncontrollably. Roger came up to her. She drew back, against the wall, drawing in her breath, then in an attempt to protect her unborn child, turned to the wall, face twisted back in an endeavour to see what Roger would do. The first slap knocked the side of her head against the wall. The second caught her head as it rebounded and she fell to her knees. As she hunched over, his shoes slammed into her stomach. An involuntary grunt came out of her mouth, as she tried not to cry out. As she attempted to run to the children's room, he caught her hair and twisted it round in his hand.

'Leave them out of this, bitch!' he snarled. 'I haven't finished yet!'

At that moment, Barbara flew in, closely followed by Colin. Roger let go and snarled at Colin. 'Keep out of this, mate, it's none of your business.'

'I'm sorry, mate, but I can't let you do this to Millie. Now calm down and lay off!' He twisted Roger's arm up his back and pushed him up to the sink. Barbara held Millie and yelled to the kids to get in her car. Michelle and Jason rushed out the front door. Barbara hustled Millie out the door. 'Come with us, Roger,' Millie pleaded. He just shook his head, then cast his eyes to the floor.

Roger yelled to her. 'Get back to the gutter you came from, bitch, you get nothing but the clothes on your back. I'll get the Welfare onto you, so watch out!'

'No Roger, that's where you're wrong. I'm just getting out of the gutter,' Millie retorted quietly, firmly, now reinforced by Barbara's arms.

Barbara drove off but Millie, huddled in the back with two silently crying children, felt her stomach cramp in an agonising spasm and the warm blood gush out. Her body stiffened, she clenched Michelle tighter. The child tightened her grasp on her mother's arm.

Millie wept for the child that wasn't to be, and for the children that were. She wept for the years past and the uncertain future now looming ahead as dark as the night that surrounded the swiftly moving car.

Snow Domes

'YOO-HOO. DORRIE.' The voice drifted over Doris's back fence; a high dry girl-voice calling from beneath a large transparent white picture hat, its brim encircled with a garland of aged silk flowers in pastel hues. Doris peered out the back window above her kitchen sink.

'Dear dear. Just when I'm busy.' With a long-suffering sigh. She put down the dishcloth and set about tidying the grey hair tied in a bun set low on her neck. 'Poor ol' thing,' Dorrie tsk tsked.

'Yoo-hoo!' The voice rose and fell, a little more insistent.

'I'll be there dreckly, Sophie,' Doris called from her back door. She brushed breadcrumbs off her large bosom, remains of the sandwich she had just eaten for lunch. Her face was broad and her brown skin smooth despite her years. A kindness radiated from her, the sort of unconditional kindness that comes from someone who has, after experiencing life's adversities, become calm and wise and strong.

Doris and Sophie had been neighbours for many years. Through all the years of their children growing and leaving home, through husbands dying and all their illnesses and crises of life they remained a familiar constant to each other. Although neither would go so far as to call each other a close friend. A more dissimilar pair you could not find. Doris, large, taciturn and kind. Sophie, small, hysterical and self-absorbed. Placement by the Housing Commission. Neighbours by chance. Doris grew larger as she aged. Sophie shrunk. Doris is Aboriginal. Sophie is not.

Carefully negotiating the low back steps, Doris walked unhurriedly over to the wide white hat at the fence.

'What's up Sophie?'

'Oh, Dorrie, you must come over this instant, I can't seem to get the gramophone to work . . . I've checked all the switches and everything . . . and I just don't know . . . you know that was the last thing Harry bought me before he ... well you know ... can you come over now?' Her voice had risen to panic pitch. Doris deliberated on this.

'Well ... don't know much about them 'lectic ones, but I'll 'ave a look. Just give me a while to check the gas is off from the kettle. I was just gettin' a cuppa.'

'Oh, don't worry about that, have a cuppa with me,' Sophie replied.

Knowing there is no way out of this, Doris agrees, only if Sophie doesn't get offended if she brings her own tea bags. The conversation about tea bags was a standard one conducted each time Doris came over. Sophie could never understand why using tea bags several times could be distasteful to Doris. Who did Doris think she was anyway, Lady Muck? It saved money, and money was too scarce to be throwing out things after using them only once. More money for the catty, Sophie said. Doris had abandoned all efforts to explain that the word was 'kitty' years ago. She had accepted Sophie's idiosyncrasies without question now.

Sophie always pointed out that she was wealthy because she was careful with her money. They both received the aged pension, both paid the same rent, yet Sophie felt superior, upper class and wealthy. Doris indulged her, all the while pitying her neighbour in a deep, sad way.

'Mind you wipe your feet, Dorrie.'

'Righto.' The 'mind you wipe your feet' ritual had long ceased to annoy Dorrie. It was just Sophie's way, she knew that.

The loungeroom overflowed with artificial flowers. Every surface was covered in lace-edged doilies and china ornaments of every kind. A collection of snow domes filled other spaces. They had scenes, some Christmas, some not. They all had artificial snow when shaken. Doris had never seen snow and was quite sure it would be just like the snow domes. All the dusting they required was unnecessary as far as Doris was concerned. All this frippery a waste of time. Too many things, she would tell Sophie. Doris had asked Sophie once why she didn't have any photographs of her son and daughter and Sophie replied that she didn't have any nice photos and even if she had they wouldn't be on display. Not the way they treated her. Doris could never understand this. She loved her children, and now ... her grandchildren, too.

'Come and have that cuppa first, Dorrie. We'll look at the gramophone in a minute. It was working last night, I'm certain. You know how I like my music. It's the only thing I've got now.'

She twisted a fine linen handkerchief between her thin gnarled fingers, appearing anguished. Doris ignored her. Didn't want to encourage this pantomime. Sophie's hair, completely white, was swept up into an untidy chignon. Her colourless wrinkled skin was paled even more with powder, cheeks rouged heavily with large pink circles, her lips made into a perfect cupid's bow with a dark pink lipstick. Her eyes were a faded watery blue. Lily-of-the-valley perfume hung in the air like an old memory. Doris always felt stifled in the airlessness of this house. The windows were never opened, the curtains always drawn, didn't want anyone, except for Doris, to come in. A tidy house was the only way to keep some sort of order in her lonely life. Her possessions, her life, were to remain just as she wanted, with no changes, no intrusions.

'You haven't heard from them then?' Doris ventured.

'Oh no! Not Little Lord Fauntleroy. No time for his poor old mother now he's got that job in the furniture place ... and Madam Butterfly is galavaranting around Queensland somewhere. Thoughtless, thoughtless children. That's what I gave birth to. Sometimes I wished I'd never had them for all the comfort they are in old age. After all I've done for them, you'd think they'd show me a little depreciation.'

Clutching her handkerchief to her breast, a hand to her forehead theatrically, she sank back into a chintz lounge.

'Oh, Dorrie, you don't know what they've put me through.'

Doris was unmoved by this outburst, she'd seen it a hundred times. Calmly patting Sophie's hand, she soothed, 'Now, now. Don't go gettin' yourself upset. Let's have that cuppa.'

'Oh. Dorrie, before we have a cuppa could you just give the oilclorth in the kitchen a rub over with the mop for me? My old heart's been jumping around so much this morning I don't think I should do it. And the lav, that needs a mop too.'

'Righto, I'll do that while you put the kettle on.' Knowing that she's been enticed over to do this, Doris, in her slow methodical way, set about mopping. The same scenario had been acted out many times over the latter years, but Doris hadn't really minded, except for just lately. There was no one else to do it. Sophie hummed a tune while she put the kettle on, moving sprightly now that she had company. As Doris mopped in wide slow sweeps, she thought of the way things went in their lives. Sophie, an old woman with husband dead, children gone and no family to visit her. Why, if Sophie fell down dead she'd be the only one to notice. Not like herself now. Such good kids, two sons and one daughter. They had all done well, she was so proud of them, and they always visited. Of course, Sophie didn't like to talk about this, had never praised Doris for raising good children. Sophie wasn't like that, only interested in her world. Doris had accepted this long ago, and limited her conversation to accommodate Sophie. Besides, she knew she'd done a good job of raising her children. She didn't need to be told. Not by Sophie, at least.

'Sophie, you plannin' on goin' somewhere, all dolled up today?' Doris had noticed the make-up over the last few months but had never raised the subject before.

'Oh, yes, didn't I tell you? Mother's coming to visit today. She does love and miss me so much, me being an only child. She says it's so lonely in the old house since I married Harry and left home. Father isn't well you know ...'

She twirled a white strand of hair that strayed down her forehead, speaking in a breathless girl-voice. Doris had sat down, slightly breathless herself from the exertion of mopping.

'Now Sophie, remember ... your Mum and Dad have gone, and so has Harry.' She stared long and hard at her to emphasise this. 'Let's have that cuppa. Dear, dear, this is just a cup of cold water, Sophie. You must mind what you're doin' now. Let me make the tea.'

'I must have forgotten to turn the kettle on, Doris.' Agitated,

Sophie attempted to regain her composure a little. 'Have you mopped the oilclorth? And the gramophone, you forgot the gramophone!'

Doris studied Sophie for a while, thinking how dreadfully sad the old woman had become. 'I'll 'ave a look dreckly. You been taking your tablets properly, Sophie? I'm a bit worried about you lately.'

'Yes well . . . I think so. Oh! I don't know. I'm always forgetting things. What was I saying? Visitors . . . I'm expecting someone. Who did I say I was expecting? Aaaah, this is a nice cup of tea.'

She lifted the cup with a small finger delicately crooked in what she considered to be correct manners, immediately forgetting the preceding conversation. Doris encircled her cup with both hands to feel the warmth soak in and pondered on what to do with this pathetic woman.

'Sophie, you have to let the sink water out after you wash the dishes you know. That water's startin' to stink, and you with a nice house an' all.' Doris thought she would try to appeal to her vanity and show that she wasn't doing things properly of late, that things weren't quite right.

'I have to save water, you know that . . .' Sophie believed that she was doing things in the most correct fashion. And who was Doris to question her?

A car pulled into Doris's driveway. 'That'll be Bunny, Sophie. I'll come back later. Mind you clean up the sink properly now.'

Doris waved from Sophie's front yard, 'Over here Bunny!' Bunny was the nickname of her daughter.

'What are you doing for that woman again, Mum?' Bunny rolled her eyes in mock despair. 'You don't have to do that you know. She can get home help.'

Doris fussed over the two grandchildren, choosing to ignore her daughter's protestations. She bustled the children inside, offering freshly baked scones, done that morning in anticipation of the visit.

'Mum, really, you know you shouldn't be doing that extra work at your age.' Bunny wanted it sorted out this time. She and her brothers had brought the subject up from time to time, worried for their mother's health. Wanting her to enjoy her time, now that they had all left home.

'Bunny, an' how many times have I said it's no trouble for me to do it. I'm not that silly to be doin' too much. Besides, I'm feelin' real good lately. Poor ol' thing. Her mind's goin' a bit lately. Think she's got that ol' timers' disease. She's got no one, you know that. Those useless kids of 'ers never come to see her any more. Mind you, can't say I blame 'em sometime.' Doris spoke in a firm quiet voice, and Bunny knew that no amount of talking would convince her mother to do other than what she wanted to do. She continued just the same.

'But Mum, it's just that we don't want you to think you still have to go on slaving for her, you know … like the old days when you were sent out to do that "domestic" work that the Native Welfare organised, as if that's all us black women could do. I really get wild when I think of the life you've had. I reckon you could have gone on with school and even uni. You gave me that chance … and it's Alzheimer's disease, by the way.' She smiled at her mother.

'Yes, I know, Bunny, and look at you with that anthropology degree. I'm so proud of you kids. All of youse. But as I always say, I wasn't treated too badly, when I think about it. Plenty girls had to put up with a lot more. If you knew your place and didn't make no trouble … you were right.'

Bunny shook her head. 'Mum. Don't you see you were at the mercy of the government? It makes me so wild, you had no choice.'

'Bun, it's no good being wild now, they were different times, those days. Anyway, old Sophie needs a helping hand, I don't think of it as work. You think I don't know the old girl cons me into things? I wouldn't do it if I didn't want to.'

'Oh, Mum!' Bunny was exasperated. It was a well-worn conversation, always a stalemate. She felt her mother ought not be working as Sophie's housekeeper, for her health as well as pride. For Bunny had learned of the 1905 Act, and the ensuing policies that affected her mother and indeed all Aboriginal people. Doris, on the other hand, saw her early days as something that was past, and best forgotten. She sometimes laughed at the thought of her children now, being so good with words and all, how they would've bucked if it were like it was in her day. No way would they let anyone push them around! There would have been hell to pay. Sometimes Doris would think of those times. Like when the farmer's wife who she worked for would make her polish the old wood stove. Time and time again the missus would find a spot that had to be redone. Doris would do it over again, never once complaining. And the missus would laugh at Doris's blackened hands and say it didn't matter because she was black anyway, so who would notice? Sometimes Doris would get angry, take a snowy piece of Irish linen from the missus' dresser drawer and wipe her blackened hands with it and then throw it into the stove fire later. Doris blamed the family milking goat, which was known to eat the odd thing or two, especially if dropped on the way back from the clothesline. A small revenge; nevertheless, a revenge.

'Remember what I said about doing too much, Mum.' Bunny waved from the car window as she drove off. Doris smiled as she waved, the smile that the children knew meant, 'I hear you, but I'm not listening.' Doris walked in her careful and deliberate way back to Sophie's.

'Mind you wipe your feet,' lilted Sophie. Doris mouthed Sophie's words silently, pulling a la-de-da face. 'Took your time, Dorrie,' Sophie snapped.

'Bunny visiting again, she worries about me.'

'Aren't you the lucky one then. No one worries about me.' Sophie's tone was sarcastic.

'You've got me next door, you know that, Sophie. Now where were we? That's right. The gramophone.' Doris felt a twinge of annoyance. Not comfortable with this feeling, she chastised herself for not being charitable. Must not be uncharitable, must remember ... a friend in need is a friend indeed ... do unto others as you would have them do unto you ... love thy neighbour. Little adages kept coursing through her mind. A legacy of her days on the mission.

'Do you think we could dust the ornaments, Dorrie?' Sophie

had softened, realising that her friend could turn around at anytime if she became more testy.

'We could. Yes let's do that first. The gramophone can wait.'

Doris found the dusting cloths and handed one to Sophie. Old cracked record, Sophie, that's what you are, a dusty old cracked record. Doris chastised herself again for having these thoughts. They dusted and polished in silence. Sophie held up a snow dome and shook it gently. She began to sing: 'I'm dreaming of a white Christmas.' Her voice was high and shrill. Doris stopped polishing and gazed at the snow-haired old woman with the snow dome. Caught up in the moment, she joined in with her rich voice, much more tuneful than Sophie's. Their voices soared. 'With every Christmas card I write.' After singing as much as they could remember, they both sat down, tired now, deep in thought.

Doris wondered if she too was losing her grip on things. No, she needed to sing to rid herself of those thoughts that had been coming quite out of the blue today. Perhaps she could offer Sophie more than her usual dose of tablets ... or maybe she could mix them all up. It would be an act of kindness, all things considered, what with Sophie having no one else to care for her. Doris certainly wouldn't be around forever, and what would happen to Sophie if Doris went first? The best idea was to wire the gramophone incorrectly. Surely that would work, but there was also the problem of her own safety and whether this was the proper thing to be thinking about at all. The more Doris dwelled upon it, the more sensible the idea became. It would be the kindest thing to do, under the circumstances. Of that Doris was becoming more and more certain. But how to do this thing, this quite awful thing really, in the safest and kindest way? Yes, that's what it would be, a supreme act of kindness. It would give them both peace.

And already Doris had the answers to all the questions she would be certain to get on the Day of Reckoning. How could anyone not see that it would be for the best? How could anyone see that there was anything but kindness in her soul? In her whole life she had done nothing to be ashamed of. Nothing that in her heart she felt was wrong. Aah, yes, good old dependable Doris. She knew that was what everyone thought. They'd know the reasoning behind it. 'It.' She didn't know what else to call 'It'. Her eyes closed and she nodded off. Sophie had done the same.

Sophie woke with a little shudder. 'I say, Dorrie, we both nodded orf for a while. Silly old things we are. Dorrie . . . Dorrie.' Her voice rose slightly. Lifting her small gnarled frame out of the chair, she shuffled stiffly over to Doris and shook a shoulder gently. 'Come on dearie, we haven't finished yet. Mind you it's getting dark, so I think we'll call it a day. Dorrie?' Doris's skin felt cool to Sophie's touch. 'My, my, you'll be getting yourself a chill old girl. Come on wake up. This is most unusual, you must be tired. I'll get a watchamacallit . . . quilt thingy . . . eiderdown for you.'

Sophie went off to fetch it, but became distracted in the kitchen, and set about fixing herself supper. Humming to herself, she finished the meal of sardines on burnt toast and limped off to bed.

Morning came with a chill. Sophie hugged a shawl to herself and switched on the loungeroom light. With a little gasp she cried, 'Dorrie! You're still here! Oh dear, and I forgot the . . . er . . . eiderquilt, and now you're froze.' With a fearful shudder, she sat down. 'Now you've always been the one to look after me, I'll look after you. I'll just sit here and wait till one of the kiddies calls by. Now what was the girl's name? Was it Squirrel? No . . . no . . . I remember, it was Possum. Or was it? Never mind. I'll remember it when she gets here. I won't move, I promise. I'll even sing to you. I'll put the kettle on shortly.'

Doris looked cold and grey. Sophie began: 'I'm dreaming of a white Christmas. With every Christmas card I write. May your days be merry and white . . . now how do the lines go?'

The room lightened with the rising of the sun. Sophie sang and sang, and thought how peaceful Doris appeared, and how the garden would need trimming. Yes, she would give the roses a good tendering today, till Possum came by . . . or was it Flossy? No matter, maybe she'd ask her, whatever her name was, to have a look at the gramophone. She then set herself to the task of dusting her beloved snow domes, realising in a detached way that her only friend was gone. Now she would have to manage this dusting business alone.

Alf Taylor

ALF TAYLOR was born in 1947 in Perth, Western Australia, and grew up in the New Norcia Mission. He is a member of the Nyoongah people, though he did not discover this till he was sixteen years old, when he left the mission to find his family. He finally traced his mother to a reserve in Cool-gardie. Alf has been writing since 1984 *and has had two collections of poetry published by Magabala Books. 'The Woolpickers' was first published in the journal* Overland *in* 1996. *He frequently gives readings of his work at writers' festivals and conferences, and participates in school tours and writer-in-residence programs. He is currently working on his autobiography.*

Nyoongah Country

Glossary

boyyah	money
bullyaka	take off
buntjie	womaniser
gerbah	alcohol
moorditj	deadly (good, cool)
munnartj	police
muntj	have sex
Nyoongah (*also* Nyoongar)	Aboriginal people of south-west WA
unna	isn't that right?
watjella (*also* wajbulla)	whitefella
yonga	kangaroo
yorgah (*also* yorga)	woman
yortj	penis

The Wool Pickers

W HEN THE WARM months take effect on the dry land, after the crops have been taken and the grass has been singed by the hot summer sun, that's the reminder of the fully fleeced sheep that perished during the bitterly cold winter. That's when Barney and his nephew Bill go wool picking (with the farmer's permission of course).

'Well,' said Barney to his nephew, 'it's a good day for wool pickin', unna?'

'Yeah, Unc,' said Bill, looking up at the early morning sun. 'It's gunna get hot later on.'

'What ya reckon, feel like comin' out?' asked Barney.

'Course, you know me Uncle, bugger-all else to do, runnin' low on tucker, dole cheque next week, hell dunno how we gunna live 'til then,' responded Bill.

'Right,' said the old fella, 'I'll get the ute ready, an' tell Auntie Florrie you an' me goin' out. You tell your yorgah too.'

'Course Unc, gotta tell my yorgah, she growlin' cruel already...'

'Get off your black hole Bill an' do somethin' solid, not wanna muntj alla time,' said Bill mimicking his woman. The old uncle laughed as he watched his nephew walk away. *When you an' your yorgah fight, even the good Lord ducks for cover*, he thought, laughing to himself, making off to tell his wife Florrie.

Barney and Florrie were in their late sixties, and fifty of those years were together. Through thick and thin, through the days of alcoholic stupor and nights of alcoholic amnesia – and they were still together. Their three children, two boys and a girl, were living in Perth. All had good jobs and, most importantly, they had lives of their own.

Barney often cursed himself for not having a clear head when they were growing up. Thankfully they understood now, stating a lack of opportunities for the Nyoongah community in a small wheatbelt town.

'Me an' Bill goin' out to see if we can get some wool,' said Barney to his wife Florrie.

'You might gotta go long way out. Nyoongahs bin pickin' close here,' she said.

'Boyyah any?' he asked and in the same breath added, 'You know, petrol.' Knowing his wife usually had some put away somewhere. Ever since they both gave up the grog, about fifteen years ago, she always had enough till next Pension Day.

'Ready Unc?' asked Bill, carrying his waterbag. Seeing Aunty Florrie he added, 'How you bin Aunty Florrie?'

'I bin good since I chuck away that stinken gerbah,' she replied, shaking her head.

'Yeah, you two look solid now,' said Bill. *Since these two gave up the gerbah, they seem so full of life. They looked better than the younger ones, still on the gerbah*, he thought.

'Boyyah wa or you gimme, unna?' Bill asked, searching his pockets.

'Take 'em here,' Florrie said, passing a ten-dollar note to Barney.

'How many bags you got Unc?' asked Bill.

''Bout five empty wheat bags,' replied Barney.

'Let's bullyaka then,' suggested Bill.

'You gottem gun?' asked Florrie.

'Yeah, under seat, you make 'em big damper. Might get yonga,' he said as he and Bill prepared to leave. He started the ute and pulled away from the house, both waving to Florrie.

As they headed north, they could see that the hot summer's sun had already done its damage to the landscape. About five months ago, the land was covered by lush green crops of wheat and a thick carpet of glistening green grass. Seeing the land now, with its lack of rain, even had the sand restless. The sands seemed to move with the strong breeze, although the gentle winds slowly stirring in the summer were very far and few between. The soil with its great patience, suffered the onslaught of the menacing sun.

Nothing was said between the uncle and nephew. Barney moved along at a steady pace, he didn't want to go too fast in this heat. He was afraid the radiator might boil.

Gotta get it fixed next Pension Day, he thought. *Come next Pension, it'll still be the same.* When he was home travelling within his own shire boundary, he never had to worry, but trips like this it always came to his attention. He cursed himself out aloud.

'Hey, wassa matter Unc?' asked Bill, wondering if his old uncle had lost his marbles.

'Nothing . . . um orright, juss diss bloody radiator. Keep meanin' to get him fixed. I don't worry about him, till I go on trips like diss,' he growled.

'How far you reckon we come Unc?' asked Bill.

Keeping his eye on the temperature gauge, 'Might be twenty miles, might 'e more,' he replied.

'Let's try the first farm we come to Unc,' said Bill, not wanting to be stuck in the middle of nowhere on this hot day. Barney slowed the ute down, it was a left turn towards the farmhouse. He could see that the sheep were thin as they ran away from the oncoming vehicle. *Rain and feed obviously very scarce out this way too*, thought Barney.

'Reckon he got some dead one's here,' said Bill, noticing the condition of the sheep.

'By gee, that cold weather we had in the winter musta downed a few,' replied Barney.

'Wonder if any Nyoongahs been this way?' asked Bill as he slowed the ute down in front of the house, only to be greeted by barking dogs that seemed to come from nowhere.

'Where in the hell these poxy dawgs come from?' called out Barney as he wound his window up. There were about five sheepdogs running around his ute, barking and pissing all over the tyres. One big bastard was standing on his hind legs, his front paws leaning against Barney's door, barking furiously at him.

'Bugger diss!' said Barney, counting the fangs on the mutt's jaw.

'Shoo! Gone! Get!' shouted Bill, also winding his window up very quickly.

Barney looked at his nephew and with a smile on his face said,

'Gone, go up to the house an' knock on the front door.'

'You gotta be jokin' Uncle. I'd rather fight ten drunken Nyoongahs than wrestle with these poxy dawgs.'

'Ni, boss comin' now,' said Barney, pointing towards the house.

'Duss him orright,' replied Bill as he watched him come towards the ute.

'Go on, piss off you bastards!' shouted the boss. The dogs slinked off on his command. Winding the window down Barney said, 'Thanks boss, I was a bit frightened for awhile.'

'Don't have to worry about them,' said the boss. 'More than likely to lick you to death.'

Duss what you reckon, thought Barney. 'That big bastard lookin' me in the eye would frighten the shit out of the devil himself. He got more teeth than a crocodile, an' more sharper.'

'Well, what can I do for you?' asked the boss.

Good, thought Barney, *no Nyoongahs been out here*. Getting out of the ute and looking to see if the coast was clear, he asked, 'Wondering if you got any dead wool around the place?'

'Dead wool?' asked the boss confused.

'You know,' said Barney, 'any sheep died over the winter months.'

'Oh, I understand now,' replied the boss. 'As a matter of fact I have. That cold snap we had at the end of May and the beginning of June, that really took its toll on the sheep.' He pointed towards the west paddock. 'There were quite a few that didn't survive.'

'Be orright if we have a look?' asked Barney.

'I suppose it's okay. As long as you shut the gates behind you and try not to frighten the sheep. I hate to see my sheep running around on a day like this,' he said.

'Duss true boss,' said Barney. 'We be careful orright.'

'Also beware of your exhaust pipe when you travel over the stubble,' said the boss pointing to the back of the ute. Barney got out and both he and the boss checked under the ute.

'Your exhaust looks safe. Okay then ... and don't forget the gates,' said the boss.

'We won't,' said Barney.

'I guess you blokes didn't win that four million in last night's Lotto draw!' said the boss, walking away laughing.

What dat yortj talkin' bout, thought Barney. 'Four million dollars. I wouldn't be here pickin' your dead wool, would I?' Shaking his head and getting into the ute.

'Choo, you solid Unc,' said Bill with dollar signs in his eyes.

'Yeah,' said Barney. 'As soon as he said, "what can I do for you", I knew Nyoongahs never been here.'

They had to go through three gates before hitting their jackpot. Barney drove carefully through the paddocks, keeping away from the high stubble. Barney himself also climbed out with Bill to shut the gates.

'Here, look Unc!' shouted Bill, pointing. There before their very eyes, dead sheep were everywhere. The winter had been cruel to these sheep, who had yet to be shorn. Barney and Bill quickly and happily ripped the wool from the dead carcasses. These sheep had been lying here for at least three months or more. Perished in the winter and dried by the summer.

The stench and the blowflies didn't deter the eager hands that shook the fleece from the bones and brushed the blowflies away at the same time. The maggots, exposed to the deadly sun, cringed at the onslaught. The crows cawed out joyfully, as the rotting flesh was to be their feast. The dead wool, when sold in all its stinking glory, would put food on the table, petrol in the tank and smoke back into the lungs of the two men.

'Dass all Unc!' cried Bill, sweating profusely as he hoisted the last of the five fully packed bags into the back of the ute.

'Gawd, diss place stink,' called out Barney, not realising he had been right in the middle of the stench for the last two hours.

'Let's bullyaka then Unc,' said Bill with a satisfied smile on his face.

'Yeah, you have boyyah till your day now,' smiled Barney as he edged his way through the gates and past the farmhouse. He wanted to thank the farmer for giving him permission to pick his dead wool.

There was no life around except the dogs and he wanted to get as quickly away from them as possible. The drive back was even slower than the drive coming out. For he and Bill did quite a job back there.

'How much we get for this lot?' asked Bill.

'Orrr, dunno. Might be hundred dollars, might be more,' said the old fella with a twinge of tiredness in his voice.

'Never mind Unc, long as my yorgah get some money. She'll be happy,' said Bill.

'The first thing um gunna do, is have a shower an' tell Florrie to get some mutton flaps,' he said feeling the hunger pangs starting to attack his stomach. He was also beginning to realise that the stench was quite powerful in the cab of the ute.

'I hope Aunty Florrie made that big damper. I wanna get some off youse,' said Bill feeling the same.

'Nearly home soon,' said Barney, not worrying about the radiator as he put his foot down on the pedal.

'Hey Unc, what that watjella said back at his farm. Something 'bout four million dollars. I thought he said four million sheep was dead. I was happy cruel, look,' laughed Bill.

'Naw,' Barney said, laughing. 'Lotto draw last night.'

'What if you had four million dollars Unc? What you do?' asked Bill.

'Well,' laughed Barney, 'first thing I do is give my kids a million each.'

'What you an' Aunty Florrie gunna do with your million?' asked Bill laughing.

'Um gunna take Auntie Florrie to dat French River place, somewhere. And next we be goin' to see that Nyoongah bloke. You know, he was locked up in jail for twenty years an' come out to run his own country. Wass his name?' asked Barney.

'Or yeah Unc, I know. Or ... Nelson Mandella, yeah. Unc dass him. Anyway Unc, what you wanna meet him for?' wondered Bill.

'Look young Bill, all I wanna do is shake his han' an' tell him he horse of a Nyoongah orright. After bein' locked up alla time. Come out an' be boss of his own country. He moorditj orright.'

'But he not Nyoongah Unc. He South African,' Bill explained to his old uncle.

'He still moorditj anyway,' said Barney. They were now driving through town and slowly making their way to the Woolbuyer's. As he pulled up outside Willie the Woolbuyer's shed, Bill said to his old uncle, 'Never mind Unc, you sit here an' rest. I'll take em into Willie's.'

Barney watched his young nephew unload and take the old wool into the woolshed. It wasn't all that long before Bill came out with a smile on his face. As he passed the cheque to Barney, Bill said, 'We got one hundred dollars for that lot, one dollar a kilo he give. Dass orright, unna?'

Barney was pleased. He headed for the bank where they cashed it. He gave forty dollars to Bill, whilst he kept sixty – fuel for the car. He dropped Bill off, who didn't live all that far, and then headed home for a shower.

As Barney stepped inside, he passed the money to Florrie. 'Here boyyah, you goin' down town an' get me some flaps.'

After he'd showered and got himself cleaned up, he sat and had a cup of tea. It was peaceful and quiet. Florrie came in carrying the shopping and put it on the table.

'Gawd, still warm outside,' she said. Florrie took off for the bedroom. Barney watched as she stopped to pick up her reading glasses and disappeared into the other room.

Within minutes the warm, peaceful and quiet humidity of the early evening was shattered by a piercing scream.

'Choo, aye wassa matta?' shouted Barney, jolted back to reality and running into the bedroom. He froze in his tracks as he saw his wife sprawled on her back across the bed, white as a ghost shouting, 'Gawd, gawd. Thank you Granny Maud!'

Barney was speechless. Granny Maud had died forty years ago. When he and Florrie first got together as pups – Granny Maud had always called them that – and she was eighty when she died. Their first child was two then.

'I think I win plenty of boyyah!' was Florrie's only response when she came to.

She composed herself and told him about the other day. She was lying on the bed, having a cry and thinking of Barney – old as he was – always going out to pick dead wool to put food on the table. Then she looked up and saw the spirit of Granny Maud, clapping her hands and smiling at her, then she disappeared.

After that she walked down town, and saw on a poster at the newsagents in big bold letters 'FOUR MILLION DOLLARS' to be won that night. She went in and bought a ticket and she had just checked her numbers with the paper, and she had gotten six numbers correct.

Still trembling, he asked, 'What Granny Maud got to do with it?'

She told him when she had the last two children her spirit was by the bed, smiling and clapping as she was giving birth.

'Look at our beautiful children now. Granny Maud only brought good luck to me,' she whispered. She was thinking of Barney and the kids. Especially Barney – to take 'im to see that Nyoongah who was put in jail an' came out to be boss of his own country before they both passed away.

Barney grabbed and hugged her. With tears in his eyes, he whispered in her ear, 'He not Nyoongah, he South African!'

Uncle Jacko

'BRICKWALL OSWALD JACKSON,' shouted the local sergeant (acting as Clerk of the Court) to a group of Nyoongahs standing around outside the courthouse. Waiting to go to court, before the local Justice of the Peace. The Nyoongahs were mainly charged with execrable offences, such as drunk and disorderly, being on licensed premises, using obscene language and, if the police were lucky, there could be a drunk-driving charge.

The Nyoongahs shouted cruel, when they heard what the Sarge called Uncle Jacko. 'More like Brickwall Bigballs Jackson' ... 'Duss a poxy name Uncle Jacko' ... 'Duss your real name, Uncle Jacko.' Laughing.

'Um gunna show these little piss arses,' thought the seventy-two-year-old, dignified Aboriginal man. Striding purposefully towards the court. Neatly attired in his five-dollar-fifty op shop suit. As he approached, the sergeant acknowledged him and said, 'You know what to do and say.'

Within thirty minutes or more, Uncle Jacko strode out and stood on the steps. Extending his arms out and addressing his multitude, he said in a loud clear voice, 'For the nine hundred and ninty-ninth time. Brickwall Oswald Jackson, I have no alternative but to caution you. For being drunk on public property.'

All the Nyoongahs shouted and clapped. He heard cries of 'Moorditj Uncle Jacko' ... 'Made em piss, Uncle Jacko' ... 'Nearly thousan' Uncle Jacko' ... 'You deadly look, Uncle Jacko.'

As he walked away from the courthouse, punching the air with a little skip and hearing the Sarge call out to the multitude of Nyoongahs.

'Quiet please, court's in session.'

'You mob lucky, orright. If you mob back in da ol' days, ol' JP would give you a month in Fremantle Prison, juss for drunk. Cause I know, I bin Fremantle,' he chuckled.

Making his way to Flo's house, he knew why they picked him up, he was asleep under a shrub, in a vacant block. He couldn't make it to Topsy's place, he was too drunk, and decided to have a rest. Eventually going off to sleep, until that munnartj shone a torch in his face saying, 'Come on Jacko, to the cell you go,' before jumping in that Rat Van. One little sleep cost him a muntj, he cursed himself rigorously.

'Never mind,' he thought. 'Topsy still got 'im with her, never sold it to anyone. I hope not.' Chuckling to himself, walking head down.

'What you smilin' 'bout,' scowled Flo. Bringing him back to now and today. 'I heard all 'bout you,' she continued. ''Magine you ol' buntjie man, sleepin' under bush. Choo shame.'

He realised he was outside of Flo's house. And hadn't seen or spoken to any Nyoongahs since he left the courthouse. Yet she knew exactly what happened. 'Gawd, what diss woman, ghost, Devil or what,' he thought. Then asking, 'How you know, what happen?'

'Yarns be told before you do it. You know diss little town, fulla Nyoongahs.'

'Dat tored it,' he thought. Shaking his head.

'Come for cuppa tea, Brickwall da Beast,' she said laughing.

'Gawd, I bin not hearin' dat name for a long time,' he said laughing. Along with her. How Toby gave him that name before he took off to Leonora, somewhere.

'Hear from Toby?' he asked. Sipping his tea, which is not the liquid required. 'But at the moment,' he thought, 'diss will do.'

'Naw, not even Brenda,' she said, feeling angry with both. Especially with Toby.

'Never mind, he get to tell Welfare. To tell you he orright,' he said hopefully.

Uncle Jacko really liked Toby. He wasn't related to Toby, but always admired him. Uncle Jacko could see that Toby was going to make it to the top. Whenever Toby knew Uncle Jacko was in jail, he was always there to bail him out. Every time he'd bail him out, he'd always say, 'Come on Brickwall the Beast, you got no shame. Promising all these old yorgahs a muntj last night.

They reckon there were five old yorgahs waitin' on you. You want that big beast of yours cut off.'

They'd both walk down to the pub laughing. Toby had a kind and caring, forgiving way. That everybody loved. 'But poor boy,' he thought, 'some day, someone will learn to love in return.'

'Who tell 'em you 'bout me anyway?' he asked, forgetting about Toby.

Flo laughed at Uncle Jacko and, being a good strong Christian lady, told him in a gracious manner exactly how she was told. 'Dey reckon you was layin' down, tryin' to do dirty, to the sand.'

'What,' he spluttered, nearly swallowing the big mug of tea.

'Duss not all, you had your trousers down round your ankles,' she said laughing. 'An' dat munnartj was shinin' da torch on your bare ring,' going into fits of laughter.

'Don't you talk 'bout me like dat Florence,' getting up from the table. Clenching his jaw and fists at the same time.

'Duss other Nyoongahs.'

'Fuck da other Nyoongahs,' he shouted angrily. Cutting Flo off in mid-sentence.

Regaining her composure, she said, 'Don't you swear in diss house. Diss is the Lord's house, you know um a Christian. I like my Church.'

That really spun Uncle Jacko out. His anger went into overdrive, his blood pressure went through the roof. Flames coming out of his mouth, nostrils, he was seething. His voice not that of a human being, as he growled at her. 'You tell me who said dat yarn to you. Cause um gonna skittle da first Nyoongah who look at me,' still growling and throwing a combination of left and right jabs.

Flo was still laughing at Uncle Jacko's antics and managing to subdue him.

Settling down on the chair, he said, 'Choo, you know these Nyoongahs. Gunna stretch that yarn, cruel.'

Flo shook her head and said, 'What for you bein' silly.'

'Gawd,' thought Uncle Jacko, 'if she don't believe me, these other Nyoongahs won't. Dat yarn already gone around Australia. While um sittin' here.'

'I know these Nyoongahs, dey like stretchen 'em,' she said smiling.

Uncle Jacko went on to tell her exactly what happened. Why he got picked up and why he was charged for sleeping under that bush.

'Dat gerbah no good for you. Gibb it away. Be a Christian like me and come to Church,' she pleaded.

'Gawd duss all I need right now,' he thought. 'No um orright. Um doin' some paintin' now,' he said getting her on side.

'Yeah dey bin tellin' me, you bin doin' some paintin'. Dat flash watjella you talk to, dey reckon he gotta flash car too,' she said.

Uncle Jacko adjusted his tie, brushed back his long silver-grey hair and said with some authority, 'Dat flash car dey call him Lambro something.'

'What duss a I . . . Talian man unna?' she asked.

'No,' he shouted. 'Duss da name of his flash car.'

'Don't have to shout,' she said sternly.

'Um sorry Flo, diss yarn make me feel no good. But something big gonna happen to me,' he said seriously.

'Only thing big gunna happen, if you come to Church. Give your heart to the Lord,' she said, hoping to break through that armour of sin.

'Diss woman don't give up,' he thought. In a more serious manner he told her of this talent he found in a cell. While waiting to go to court for drunk and disorderly. Toby wasn't there to bail him out, so he asked the old Sarge for some paint and paper. He had three hours to kill, so he did some paintings. When the Sarge saw the paintings he was very impressed with Uncle Jacko's work. And kept them, saying he would pass them on to this art dealer he knew in Perth. He had done some more paintings and the art dealer himself was very impressed. He encouraged Uncle Jacko to keep painting. The art dealer had taken his paintings 'overseas'. Even the world was impressed with his work. His dot paintings, seeping with his Aboriginal culture and stories, going back thousands of years.

'So you see, I bin painting in da quiet. I don't want these other

Nyoongahs to know what um doin'. Duss why I got off with a caution. Ol' Sarge, tell 'em JP I might be goin' overseas soon,' with renewed vigour in his voice.

Flo looked at Uncle Jacko in awe. 'No not diss ol' buntjie man. Why he only drunken ol' sinner,' she thought.

'Look Florence um seventy-two now. Come next rain I be seventy-three,' he said, feeling very proud of himself for living so long so far. A lot of his relations and friends did not reach the age of sixty. 'Sometimes younger,' he thought. 'Dat stinken gerbah kill em all.' Then saying 'Yeah Florence, I want diss world to know who Brickwall Oswald Jackson is. Before he die,' with a lot of meaning in it.

'What, you keep drinkin' dat flagon. You be finished, only us fellas here know you, duss all,' she said.

'Yeah duss what I bin thinkin',' he said solemnly.

'Yeah be good if ol' Sister bin livin' today. She be proud of you,' she said, feeling sad for Eunice.

'Yeah,' he said. Thinking of all the good times he and Eunice had. But he knew their Aboriginal custom was not to speak of the dead and he and Flo respected wholeheartedly.

'You know diss watjella, he comin' round here,' he said to Flo.

'Where here?' she asked.

'Here, right here,' he said, indicating her house.

'What for you tell 'em to come here?' she snapped.

''Cause um not gunna tell him to pick me up under some bush,' he said laughing.

'Choo you got no shame, tellin' 'im to come to my place. What, he comin' in his flash, car?' she asked.

'Course, what you think. He comin' in a horse and cart?' he said laughing. And could see that Flo was looking at him in a different direction. 'Not da ol' drunken buntjie man sinner.'

'When he comin', today?' she asked.

'Any time now, soon be today,' he told her.

'Choo, I gotta clean my place up,' she said nervously.

'Don't worry Florence, diss house cleena den da Buckingham Place. Where da Queen lives,' he said laughing.

'Yeah Brickwall, if you see her over there, you'll be asking her to have a drink from your flagon,' she laughed, calling him a buntjie man.

'Ni ni, motor pulled up outside, unna?' he asked.

'Yeah duss him,' she said. As Flo and Uncle Jacko rushed to the front door, to see a gleaming red Lamborghini parked outside her house. What she couldn't get over was how the door was opened from the inside and lifted straight up. Like the top of the car was holding the door up. Like a big eagle with one wing lifted up. And a well-dressed man got out, and Uncle Jacko approached him smiling.

'Mr Jackson, nice to see you again,' he said.

'Call me Jacko, an' what your name again?' he asked.

'Mario, Mario Muntjama,' he told him.

'Or yeah, duss right. Look I want you to meet my ol' friend,' he said, nodding towards Flo, who was standing on the verandah. Couldn't believe what she saw. A flash car that look like it came from out of space. And a man, with over a thousand dollars worth of suit on. With all those gold trinkets hanging off of him. Standing and shaking Uncle Jacko's hand, with his five-dollar-fifty op shop suit on. 'No,' she thought, 'diss muss be dream.' As she watched Uncle Jacko and the man approach her.

'Flo, meet diss here Mario,' he said. Introducing them with a smug smile on his face. He can see Nyoongahs along the street peeping out of their yards. They couldn't believe what they were seeing.

Flo and Mario acknowledged each other. Then Mario turned to Uncle Jacko and said, 'You'll have to come to Perth with me, then we fly off to America.'

Uncle Jacko went into the staggers, grabbing his chest. His mouth was open, but no words came out. While Flo grabbed the verandah post, for support. She too was in a state of collapse.

'I am sorry, I should have told you while you were sitting down,' he said, grabbing Uncle Jacko to support him.

Regaining his composure, words came flowing free. 'What you talkin' 'bout 'Merica for?' he asked, wanting Mario to repeat himself.

''Merica, 'Merica, what you gunna do there?' Flo asked, getting over her shock.

Mario did repeat his words after making sure Uncle Jacko and Flo were in a stable position. Like on a chair. He told them he had arranged an exhibition at the Museum of Contemporary Art in New York City. The curators were very impressed with Uncle Jacko's work and they wanted him to be there in person for the opening.

'Ol' man like me, Brickwall Oswald Jackson. Goin' 'Merica, seventy-two years old, I be blowed aye,' he said in a trance.

'Those paintings are of your wonderful culture, the world wants to know of your work. Eagerly the world awaits you and your culture,' said Mario. Sounding very impressive.

'Um gunna tell Toby an' all these other Nyoongahs here dat you gunna be big shot,' said Flo. Coming to her senses.

'How um goin' again?' he asked.

'We'll be flying out at the end of the week but we'll need to get your passport fixed up and you'll have to get a new wardrobe. Then we're off.' Mario told him.

'What wardrobe?' he asked, wondering what he was going to do walking around with a wardrobe on his back in the middle of Perth.

'You know, new clothes, a suit,' Mario said. 'But you are not to worry about a thing. I'll fix all that up,' he added.

'What, we goin' now?' asked Uncle Jacko, still in a daze.

'Yes we've got to be in Perth soon,' he said.

'C'mon den,' he said, hugging and kissing Flo, then headed towards the car.

The last words Uncle Jacko heard from Flo before disappearing from the town was ''Member me, when you be big shot.'

Jared Thomas

JARED THOMAS is a Nukunu man, born in 1976 in the South Australian town of Port Augusta. Always keen on writing during his school years, he moved to Adelaide at age seventeen to undertake an Arts degree and further his writing skills. In 1997 he won the Tandanya-National Aboriginal Cultural Institute Artists Award  *Fellowship and is currently undertaking a graduate diploma in creative writing under Professor Tom Shapcott. He is also developing a play, Flash Red Ford, for production in Kenya and Uganda.*

Glossary

boogadis	boots
murntu	backside
thitnas	feet

Westies vs *Bungala 1981*

J ACK ALWAYS WOKE early on the day that he played footy.
He'd wake at six, though he played at nine, put on his purple
West Augusta football shorts, socks and guernsey and then jump
back into bed. Jack would then dream the day's game over in his
head, what he would do when he got the ball, how many kicks
and marks he'd get. Jack was especially anxious when his team
played Bungala because their oval wasn't a part of the town that
he lived in, but a part of the Aboriginal mission. Bungala was
also the team and home of a few mates he affectionately called
cuz.

Jack and his under-ten team mates would always arrive on
time at the mission in their parents' flash cars. When the little
white boys jumped out of the cars, they huddled together and
laughed at what they could see around them. Jack and his dad,
William, stayed clear of the young giggling pack. Jack felt
embarrassed to arrive at his friends' place in a car, he thought
his friends would see his not walking there as a sign of weakness.
And Jack didn't understand why his team mates were laughing,
because he thought Bungala, being right out in the bush, was a
fantastic and adventurous place, which showed how tough the
Bungala people are. He also knew that a part of him belonged
there.

From the boundary of Bungala mission one could see the
Flinders Ranges, they cradled the mission. A thick cloud of fog
partially covered the crimson hills and floated in a large dis-
persing hue across plains of thick red dust and dry bristly buck
bushes. The mist would always lie in this way, a nightly blanket
which slowly removed itself in the morning, as it drifted from
the chilled south seas to the hot red centre. Its presence still
remained in the winter morning sunlight, a cold and slippery
residue upon the make-do prickle-ridden oval. Corrugated iron,
rust-encrusted tangled cars and parts of houses were scattered all

over Bungala. The old-fella residents, kids and women had made their fires and warmed themselves and their billies with the sacred flames.

The boys from Westies laughed with fog bellowing out of their mouths, as their opposition woke one by one beneath small gum trees with their camp dogs. The Bungala boys wore no shoes or socks, just shorts and shirts, as they made their way across the oval, dodging cow pats and prickles on the way. One Bungala boy's job was to scare the dogs and cattle off the oval and point out the prickles and cow pats to the other Bungala boys on his way across the oval. The Bungala boys appreciated the cow pat spotter if he prevented others from stepping in fresh globs of shit. The Bungala boys approached the Westy mob to organise the game, as they always started short of a team until other team mates woke up. As the Westy boys could make two teams the coach of Westies gave Bungala some of his lanky limbed or slower players.

William cringed when realising Bungala were short of a team as he knew that Jack would volunteer to play for them immediately. As Jack changed out of the guernsey that his father was so proud to see him wear, William would wait for Jack's team mates to tease him. William remembered being Jack's age, a little 'half-caste' Aboriginal boy, living amongst the sandhills, on the outskirts of the mission. Sandhill Savage they called him, they pulled his hair mockingly checking for nits, and when he was old enough to be with girls, their love for him declined once realising that his deep tan wasn't due to the sun that shines on all Australians, but in fact a sign of his Aboriginal ancestry. It was because of the things that happened to William when he was a boy that he tried so hard to guide Jack through life devoid of heartache. William found his long association with Westies to be a ticket to status and a rewarding social life in his later years. William hoped that a sporting career would provide the same opportunities for Jack.

As soon as Jack started kicking the football around with the Bungala boys the Westy men started ridiculing him and his father. Two men shouted spontaneously, 'Like father like son.' Another said, 'Once a Sandhill Savage always a fucking savage.' And another, 'Don't know how we kept you with the club so long let alone your son. Thought you would have gone walkabout long time ago.' William bit back his anger, his body trembled and he could feel a wave of heat overcome him. He could have torn the men apart, they knew it and he felt like it, but instead he buttoned his lips back over his grinding teeth trying to mimic a smile.

Westies had placed two goals on the board within the first five minutes of play. Bungala played hard, attacking the ball with speed and desperation. Despite the Bungala boys' zest, the Westy boys' kicking ability gave them an advantage. They kicked very long and this enabled them to keep the ball closer to their goals and in turn increase their chances of scoring. When the Bungala boys kicked the icy water-logged ball, it left a deep sting on their bare feet and the ball only travelled several metres. Westies dominated until Ringo and Archie made their way onto the field. Ringo and Archie were two of Jack's good friends.

'G'day cuz,' they both said when they spotted him.

'Eh bruddas, where ya's been?' replied Jack.

Both the Bungala and Westy team players were always mystified by Archie and Ringo's football ability. This day was no exception. As soon as Ringo began to play, he retrieved the centre bounce, broke the tackle of a towering ruckman, dodged the rover and ruck rover and then boomed a kick which travelled a whole twenty-five metres, as far as any footy boot wearing Westy boy's kick. Instead of bouncing as a projectile tends to do when hitting the ground, the football skidded through a deep puddle on the oval sending splashes into the air. Eight players swooped onto the ball at once. Jack was near the centre of the oval looking desperately to see who in the pack had possession of the ball.

Everyone at the game was amazed to see little Archie come speeding out of the pack with the other players chasing him as he lined up and speared a kick straight through the middle of the goal posts. All of the Bungala boys jumped up, punching the air and screaming, 'He don't muck around, Archie and Ringo, no messin' with them.' Jack became inspired, so much so that he decided he had no need for football boots.

'If Ringo and Archie could play so deadly without them, why can't I?' he thought. He ran to the boundary and chucked one boot at a time back at his father. The Westy men laughed hysterically at Jack's act and William felt embarrassed like he had never been before in his life.

'Jack, what in the hell do you think you're doing? Get here immediately boy,' growled William.

'Na, can't ya see I'm tryin' to play footy?' responded Jack as he turned to run to the centre of the ground.

'Jack, get your little murntu here boy before I come there and kick it for ya.'

When William started using his own words Jack knew his dad was angry and it was time to listen up. Jack turned slowly and walked towards his father, stopping cautiously several metres before him.

'Now Jack pick those football boots up and put them back on your thitnas boy.'

'But Dad,' whinged Jack, 'Archie and Ringo ain't got 'em, and look there, they playin' real deadly unna?'

'Don't you ever answer back to me boy,' and with this threat he picked Jack swiftly off the ground by his wrist, and tanned his murntu so hard, that the crimson fingermarks from William's handprint rose from Jack's exposed skin. Jack broke his father's hold and stepped away from him clenching every muscle in his body to hold back the pain.

And then it gushed from his mouth: 'My name's Jack not Jacky Jacky's son! Now hold onto my boogadis cause I'm goin' to play me some football.'

Jack spoke involuntarily, but so assertively that Jack's dad was stunned to laughter. Jack was not only surprised at what had just slipped through his lips but surprised at his father's response. Initially he put his hand to his mouth and his eyes beamed with anticipation as he awaited another hiding. When William laughed, Jack took his wet, muddy socks off, and placed them in his father's open hands with caution.

'Well go on, go chase a kick then,' said William, and with his father's approval, Jack sped back onto the oval.

The game ended with Westies winning as they always did. But this time Bungala had got within five goals of Westies, which was something they had never done before. The boys from the teams shook each other's hands as they made their way back to the boundary of the oval.

Rosemary
van den Berg

ROSEMARY VAN DEN BERG was born in 1939, a Nyoongar woman from Pinjarra, a small country town in the south-west of Western Australia. She is a mother of five and a grandmother of twenty-one, and now lives in Armadale, WA. Rosemary has been writing since 1988 and her first book No Options, No Choice! *was*  published in 1994 by Magabala Books. She has two other manuscripts, including a collection of short stories, awaiting publication and has had several academic papers and articles published. Rosemary is currently studying for her Doctorate in Philosophy at Curtin University and working on her autobiography.

On My Own

FOR THE LAST two weeks I have been on the go, travelling solo around the south-west of this State, keeping one step ahead of my pursuers – loneliness and fear. I am not used to being alone. I hate being alone. It is debilitating for me to be so alone. I want to go home, but I cannot, not yet.

I left my husband and everything that is comfortable and familiar to me at home. I wanted to prove to him and my children that I could survive without them. I wanted to prove that I could survive without hearing my grandchildren's voices playing happily in my back yard one minute, and having a ding-dong squabble the next. Of being the referee to their disagreements and making sure the problems were solved to both parties' satisfaction before their respective mothers took them home and peace and quiet reigned in my house once again. I am a grandmother of many and I am feeling my age. People tell me I am an independent woman in my own right. And yes, I am. I worked for this position and travelling around with this job is a part of the requirements. Thank God it is only for two weeks. I don't think I could stand it any longer. I'm not used to this loneliness, but must pursue my course of action.

I am not a young woman by any means. The first flush of youth left me years ago and the gauchness of being a teenager, tripping through adolescence, has long since past. When I became a wife and experienced the joys of motherhood, I was on top of the world and could handle any situation which confronted me. I was in my prime and, with my husband, faced the world head-on. Nothing was too daunting. I had always been around people, had their support and love, and company.

My daughters did not want me to leave. I am a gun babysitter at times. My sons were impartial, probably because their wives were psyched up to the mother-in-law syndrome. My husband told me my going was my own choice. I would have to live with it. He would be lonely and would miss me, but he could not change my mind. I had to go. For me, the time had come when I had to assert my own authority and my own identity, and to be a woman in my own right. I have that responsibility to myself. Over the years, I have become too dependent on my husband. When the children left home to lead their own lives and raise their own children, I became more and more reliant on my husband's company and was frightened to be alone for any length of time. I became a clinging vine, a wimp, and I did not like it one little bit.

Yet it is understandable that I did not like being alone, for I am an Aboriginal woman and our culture is family orientated. We like company and having family and friends around us. It keeps the unknown at bay and night fears are less threatening when you have someone near. The sound of another voice allays my fears and having my husband close at night is especially comforting. So why did I put myself in this position where I have to sleep alone, eat alone and pretend I am a single person? I suppose getting a big pay packet at the end of the two weeks is good enough reason.

Now I am alone and I do not like it one little bit. As I sit here in my motel room, I think of my journey so far. While the daylight hours bring relief from the night, all the inherent fears of the dark come to the fore and my imagination runs wild as soon as the sun goes down. Unknown possibilities of terror, of something coming to get me, make the night a fearsome obstacle for me to hurdle. I must be brave and calm myself.

For the past ten nights I have been sitting up in bed for as long as possible, reading my study books or magazines to pass the time. I read until my eyes are so strained from the tiny letters in the book that I wipe my glasses to enable me to see clearly. I go to the toilet, wash my hands with my head down, afraid to look in the bathroom mirror for fear that a ghoulish face may be looking back at me. Nervously, I wipe my hands, turn around and walk out the door. In the bedroom, I wonder once again why I put myself through this ordeal.

I know I must turn off the lights for I cannot sleep with the room lit up like the proverbial Christmas tree. I must be brave and face the night. I jump into bed and pull the blankets right over my head. My arm snakes out to turn the nightlight off and quickly returns under the blankets. I huddle under the covers like a ball, making an opening just large enough for my nose to breathe fresh air. I lie there in agony listening to the sounds of the night. Slowly I relax and sleep overcomes me.

During the day I can cope with being alone. I keep busy talking to people in the course of my work. I talk to children and adults. I don't care, for they are all human beings and I am communicating. I am not alone but am a part of this world. When I have finished my talks for the day, I head back to my hotel room in whichever town I've visited, sit and read again or, through sheer boredom, I go window shopping until it is time for tea.

Tonight is my last night by myself. Tomorrow I return to my husband and my home. My tour will be over and I will once again be with the people I know and love. As I book into the last hotel on the agenda, I wonder if all my fears were unfounded. Outwardly the hotel looks warm and inviting and I was sure my room would be the same.

After booking in at reception, I am told my room number and how to get there. I climb the stairs thinking, 'Wow, this looks alright!' But as I reach the landing, I see dark corridors. I console myself that the lights haven't come on yet and when they do, the place will be brightly lit up. No matter, my room must be okay. Surely they would not put me in the attic. No, here's my room. All I have to do is go in, close the door and watch some television until tea time.

~

As I put the key in the lock and opened the door, I was overcome with a feeling of unease. The room was in darkness and the atmosphere was not welcoming. Quickly, I turned on the light and looked around. The curtains were a dismal green colour and the bedcover was a tacky brown. The bed, wardrobe and bedside table looked as if they belonged to an opportunity shop and the carpets were dreary and dark. There was no television. I felt like running there and then.

'God help me,' I thought, as I carried my case and bag into the room. 'Let me be strong enough to last this night.'

A primal fear came to me and I knew this night would test my mettle as an independent woman with common sense and fortitude.

After following my usual ritual at bedtime, I managed to fall into a restless sleep. I kept waking up, then dozing off again. It was after midnight when I fell into a deep sleep. I lay immovable until, at three-thirty in the morning it happened. First the soft scratching, then the muted knocking. I lay there dazed at first, not comprehending what was happening. Suddenly, the bedside digital radio turned on and a voice from the tourist station was extolling the virtues of the coastal plains. I froze. As the voice on the radio continued its spiel, I lay in the foetal position, blankets and pillows pulled right over my head.

'For God's sake, who turned that radio on,' I said to myself.

I lay there for many long minutes shaking under the covers until a sense of the ridiculous got the better of me. The room had no bedside lamp so, flinging back the bedclothes, I made a dash for the lights near the door. After turning the lights on, I looked around the room and saw nothing. I stood at the door for a while making up my mind if I was imagining things and perhaps the radio had been pre-set for that time of the morning. I decide, while I was up, I had better go to the toilet, but as I took one step, the wardrobe doors opened, as if someone, or something, was going to get an article of clothing from within.

'Fuck this! Stay shut, you bastard!' I said out loud as I slammed the wardrobe doors shut. I stood there watching the doors for a moment, making sure they couldn't open of their own accord. Nothing happened. By this time my bladder was fairly screaming for attention, so I ducked into the loo. I told myself not to be stupid. There was an explanation for everything. On my return from the bathroom, I found the wardrobe doors had opened again. The hairs on the back of my neck tingled as I swore aloud once more then hurriedly walked to the wardrobe, shut the doors with a bang and got a chair from near the bed to jam them shut.

I jumped back into bed, leaving the lights to the bathroom and the main room on. I left the radio on also. Listening to the announcer's voice was comforting, I thought, as I snuggled under the blankets. Everything was getting back to normal. I was being lulled back to sleep by the droning sounds of the radio, when, all of a sudden, it was switched off. Just like that.

I flung the blankets off me and jumped out of bed, ready to do battle with whatever was teasing me like this. I checked the radio to make sure the automatic setting wasn't on. It wasn't. I checked the wardrobe doors to make sure they weren't open. I checked the toilet and shower recess and the windows. By this time I was well and truly stirred up. My fear had given way to anger and I was hopping mad. I swore at that thing until I had no more words to say.

Sleep had vanished and so had that frightening presence in that room. By this time, it was five o'clock in the morning, so I turned the radio on to a station with music, got out my writing pad and started writing until it was time for me to shower, get dressed, pack my case and bag and leave that miserable room with its unknown, unseen, resident. I never looked back.

Herb Wharton

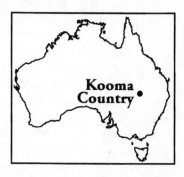

Kooma Country

HERB WHARTON is an unstoppable writer, storyteller, traveller, yarn spinner, a welcome speaker at conferences and literary festivals, and an oft-invited guest on the international circuit. His first book, Unbranded, was published in 1992 by University of Queensland Press, followed by Cattle Camp in 1994 and Where Ya' Been Mate in 1996. He was awarded the 1998 writer's residency at the Australian Council's Cité Internationale des Arts studio in Paris. His next book, Yumba Days, for young adults, will be published by UQP in 1999. Born in Cunnamulla, Queensland, in 1936, he is a descendant of the Kooma people. 'In the Yard and Round the House' has been developed from a talk he delivered to a Queensland Museum conference at which a number of writers reminisced about their yards, back and front. Needless to say, Herb's experiences were somewhat different from most.

In the Yard and
Round the House

O UR HOUSE, OR HUMPY you might say, was a *real* Queenslander, made out of reused galvanised iron and bush timber, and a few cut boards, mostly pine, for the front wall. My father built it himself in what we called the Yumba, where later on many Murris lived, segregated from the town by the cemetery and the big red hopbush sandhill that ran around it on the eastern side. Our home was about one hundred yards from that sandhill and about the same distance again from the cemetery fence. On the western side about half a mile away was one of the very few permanent waterholes in the Warrego River. That was the boundary fence of our back yard.

The house had only a dirt floor, about three rooms, a half-enclosed verandah and a big boughshed made of saplings and bushes. There were a couple of windows in the front and the back windows were two pieces of tin, propped open with saplings and quickly closed when it rained or there was a dust storm coming from the west. We would pull the props out, then wedge them against the tin windows.

The water tap, about sixty yards away, also served five or six other camps. Water was carried in a billycan or bucket made from a kerosene tin. There was no such thing as electricity. When the old kerosene lamp was out of commission we'd make our own from a small treacle tin filled with animal fat and a strip of felt cut from a discarded hat as a wick. I still recall how us kids were fascinated by the flickering flames from those lamps, which shed a light so dim that older people would say you needed to strike a match so you could see where you were going – certainly not enough light for homework. Dad told the teachers that if they couldn't teach us enough at school too bad, for he had plenty for us to learn at home carrying water, gathering horse and cattle manure when the mossies were bad, and collecting kindling wood from the dead hopbush on the sandhill. The green hopbush made ideal brooms for sweeping up the rubbish without wrecking the packed-dirt floor.

There were no streets in the Yumba, even after the shire council decided years later to build six houses, some only a few yards apart, like in the towns and cities. Earlier houses, and shacks and tents before then, were built far apart from each other, even among the same tribal groups. Later, when other mobs from down the river or from further west came to town, they would camp further away, grouping together by themselves. A sort of them-and-us-fellas attitude I believe. Yet there was no differences. It was just natural to do. Luckily our nearest neighbour was still a hundred yards away.

I recall when they built those new houses, still with dirt floors, no electricity or running water, they just extended the water line and put in another two taps to service the new houses plus all the other shacks that were to spring up. Two or three council houses all shared one outside dunny. Later they built a toilet block and showers. Oddly enough I believe Cunnamulla township was the first town in Queensland to be completely sewered, long before we got that toilet block down the Yumba. My Dad, I remember, was offered one of them new houses but he declined, saying he could look after his own. I am still mystified how people ever came to camp closer and closer together in the city, all forever arguing with their neighbours, while everyone's best friend lives a hundred or a thousand miles away, never next door.

From the Yumba we walked barefooted to town and school in freezing cold and searing heat. My first pair of shoes were white sandshoes. I took one look and hated the spotless white things. Bugger if I could imagine wearing them, a Murri striding to school in white shoes, no socks. Besides, they would have been useless when playing on the sandhill. I don't know what became of them but they never wore out. At school I remember I liked doing the things that interested me, lots of fights and lots of good times. The fights I think might have been part of the good times. Even down the Yumba among ourselves we fought. Freedom of speech was integrated maybe with freedom of action.

At school we learnt mostly about white explorers in a so-called unexplored wilderness, and English and European history, not Australian history, or only in part. Yet at night time in the Yumba we sometimes had different lessons about the land, animal and bird stories of creation. More creative than any of the stories at school about golden apples, angels, flying horses, lizards breathing fire – all belonging to another make-believe world. What was fact, what was myth? I would wonder about all these things, growing up with a front yard playground that could stretch as far as your imagination.

Our back yard was mainly the river. I recall how we fished and hunted down there, and in drought time watching a big red cloud of dust appear in the west, growing higher, spreading wider and wider as it drew near, until it hit the Yumba and the countryside was engulfed in a reddish-brown world of dust and sand. And while parents yelled for everyone to take cover, us kids tried to remain outside, bracing ourselves against the forceful wind-blown dust and sand. To me there was something magical about the feel of the sand hitting my bare legs – a stinging, tingling sensation.

One Sunday playing in front of our home with my shanghai I heard a droning sound. Looking up I saw the weekly mail plane from Sydney approaching from the south. Low and very slow it was flying, giving the passengers a bird's-eye view of the Yumba. I must have been about eight at the time and decided I better give these bastards something to remember us by. So as that old cumbersome aircraft approached, I took aim, I pulled hard on the shanghai strands, then let fly. Imagine my astonishment when I heard this loud rifle-like crack as the missile from my shanghai hit the propeller blade. Then I stood unblinking, motionless, expecting any second to see the plane nosedive and come plummeting to earth. 'My God what have I done.' Hastily I buried my shanghai as the plane flew on over the hill to the dirt airstrip on the other side of town. I stayed close to home for the rest of the day, expecting at any moment to see the old funny-looking ute the police used. Surely the pilot must have reported the incident, but as sundown came and no police car appeared around the corner of the cemetery fence I felt relief. (Perhaps that pilot was flying too low and unsafely to complain.) Years later, when I heard Rolf Harris singing about some old Murri outback throwing his boomerang into the air and bringing down the flying doctor, I really could visualise such an incident. And I like to think my hostile actions did have some effect, because I don't remember that mail plane ever flying so low over the Yumba again.

After the other houses were built, with plenty of people around, there was always a game of rounders – something like baseball – yet there was no limit to the number of players and no age limit, old and young played. So while others grew up with cricket, we grew up with rounders. All we needed was a tennis ball; the bat was a piece of board or a pick handle – any solid piece of wood. This was a real community game. But later came the building of that modern toilet block, on top of the first base, restricting our game of rounders. Just beyond the third base was an old ironwood tree. Someone I suppose could have chopped down that tree and we would have had the space, with the toilet block for home base. But it was as much of the Yumba as us and it stayed, sounding a death knell for rounders. Although a few other games were played in other places in the Yumba, in our front yard, it was not the same.

Yet our real front yard was a small fenced-in area where Dad had at times grown a few vegetables. Getting water to the garden was long hard work: no hoses, so Dad dug a trench the hundred yards from the tap to a small iron tank sunk into the ground a few feet deep. Then late at night when others were not using the tap he would let it run until the small tank was full. Overnight the hot artesian bore water would cool to be used to moisten the parched dry earth, enabling a few cabbages, pumpkins, or whatever, to grow, to help feed the many hungry mouths he had to fill.

There were nine boys and two girls in our family so when it rained, or in winter, our home was crowded. Sometimes even visiting relations would stay a few days. But space was never scarce, especially in summer, as you could roll out a swag anywhere on the ground outside. Inside was a small wood stove to cook on but we often sat around and cooked on an outdoor open fire, even in winter. But when it was really cold a fire bucket, made by cutting a few deep gashes in an oil or flour drum, was lit inside.

Our back yard, the river, was equally important – the home of the Munta-Gudda that ruled the river, the land. If you misused your resources it would punish you in a strange way. Our myths, legends and beliefs have been handed down for centuries, telling us how to look after our country. Yet it is only in recent times that so-called Christian-civilised societies passed laws to protect our resources and Mother Earth.

Growing up in the Yumba had advantages and disadvantages for a lot of Murris. We escaped the mission handout and total oppression. There were no dole cheques so we often hunted, learning to track animals and to read the land, for to Aboriginal Australians it was a book. So when I started droving and roaming the stock routes of the inland with mobs of horses, cattle and sheep, riding along I could clearly see how history was etched upon the ground in many places. And I began to understand why some so-called superior white explorers died out there, simply because of their ignorance – of being unable to read the land or understand the people who were part of it.

Growing up with a back yard like that I realised later was a sort of privilege. The most important part of going to school was learning to write. But then in the Yumba I had lessons never taught in schools. Many might say we were disadvantaged. Oppressed we may have been, by unjust laws and attitudes, but downtrodden never, because we learnt to express ourselves with the power of words, which gave us independence, teaching us how to think, not what to think.

The Yumba, Bourke Road, Cunnamulla, was my first permanent address. Today it's Bedford Street, Cunnamulla. I've actually moved from one hundred yards south of the town cemetery to the same distance north of the cemetery. My home now has electric lights, running water, a board floor and glass windows, built on the edge of a sandhill. The nearest house is still sixty or eighty yards away.

In between the move from south to north of the cemetery were years of wandering, working in the outback at different jobs – an ongoing education you might say. Then came my involvement in writing, then more roaming, not only Australia-wide but overseas. Always something new to learn: different people, ways of living, many houses with no front or back yards. Bedford Street where I now live has the best weed garden in the world. Sometimes religious groups visit, trying to sell me books and religion. Well over the years from my verandah I have managed to sell them two of my own books. So at this rate it will take a million years for me to convert these people to my way of believing in an earthly mother rather than a heavenly father.

Bedford Street is becoming well known. Peter Carey, the writer, also lives in Bedford Street, but in New York. I gave him a photo of the real Bedford Street to show him how far away from the centre of the universe he lives. I have a photo of his Bedford Street. And perhaps, too, it was just coincidence that on the couple of times I have visited London my address was Bedford Square. I have come to realise I can live anywhere in the world.

Back yards and homes certainly bring back memories of days long past, many that are related to the present. Our home was no mansion but it was ours. I still don't think of owning it – we belonged to it and the landscape.

The Yumba is long gone now, the big red hopbush sandhill is fast disappearing because of misuse. The riverbanks that were once accessible to everyone are now privately owned and fenced off. The places where the Munta-Gudda lives are covered forever since the building of a dam. Yet the Munta may well live on, punishment yet to come.

I still return to the site of where we lived. There used to be a cedar tree growing in our yard. After all us mob moved into houses in town the Yumba site was dozed and became a rubbish dump. Our cedar tree still stood. Until one day a young kid told me, really worried, 'Hey, you know the council bloke with the bulldozer, they been push down that tree and try to burn it.' I was touched that this kid was so concerned. Yet I could not fathom the small-minded politics of those who thought by getting rid of the tree they were getting rid of the past, in case of future land claims. For I knew that even without the tree I could walk directly, unaided, even in the dark, to where our home and cedar tree once stood. Where memories linger. A place that gave me identity, helped shape who and what I became. It gave me the sense of belonging too, being part of, not owning.

Today my back yard is the world. I have visited many Yumba sites lately; history almost asleep, untold. I have come upon a Yumba in what was the no-man's land that once divided East and West Germany in Berlin. What a discovery that was for me. Now I wonder – is outback isolation really a myth? For it seems the *rest* of the world still lives in isolation from the Yumba site just south of what some refer to as Cunna-bloody-mulla.

Alexis Wright

ALEXIS WRIGHT is one of Australia's rising Indigenous authors. In 1997 her novel Plains of Promise was published by the University of Queensland Press (a second novel is in progress) and her non-fiction work Grog War by Magabala Books. She is also editor of Take Power, an anthology of essays and stories on twenty years of land rights in Central Australia published by IAD Press, 1998. Her story 'When Devils Call' won the 1994 Northern Territory Literary Award for Aboriginal and Torres Strait Islander Writers (and was subsequently published by Northern Territory University Press in Extra Territorial, and 'The Chinky Apple Tree' was highly commended in the 1996 NT Awards. She has held a diverse range of positions in Aboriginal agencies and government departments around Australia as a manager, educator, researcher and writer, and now lives in Alice Springs with her husband and three children. Alexis is of the Waanyi people of the highlands of the southern Gulf of Carpentaria.

The Chinky Apple Tree

MOMENTS BEFORE HER death the old woman had difficulty in pinpointing the exact image of what happened first, or place into a precise order a series of events that had triggered her dying. Around and around, the unsorted pictures flew in her mind to the rhythm of her hair caught in the dust of a wild wind. Jumbled with an image seen time again in dreams over a lifetime which was now clouded by a tangled web of events.

She always saw the same tree. The sea of pale green leaves known to her from almost every conceivable angle. Round. Like the bellies of small fish. In those dreams she does not see herself but she is always present, almost as if she is inside the person in the dream, but she knows it is not her. Why she knows it is neither herself nor her body remains her mystery. She has often tried to capture their life without success. To identify the body she invades in these dreams to see the tree through their eyes. Neither was she able to locate the tree, although she had seen enough Chinky Apple trees to know it could have been any, but not the one from her memory of her grandmother's back yard.

In the mind of herself as a small child laying on her back on the cool ground, the wind sent the small silvery fish streaming down, one behind the other, from the pale understorey. A touch so slight that hits her on the forehead before falling onto the ground. Afterwards, only her outline remained on the ground uncovered from the fallen leaves.

At the point of dying at her grandmother's age, she is still trying to piece together the same images into a sequence of events. Where she once stood on the dirt floor at the door of her grandmother's house, made decades ago from rusted tin, she had smelt the dust storm in summer hitting the top of the tree and bending it. Swish! Swoosh! The tree waved to and fro, as though waving goodbye. One day she left during a storm and never came back. Whenever she has returned, which she has done many times over the years, to the childhood memory, she becomes the swarm of grasshoppers that emerge after rain like a green cloud from the fresh grass outside the yard. A swarm that turns as sharply as a guitar is plucked when played with precision, as if returning a memory to the tree while devouring every leaf.

~

From the wooden bridge the two men fish over its side by moonlight tonight. Nearby, where the old woman is standing, she relies on the familiarity of habit to comfort herself. She feels relaxed in the expectation of being together every night with the two men. A habit that binds them together. She is long blind to understanding the reality of her presence on the bridge by her fading eyesight. While she looks over the rail, she sees by remembering the water's shine in a million ripples from the light of stars while passing under the bridge. It was like a bridge of the woman's world of long ago that stretched out over a spinifex landscape where on nights such as these only stray cats prowled around snarling at each other in that dry stony creekbed. Long ago when she was a child she might have wished for these running waters where the men fish.

In her mind her eyes are alongside the men who can see upstream the cod sitting, suspended, almost motionless in the shallow water. The water with stripes of purple and blue and silver fish. It is the way it has always been since they were boys. They sit with damp trousers on a mossy bridge. Slippery from fish guts and the stench of decades of yesterday's dead fish. She gets lost in the hours of stooped, bristly faces that sternly scaled fish on the wooden planks. And the stench of fish. A sign of well being and relaxing in all that is familiar and as strong as a bond between two men.

~

Where was the woman? Were they really waiting and waiting for fish? Waiting for the fish to move? She knew it was up to her to make it happen. Yet when the heavy clouds set off a drizzle that felt cold on her face, she still waited before deciding to take the slow walk home. She sold grasshoppers for bait. Before, when the two men were boys she decided to only sell them one grasshopper every day. And the boys grew into men. And the grasshoppers came and went with the years. Sometimes in hues of green, or grey, or white or a mixture of all. Today the green one with its grey tints stood on the twigs of couch with dry roots. She thought its eyes were like glass, staring out through glass, and from inside the glass jar at her. This morning when the dew lay on the dead grasses outside, she thought it should have flown when it wriggled to set itself free under her foot. It had the chance. What bigger handicap was there than old age? What would it have seen as it jumped towards the glare of the sun, the blue sky glistening through transparent wings as its flight whispered past the mulberry tree? The men took it with a scowl. They paid her reluctantly. She smiled. They always had to pay. Ever since they were small boys neither knew how to catch his bait, so they had to pay.

She had watched the creature struggling for hours with its stick legs, trying to stay afloat, impaled on a hook at the end of the line. A struggle that is so close to her now. From the bridge she watched the men smoke and exhale. The men talked and laughed and reckoned it was a narrow escape and smoked and exhaled. They could not remember all of the times that they had tricked her. There had been so many times in a lifetime.

'Remember ... must have been when we were seven? ... was it seven? Yes! That's right. When I stole money that time and got into trouble.'

'We were getting ripped off even then.'

'Extortion, I reckon, making kids pay for grasshoppers.'

They talked about other times when she had refused to sell one more even though it might have made the difference in landing that big cod that was just waiting to be caught. That fish must have been the subject of talk between the two boys for years. It lived its life many times over in their minds. They grew into men on the same story. In their minds it was always the one that got away. Like the good times in life that were always there for the picking for anyone else but always just out of reach for them. Only if there could have been one more chance.

It happened so many years ago and she still did not know why. She had one more at the time and she could have just given it to them. After all, they had seen it all wrapped up in a hanky when she had dropped their money into her purse. She had watched a sweat of frustration on their little boy faces as if to say 'go on'. But she walked away. She had thought them wasteful. They were always wasteful. From that day on she only sold them one live grasshopper each day for five cents. It was the price that paid for and ensured the constancy of their companionship on the bridge continuing for over thirty years.

She heard all of their conversations and was implicit through silence. They watched while she stood at the end of the bridge, watching them, sipping from a port bottle, the cheapest, in a brown paper bag, laughing at the little boys growing into men. Waiting for someone to come by and take her home. And someone always came. Someone she called 'Angel', or 'Love'. Someone to replace the love that had broken her heart over thirty years ago and whom she still called 'Love'. Now 'Love' became anyone. And over the years she worked hard to look nice, smell nice to the 'nice' men who came by and dragged her over the bridge. They jeered 'Yer just a Black Mole' and 'Gin' when she insisted on being treated like a lady as they knocked her small frame onto the ground. Most times finally dumping her amongst the prickly bushes along the way.

'Keep going,' the boys had whispered in earlier days, bowing their heads and nudging each other forward. Pretending they didn't see or smell stale alcohol on the downwind as they hurried past with their fish.

By the time they were men they could walk past without a glance or a single acknowledgment if they saw her there. By moonlight, the landscape served no interest past the fish under the bridge. The path was simply a corridor through the dead prickles and grass killed on either side by a poison spray owned by the council men of the municipality. Neither man cared about the job done by day over every footpath in town. Money in the shirt pocket paid for that.

Either man might have wanted to make his individual

comment from time to time whenever they saw her passed out indecently in the dead bindies, but thought it was not worth it. In any case, each knew what the other thought so that their conversations could take place in the head without either wasting his breath.

'It's hot,' one might say finally.

Then after a while.

'Too right by jove,' might have been the reply.

She fumbled with the key in the lock in the dark. She depended only on familiarity and touch. Sight a blurred vision made clear with a distorted memory of pictures that formed slowly from the past to match familiar sounds. She knew they had never come this far before. Her ears strained while listening for the next and the next sound of gravel crushing behind her. She had given them the one grasshopper in a glass jar. She did not understand their sounds coming from behind. Sounds not being made by her. Sounds she recognised from the passage of time to belong to two sons of a woman who once had love. Stopped whenever she stopped. Then extended the sound of her sound when she started walking again. When they had shoved her aside and begun to forcefully open the door she had not realised what was happening to stop it.

The thirty-year growth of insects which she had horded inside her house grew restless. Over the years the few grasshoppers that originally had a home in 'Love's' shoebox were allowed to spread as their numbers increased until every lonely room in that house was full again. Together they had watched her leave through the glass windows in the morning. In the dark house they had heard the sounds coming from a distance. Known she had not come alone and grew more fearful with each hesitation of fear in her step. Panic spread like an electric current moving down a cable that connected them as one unified force. In an instant they formed a cloud ready for flight. The moment that the moonlight shone through the narrow crack of the opening door the insects swarmed. Their cloud of strength pierced itself through the narrow opening, forcing the door to slam back against the wall. The spikes on a thousand outstretched legs lacerating the faces and arms of the men while at the same time knocking them to the ground.

The old woman did not realise that the speed of life lifted from a memory of her childhood had overtaken her. She tried to piece together jumbled images of life from the images of dreams and place them together into a logical sequence of events. The sound of the drone grew louder until she could not piece anything together. The noise did not stop lifting her away into the swarm that lifted higher into the air, while turning to and fro as sharply and with such precision as a musician strumming his guitar.

The swarm flew away over the bridge of a world stretched out over a spinifex landscape and from the sky came down to land on a Chinky Apple tree where the understorey looked like the bellies of small fish. The leaves fell on the old woman laying on the ground. And the tree was left bare.

When Devils Call

A ND THE RAIN splashes on me. Unseen rain falls in the darkness on smooth and slippery rock. And her voice, wasp-like, knifes over the wet rocks, through the crevices far into the night. She penetrates with sharp jabs through the soles of my feet. On and on she coos, 'God loves you,' her voice new with authority. Increasing authority, snaking along and up the surface of the sandstone cliff. Loudly her words reverberate, hitting out, cruel hands slapping my face, before piercing needle points jab inside my ears, into the depths of my mind.

Insistent, she continues her lies. 'Truly, can't you feel it?' she is singing. Sing-song. What a cracked bitch! I feel like hissing back, but it would make no difference. No difference at all. Nothing silences her. Even now, in the black night, she continues her lies. Frightened? Of nothing. Now. Poor dead cracked bitch.

Black droplets of rain fall from my hair, hair too frizzy, too thick for rain to soak through. Each drop glides over the oily surface of my workday face, catches the tears and forms the liquid boulders that roll heavily downwards to join the blood, escaping from my inner wounds, through and over my swollen lips. Workday face my foot! Work round here? What a bloody joke! Bitch! I hope you are happy tonight. Are you?

She continues beside me. Tries to get inside me. She had tried now for seven years, never leaving my side. Ever since that day she died. She stays here, singing her lies. She makes it harder to negotiate, through the darkness, the narrow track home, now slippery from the storm. The rain intensifies. I should have thought about the clouds building up earlier. Swirling together. When the air was thick with humidity. My eyes, injured from a drunken fight over her, are forced shut to ease the stinging pain of my tears. Blindly I climb onwards. I will get home and show her she can't stop me. The rain pelts onto my wet body, while I cling to the sandstone walls of the cliff face. I caress the cold smoothness of her as I continue to move, while at sharp corners, receive her cutting nails, slowly tearing into my face as she sees fit.

I force each step down hard and trample the mud underfoot to wipe her out. I will wipe her out. Her voice rings back, keeping time, trampling against the wetness of my face. I slip frequently and each time remind myself to take more care. I must fight her back. Oh my God, I'm slipping. I see myself falling, but I don't feel like I'm falling. The waves scream up at me from far below, ordering, pulling me to them. I have become connected to her. Connected to a million years of waves crashing into their manufactured, indented sandstone walls. I am drowning far below in the blackness of the swish and fro of angry waters.

It's not good to drown when you don't want to go that way. But on the other hand, death will be the last thread of all before me, who made me. It will be finished. This will not be a problem. I will not be responsible any more for the evil they control inside me. Let the air be dragged out of my body and end them forever. I wait suspended in the liquid mass. Death will come soon.

But I am not drowning. I am still clinging to the rocks while the waves crash around me. Suddenly I feel arms that roughly grab my legs and hold them firmly together. I shake with fear. I am unable to move but my arms grip the overhanging rocks of the cliff's edge while her arms drag me outwards. I feel the pressure of her new strength gradually force my arms over the slippery surface.

Slowly she pulls me back into the sea then releases her hold over me. I'll fight you back, bitch! But I sink further. I am pulled to the surface for a moment's breath of air, salt and moisture laden, before I am dragged under again and feel the pressure of being dragged further outward into the sea. The waves splash a repeated christening onto my bobbing head. Still she remains, singing, 'God loves you, truly he does.'

Her words make me strong to keep fighting her. She won't get me. But the water quickens its pull of me into the outgoing tide, and I am dragged downwards onto the sea floor debris, and further out. Through the roar she swoons. 'If you only take your time, you will see more clearly.' Her voice laps continuously. She is trying to get me, but she forgets I can outsmart her. I stop struggling. I wait for the inward tide to take me back. Finally I am thrown back onto the rocks, exhausted, to make my own way up the path.

~

No one could forget. They all blamed me for killing Anita. I was jealous of her and I drank too much. I don't remember killing her, but I must have. My jealousy settled her once and for all and I drank too much. But everyone did. Well, almost everyone. Though not everyone could be called 'drunken people'.

Anita and my mother were 'sober people'. Didn't drink. Church every Sunday while I lay in bed sleeping it off. But I'd be up by the time they got back. You could watch them, through squinted eyes, coming along in the distance under the midday sun. They were part of a mirage ascending from the brown, dirt road. Hallelujah. Two black saints coming home. They certainly acted that way when they got home after Mass at the mission church on Sunday. Both would glance an icy stare at me, in silence, as they walked into their chicken-wired yard and up the path, divided by their pink and white nanny-goat flowers. Behind them their heavenly trail of dust drifted back towards their God in the mission church.

'Another nice day,' I'd offer them from my spot, my upturned kerosene tin in the shade of the cedar tree, positioned where I could see down the main road on 'the lookout' for any action. The two sullen glances continued walking past me and walked on inside.

Life might have gone on this way if Anita hadn't tried to make things different. 'Better' is how she described it. For her, that is. At least that is how I thought of it at the time. She was right for wanting to get away from me. Anita was smart but I didn't want her that way. I tried to beat it out of her then. I hated her for being weaker and taking my punches like a broken doll. I made her give up wanting to learn book-keeping and typing so she could work in the community office. I wasn't going to let that happen. Not while she was the one handing out my dole money or while I was employed to cart the garbage away.

Anita gave up pretty good and made sure she became what I wanted. Devoted and there at home at all times and beneath my body at nights after the canteen closed. Other men found her passiveness attractive but for me I couldn't tell what she wanted. That caused me to wonder if she cared for me, or what she was really up to. I couldn't trust her so I had to always make sure she wasn't thinking of other men. Perhaps this is what she did all the time while I was sitting at the canteen at nights. Sitting at home thinking of other men. Or maybe that is what she thought and prayed about at church on Sundays.

Pummelling the broken doll was easy. Hateful. Yes, I hated her then. I knew that, even though my mother tried to pull me away. I just forgot to stop. But I didn't want to harm her or kill her. Afterwards, I held her in my arms all night. But she was dead. When I left, Mum had no words, not even a farewell. She died too, and sat and waited for death. She was well and truly dead by the time my term in jail was completed, although they only gave me two years. That was nothing. The punishment commenced when I came back here to nothing. I was nothing. The community was unable to stop the police from returning the 'mission boy' back home.

Only dead voices spoke to me here. And her voice that followed me to jail and back home again. Her dead voice full of compassion and hiding the lies. Cast out by my own community I could no longer live in my mother's house, so I live away from all of them. I have a cave along the coastal cliffs. Hidden in a cave, just in case. In case of her dead voice. Anita. Her family wanting to get even. I feel them listening for me. I am always on the lookout. I didn't kill her. You killed yourself. Bitch.

I mind my own business. I don't go looking for trouble. Tonight I walked into town to get a few beers to take back to my camp. In the last light it is one of the old aunties who still sees me, has watched me slip by. Already in the canteen like a large-sized lizard marooned, visible in fright, up amongst the whiteants, gripping a rotten frond in a dead pandanus tree. She strides up and down, eyeballing the prey. Revving up a froth of accusations. Everywhere drunken women are crying. An explosion of words hits the tin walls from every direction. The sounds of yelling and screaming let the evil spirits fly straight out of the mouths of drunken people. The air is spinning. Whirlpools tear through the building, colliding with one another in mid-air, under tables and through the drunken throng. 'We don't want any killers walking around here. Murderer. Why don't you get the murderer. Kill him. Kill him.' I cannot defend myself. I belonged to them. I have been beaten and left for dead.

But she stayed watching. Her lies forced me to get up and stumble my way back along the coast.

I escaped her death. Now I cling tightly to the cold face rocks. Still her voice coos, 'God loves you,' while the waves roar and curl outstretched arms around my legs. She lies again and again but I have lost the fight and allow the seduction to take place.